ROBIN THORNBURGH
824- 0203

CLOUDS

CLOUDS

Robin Jones Gunn

Five Star
Unity, Maine

Copyright © 1997 by Robin Jones Gunn

Scripture quotations are from:
The Holy Bible, New International Version © 1973, 1984 by
International Bible Society, used by permission of Zondervan
Publishing House.

Also quoted:
The Holy Bible New King James Version © 1984 by Thomas Nelson,
Inc.

The Revised Standard Version © 1946, 1952 by the Division of
Christian Education of the National Council of the Churches of
Christ in the United States of America.

Five Star Christian Mystery.
Published in conjunction with Multnomah Publishers.
Cover courtesy of © Multnomah Publishers.

October 1999
Standard Print Hardcover Edition.

Five Star Standard Print Christian Mystery Series.

The text of this edition is unabridged.

Set in 11 pt. Plantin by Juanita Macdonald.

Printed in the United States on permanent paper.

Library of Congress Cataloging-in-Publication Data

Gunn, Robin Jones, 1955–
    Clouds / Robin Jones Gunn.
      p.   cm.
    ISBN 0-7862-2137-2 (hc : alk. paper)
    1. Title.
    [PS3557.U4866C58 1999]
    813′.54—dc21   99-22270

To Beckie Melli, who walked with me
in the hushed woods that led us to St. Annakapella.

And to my dear grandma, Gertrude Rudi Clawson,
who has prayed for me since the day I was born.

Thank you both for teaching me
to treasure my godly heritage.

Sing to God, sing praise to his name,
lift up a song to him who rides on the clouds.

PSALM 68:4, RSV

1

Shelly Graham placed her hand on the doorknob and turned it
slowly. A creak echoed from the hinges, and she smiled. Everything about this room felt familiar, friendly, welcoming. She
stood in the doorway and surveyed her childhood bedroom.
Two twin beds with white wrought-iron frames stood their
ground as they had for more than twenty years, like faithful sol-
diers guarding the window between them.

Shelly noticed the new blue-and-white bedspreads Mom
had bought after Shelly and her sister Meredith had both
moved out. The painted pine desk in the corner was the same
as it had always been. The white wicker chair hadn't been
moved from beside the closet. Even the color of the room was
the same: sky blue. On the ceiling, the white clouds Meredith
had painted there eight years ago hadn't moved an inch in
their journey across the solid, latex-covered heavens. Shelly
gave these familiar images only a sweeping glance.

It was the window that beckoned to her. Sheer, ivory curtains billowed in the afternoon breeze. The cobalt blue glass
vase that held a giant snatch of color from Mom's garden
rested on one of Grandma Rudi's lace doilies. The vase was
placed in the center of the old pine bed stand that stood under the inviting window. Shelly drew closer. The daisies,

snapdragons, and carnations shivered their greetings as the breeze came through the open window, brushed past the bouquet, and, with invisible, feathery fingers, touched Shelly's long hair.

She stood before the window, eyes closed, face tilted toward the breeze. The sun slipped over the neighbor's rooftop and spilled its hot gold all over Shelly without the slightest apology. She didn't mind a bit the way it instantly stained her white shirt a glorious, pale yellow. She remembered this feeling. She remembered these fragrances.

From down the street came the ripple of children's laughter. The squeals escalated when the faint melody of the ice cream truck came the children's way. Shelly couldn't see it, but she knew the white ice cream truck had just rounded Sycamore Drive and was headed up the hill to Duchess Place.

437 Duchess Place. This was home. Just as it had been from the day Shelly was born until five years ago, when she moved from Seattle to Pasadena, California, and began her career as a flight attendant. And now, due to a transfer, Shelly was home again.

She opened her eyes and gazed out the window at the Renfields' house next door. Nothing had changed there either. It was still gray with white shutters and that wonderful oval attic window that faced her bedroom. For years a rope had run between her bedroom window and the oval attic window. For years a green plastic bucket had hung from that line. The bucket carried messages, candy, and secret treasures from one best friend to the other.

"Jonathan," she whispered. Shelly could almost see his face there in the attic window, his light, sand-flecked brown hair, about the same color as hers; his gray, stormy eyes; and the mouth that never stopped smiling.

Shelly tried to remember the codes to their secret whistles.

She puckered up and blew. Two short, one long whistle, with the long one a note lower. That meant "Come to the window." She tried again, this time blowing one long, one short, and one long, with the short one a note higher. Her whistle echoed off the side of his house, and she remembered its meaning. "Meet me at the tree house," she said softly.

There were other signals, other whistles. But she had forgotten them, just as she had forced herself to forget so many other things about Jonathan.

A wash of uneasiness came over her. Without meaning to, she had opened a treasure chest of memories that had been locked up for many years. Shelly wasn't willing to open it any farther. Instead, she tried to tuck all the memories neatly back inside the chest where they belonged. Only it seemed the chest was refusing to be shut and was spilling its wealth all over the hardwood floor of her childhood bedroom.

There, shining in her mind, was the memory of her third birthday party. It was time for the cake. The candles were lit, and all her little friends were singing. She was just about to blow out the birthday flames when Jonathan Renfield leaned forward and, with one mighty puff, blew them out first.

Shelly remembered crying and refusing to be consoled. Her mother had tried to explain that the party was for Jonathan, too, since his birthday was three days after hers. It didn't matter. As far as Shelly was concerned, this was her party, and Jonathan should go have his own party and blow out his own candles at his own house.

Her dad had captured the scene on his old movie camera and had it transferred to a videocassette along with Shelly's fourth birthday party. This birthday was celebrated with Jonathan also. Only this time the mothers had wisely provided two cakes. Jonathan and Shelly both stood on their chairs and blew out their own candles. Then they turned and, unprompted, gave each other a not-quite-on-target kiss. The parents had laughed hard. Jonathan had smiled that unstoppable grin of his, and Shelly had adjusted her gold birthday crown for the camera.

A gentle rapping on the door brought Shelly back to the present. "How's it going up here?" her mom asked, stepping into the room. Shelly felt as though her mother had just stepped on the spilled-out memories, squashing them as she walked across the floor.

"You okay?" Mom asked. Ellen Graham was a tower of a woman, in stature and in character. At five foot eleven and a half, she stood several inches taller than any of her four daughters. Shelly was the third in birth order and resembled her dad more than her three sisters did. Mom was strong, old-fashioned in her ways, as practical as a pair of loafers, and as soft as a cupcake. She made the perfect pastor's wife, and for thirty-one years she had proved that.

"It's strange being back here," Shelly said, facing her mom and noticing that she had changed into a skirt and pastel blue blouse. "Are you going to church?"

"No, we're having dinner at Meredith's. Did I forget to tell you?" Mom looked out the window as if trying to see what Shelly had been gazing at. Shelly knew her mother didn't see anything.

It wasn't that Mom hadn't tried to see the things Shelly had seen throughout her life. Maybe Mom tried too hard. She had the same difficulty with Meredith. Mom never quite saw what Shelly and Meredith did. The two girls were the dreamers and the opposites of Megan and Molly, the two older Graham daughters. All their lives Shelly and Meredith had been kindly left to their own world of imagination.

"If you're too tired from your trip to come to dinner, I'm sure Meredith will understand."

"No, I'm fine. When are we supposed to be there?"

"Meri said about seven. She has some big news for us."

Shelly looked at her mom for a hint. "Did she meet someone?"

"She didn't say." Mom sat on the bed and surveyed the room. "Are you going to be okay here? Would you like the room changed around?"

"No, I love it just like this. What else did Meri say? Any clues at all?"

Mom shook her head.

"What if I unload the car and trailer tomorrow?" Shelly sat on the opposite bed and faced Mom. "Most of it is going to have to be stored in the garage anyway."

"That's fine. How are you feeling about this move? I know it won't be easy for you to adjust to being back home. Dad is as busy at church as he always was, and I have a full calendar, too. If anything, the three of us will probably have to schedule time to see each other."

Shelly smiled. When she did, the worry lines in Mom's broad forehead began to disappear. Shelly's smile had that effect on people. It was one of her most distinctive features. Her full lips and wide, straight teeth gave her a smile that blasted out, "Apple pie, Mom, America!" It was a nice feature to have as a flight attendant. She could put elderly passengers at ease and make crying babies coo.

"I'm going to be fine, Mom. I really appreciate you and Daddy letting me move back in. It's only until I straighten out my finances and get on a regular flight schedule. I'll hardly be home at all."

"We're glad you're here," Mom said. "And you know you're welcome to stay as long as you want."

"Thanks." Shelly brushed away the insecure feeling that floated around her. None of her three sisters had ever had to move back home. Megan and Molly were both married and lived on the East Coast. Meredith worked in Seattle and had her own apartment across town.

The sun's warmth and the closeness of the room were lulling Shelly to sleep. She stretched out on her once-familiar bed and said, "I think I'll take a short nap." The motionless clouds on the ceiling stared back at her.

"Sounds like a good idea," Mom said. "Would you like me to wake you?"

"Sure. Wake me about twenty minutes before you're ready to leave, okay?"

"Will do." Mom rose and stopped at the door. "Would you like the door closed or open?"

You never could remember, could you? Meredith is the one who likes the door open; I like it closed.

"Closed, please."

The door shut softly, and Shelly was alone with her thoughts. She rolled onto her side and curled up. Her memories wouldn't let her sleep.

She closed her eyes and there, painted on the inside of her eyelids, was the tree house. It was the day after Jonathan's dad had finished the masterpiece in the woods at the end of Duchess Place. Ten-year-old Jonathan stood at the entrance and called down to her, "What's the matter, scaredy-cat? Afraid to come up here?"

"No!"

"Then why don't you grab the rope and climb up?"

"Because . . ."

"Because you're scared, that's why."

"I'm not scared of anything," Shelly yelled back.

"Yes, you are. You're scared of heights."

He was right. She had gotten spooked one time when she was five. She had been standing at the top of the Seattle Space

Needle looking down on the world below. Some kid twice her age leaned over and said, "If you get too close to the glass it'll pop out, and you'll fall all the way down."

"Come on, Shelly Bean!" Jonathan had pleaded with her. "You've gotta see all the neat stuff my dad built in here."

Shelly remembered that moment as a turning point in her life. She had trusted Jonathan more than anyone, and with that on her side, she grabbed the rope and pulled herself up to the first step. Holding tight, she climbed the thick planks nailed to the tree trunk and entered through the trap door in the floor.

"Look," Jonathan had said, unimpressed with her major accomplishment. "There's a secret compartment." He pulled one of the wallboards to the side and revealed a small, built-in box in which he had already stored two Milky Way candy bars, his favorite.

Her memories flipped a few pages to high school. She and Jonathan were sitting together in biology lab. She had set up an elaborate prank and was waiting for Jonathan to discover it. He brought his frog in its tray over to the lab table and was preparing to finish the dissecting project. But he stepped away long enough for Shelly to rig the frog with a nylon string so she could give it a tug from the next table over, making the frog's leg kick.

Jonathan kept talking to everyone and took forever to get to his frog. When he finally did, Shelly pulled the string. The leg flexed. Jonathan froze. She pulled again, harder. This time the frog seemed to leap from the pan. Jonathan let out a yelp and jumped back, knocking over his chair. His arm caught on the string, which yanked Shelly's finger hard, causing her to screech. The whole class burst out in laughter, but their teacher docked both of them half a grade on their frog-dissecting projects.

As a peace offering, Shelly had put a Milky Way in Jonathan's locker that afternoon with a note that said, "Sorry." After school she found the empty wrapper in her locker with a note on it saying, "Yeah, right. Just you wait, Shelly Bean."

She knew he was only kidding. Jonathan was quicker to forgive and forget than anyone she knew. He was also as steadfast as the Seattle rain.

In the quietness of her room, Shelly could feel the afternoon heat dissipating as the breeze brought with it a soothing sweetness. The garden flowers were releasing their fragrance confetti into the evening air, and the wind was the messenger assigned to bring the intoxicating scent to Shelly.

Instead of examining any more of the bounty in her treasure chest of memories, she forced herself to stop. *Why are you doing this to yourself? You've been fine for more than five years. What happened, happened. You can't change anything, so why are you even thinking about it?*

"Shelly," Mom called, tapping lightly on the closed door, "time to wake up. We'll leave for Meri's in twenty minutes."

"Thanks, Mom. I'll be down in a few minutes." She rose from the bed, still feeling the heaviness of her suppressed memories. They would go away soon. They always did. All she had to do was ignore them.

Shelly opened the closet door and checked to see if she needed hangers. No. Hangers were there waiting for her. Mom had thought of everything. The dresser drawers would be empty, but she double-checked to make sure. They were empty. So was the drawer in the end table.

That's how she wanted her thoughts to be, emptied of the past. Cleaned out. Ready to be filled with new thoughts, new memories made in this room, this house, this neighborhood. Jonathan was gone. It would be best if his memory disappeared as well.

But curiosity caused her to push back the sheer curtains and take one last look out the window. Craning her neck, she saw it. Just on the other side of the screen, protruding from the corner of the window ledge, was the large eyebolt her dad had affixed there so long ago. Through that loop had passed the thick, prickly rope, and from that rope had hung the green plastic bucket that had traveled those twenty-seven feet between Shelly's bedroom window and Jonathan's attic window more times than anyone could count.

All that remained was the bolt. No rope. No bucket. No Milky Way bars at midnight. And no Jonathan.

No Jonathan, Shelly reminded herself. *No Jonathan.*

2

"Okay, okay," Shelly said several hours later at Meredith's apartment. "We've eaten your lasagna, and we've endured your Vivaldi music, but before I eat a bite of this cheesecake, you must tell us: Who is he, and do I know him?"

"What are you talking about?" Meredith flipped back her straight blond hair. It was cut in a bob with the ends running along her chin line. Her hair was naturally as brown as Shelly's, but Meredith had begun to color it in high school and had kept up with the "midnight sun" shade of blond for so long that even her family members had a hard time remembering what she looked like as a brunette. The blond fit her personality — artistic, sweet, and feminine. Meredith had always had her choice of boyfriends. Shelly could only imagine which one had finally caught her sister's attention long enough to win her heart.

"Mom said you had some news for us," Shelly said, putting down her fork and giving Meredith an engaging smile. "So? We've waited long enough. Tell us. Who is he?"

Meredith giggled. "Only you would think it's a 'he.' There's no romance involved. It's all *work.*"

Dad leaned back in his chair with a satisfied look on his face. He had a broad smile like Shelly's and warm brown eyes

16

like hers. Perry Graham was the same height as his wife, but she looked taller now that they were growing older because Perry was balding and Ellen wore her short, gray hair full on top.

"You got the job," Dad said, quickly taking Meredith's clue. "Good for you, darlin'. We're proud of you."

"What job?" Shelly asked.

"At G. H. Terrison Publishing. You're talking to their newest acquisitions editor for children's products."

"Good for you, Meri!" Shelly lifted her fork in a salute before plunging it into her cheesecake. She knew this had been her sister's dream for some time, and Meredith had been diligent in pursuing the position.

"When do you start?" Dad asked.

"Next week."

"Is this the New York publisher?" Mom asked.

"No, that one never called back. Terrison Publishing is headquartered in Chicago."

"Will you have to move there by next week then?" The worry lines started to form on Mom's forehead.

"Yes and no." Meredith got up and brought the pitcher of water to the table to refill everyone's glasses. She seemed to be enjoying her little cat-and-mouse game much more than the rest of them. "I'm moving but not to Chicago."

They waited.

Meredith sat down and spilled all her news. "I get to work at home. I'll only have a few trips to Chicago every year. But I'm not going to live in this apartment. Remember that little cottage by Camp Autumn Brook on Whidbey Island? It's available! I can move in next week, and the best part is the rent is less than I pay for this little box."

Something inside of Shelly did a flip-flop. She loved that cottage. She was the one who had found it years ago when their family went over to nearby Whidbey Island for a picnic. Shelly had taken off on a hike with her elder sister Molly. That's when Shelly had found the cottage at the end of the lake.

Happy purple pansies and slender white Shasta daisies popped their heads out of the flower boxes that lined the front porch. Two rocking chairs waited for company. The window on the second story had shutters with a cutout in the shape of a tulip. Shelly christened it "Tulip Cottage" and for years talked about it as her cottage by the lake.

"How in the world did you manage to rent Tulip Cottage?" Shelly asked, an edge of hurt in her voice.

"Didn't I tell you? I called the camp. They have a new director, and he said he would keep his ears open for me. That was about a year ago. Then a realtor called today and said someone had given her my name regarding the cottage. The tenants are moving out tomorrow." Meredith laughed. "It's all too good to be true. Somebody pinch me!"

Shelly wanted to pinch her, all right. Ten years ago she would have. But they were grown women now. Friends. More than friends. Sisters. She should be happy for her sister. Her friend. After all, Shelly had been living her dream of being a flight attendant for five years now. Wasn't it time Meredith had her share of fairy dust sprinkled on her?

Mom, Dad, and Shelly stayed long enough to congratulate Meredith, help with the dishes, and hear the details about her new life. Shelly did a commendable job of being supportive and excited for her sister.

When they drove home, it was dark. Shelly felt strange sitting in the back seat of her parents' car again. It was as if her adult years had vanished and she was once again the child. Dad had always driven a Buick. This one was new, but the view from the back seat felt the same as it had that night when she was thirteen and had sat here on the way home from her junior high graduation party. Jonathan had sat next to her, nervously fidgeting in his black dress slacks and white starched shirt. He had taken off his necktie, tied it around his head sometime after the group photo was taken, and worn it that way during the entire party.

Shelly had chosen a blue dress for her graduation and the party. She had loved that dress. It was one of the few that hadn't been a hand-me-down. She had found it at the mall on a shopping trip with Mom, and it wasn't even on sale. Mom watched her try it on and then in her matter-of-fact way, she stated, "This is your graduation dress, Shelly."

Shelly remembered sitting in those stiff folding chairs at graduation and then walking up to receive her diploma in that ravishing blue dress. That's what it was, ravishing. Gorgeous. Stunning. She was sure it was the most elegant dress ever made. She was Princess Shelly, and at the graduation party she had believed it to be so.

Even in the back seat of Dad's old Buick on the way home from that party, Shelly remembered sitting demurely, sure that Jonathan would finally notice how stunning she looked. The scent of Dad's pine-tree air freshener collided with Jonathan's adolescent sweat. Mom rolled down the window an inch.

Just as Dad turned onto Sycamore and headed up the hill to Duchess Place, Jonathan faced Shelly and said, "Why do girls wear stuff like that?"

He might as well have told her he hated her dress, that he hated her. His hapless comment crushed her. She decided then and there that she would never speak to this insensitive male again.

Of course, she did speak to him again. They ran a neighborhood business together that summer. Anyone going on vacation who wanted his pets fed, plants watered, mail collected, or lawn mowed could hire Shelly and Jonathan. During one week they had had eleven houses to watch, which included seven dogs to walk and feed.

Shelly looked out the window of Dad's car as they cruised down Sycamore Drive and remembered the Klackameyer family, who used to live there in the white stucco house. Their dog, Mac, discovered the neighbor's trash the week Jonathan and Shelly were watching him, and the silly little Scottie nearly choked on a chicken bone. Jonathan had been so worried about the dog that he had taken Mac home and kept him in a box in his room.

The next morning Shelly awakened to Jonathan's whistle: two short, one long. She went to the window and pushed it open the rest of the way. The green bucket was coming toward her, swaying on its tight rope. Inside was a note: "Send dog biscuits."

Shelly signaled that she understood and ran downstairs for the box of doggie treats. Certainly Snoopy, their dachshund, wouldn't miss them, not at five-thirty in the morning. She loaded the box into the bucket and hoisted it back over to Jonathan's attic window. The bucket disappeared inside. Shelly went back to bed.

That afternoon the Klackameyers had come home early and, in a panic that their dog had been stolen, called the police. Shelly heard they were home. She got Jonathan, and they ran over with the dog. Jonathan told the police and the Klackameyers about the chicken bone and how he saved Mac's life. Right then, the little Scottie decided to regurgitate all the dog biscuits Jonathan had been feeding him since early that morning. That was the last time Shelly and Jonathan watched the Klackameyers' house and the last time they were let near the naughty Scottie.

Their summer business hadn't been a complete disaster, though. They each managed to walk away with more than two hundred dollars. Shelly saved hers. Jonathan bought himself a puppy. It was a cocker spaniel he named Bob. Bob had more personality than any dog Shelly had ever known. He loved to go to the tree house with them and he barked at every bird that ever came across his path. The only thing Bob didn't like was the one rather traumatic ride Jonathan gave him the week he bought Bob. Jonathan wrapped Bob in an old towel and sent him in the green bucket down the zip line into Shelly's bedroom. Bob was so frightened, he nipped at Shelly's hand when she tried to take him out. They never told either of their parents, and they never tried to pass live creatures down the zip line again. Except the one time Jonathan sent a toad to Shelly inside an empty Chips Ahoy bag.

Shelly snapped out of her reverie as Dad edged the Buick into the garage, carefully heading for the lemon yellow tennis ball hanging from the ceiling on a long string. He had put it there years ago so Mom would know how far to pull the car into the garage. When the tennis ball touched the windshield, the car would be in perfect position.

"Such good news about Meredith," Mom said as she climbed out of the car. "Looks as if we'll be able to move some of her things out of here just in time for you to move your boxes in."

Shelly looked around the two-car garage, which was an unusually large size for their forty-year-old house. Still, only one car could fit inside because the rest of the space was devoted to storage.

"I don't really have a lot," Shelly said. "I left quite a bit behind in Pasadena for Alissa." At the time she had packed quickly, and it seemed logical to simplify her life by bringing back home only what she absolutely wanted to keep. Now she was having second thoughts. Her old roommate would give back some of the furniture, Shelly was sure, but it wasn't likely to fit in the garage. Even after Meredith pulled her extra boxes out.

For the first time, Shelly felt a sense of loss from this move. She had never thought of herself as materialistic. Her life as an on-the-go flight attendant didn't give her much time at home to become attached to her belongings. Now that they were gone, she missed them.

"I have an early morning breakfast," Dad said, once they were inside the house. He hung his keys on the wooden holder by the back door and turned on the night-light in the hallway. "Do you ladies have plans?" Before they answered, he walked into the family room and turned on the television, clicking the remote to channel eight. His favorite news team was already five minutes into the nightly report. Shelly knew it would be useless to try to talk to him now. This was where he gleaned his best opening material for his Sunday morning sermons.

Shelly gathered the few bags she had brought in from her car earlier that day and carried them up to her room. With each step she wondered why this move had seemed like such a good idea a few weeks ago. It would have felt different if she had been coming home for a visit. Then everything would be wonderful and familiar in a charming sort of way. But with the thought of this being her abode for awhile, everything felt stagnant. She had fallen into a routine that was someone else's, not hers.

Shelly flopped onto the bed in her room, feeling much more exhausted than she should.

What's happening to me? I'm home for less than eight hours, and I've turned into a different person.

She felt the same way the next morning as she unloaded her rental trailer, stacking her boxes into the already full garage.

It's as if I'm admitting defeat. I left here determined to see the world and to make something exciting out of my life. Look where it got me. Right back where I started. The worst thing is, the only part of the world I've seen is Hawaii and Canada. Things certainly didn't go the way I had planned.

The exercise of unloading and the task of returning the trailer did her mind good. She needed to be busy. Shelly thrived on activity. She had a quick metabolism and could eat anything and not gain an ounce. She could stay up all night and still function at full capacity the next day. She even talked fast when she was excited.

Ever since she had driven into Seattle the day before, her metabolism seemed to have slowed down. She didn't want to eat. All she wanted to do was sleep. She even kept her shoes on when entering the house. In Pasadena Shelly was fastidious about leaving her shoes at the front entryway and requested her guests to do the same.

Even though she wasn't scheduled to fly for three more days, Shelly decided to go to the airport that afternoon and unofficially check in. The traffic into the airport at three in the afternoon was much thicker than she had remembered it. Parking was a bear, and by the time she arrived at the Sunlit Airlines office, she realized she would now be fighting the five o'clock traffic to reach home.

"I'm Shelly Graham," she said to the clerk at the front desk, showing her ID card. "I transferred from LAX. I'm not sure about my schedule. They told me it would be updated. Do you have a new schedule for me?"

"Let me check," the young man said. He went into the back office and returned with a handful of papers for her.

"Thanks." She turned to go and then decided to sit down on the couch and quickly check the schedule. It would be better to discuss changes while she was still here. The papers included a copy of her transfer forms along with a questionnaire. The last paper in the bunch was her schedule for the end of August and September.

"Reserve?" Shelly said aloud. She rose to her feet and marched back to the clerk. "I need to talk to the supervisor. This can't be right."

"First cubical on the left," he said. "You can go on back."

Shelly made her way to the cubical and looked around the corner. "Excuse me."

A short woman turned from her computer screen and looked at Shelly over the top of her half glasses. "Yes?"

"Hi," Shelly said, trying to win a new friend with her smile. "I'm sorry to bother you. I'm Shelly Graham. I just transferred from LAX. My schedule doesn't seem right. They listed me as reserve only. I have five years' seniority."

The woman took the paper from Shelly and looked it over. Slowly taking off her glasses she looked up at Shelly, scrunching her nose as she did. "This is right. They didn't tell you in L.A., did they?"

"Tell me what?"

"About the downsizing."

"Yes, they did. That's why I transferred up here. They were cutting back twenty percent of their flights out of LAX."

"Right," the woman said, "twenty percent out of L.A., twenty-two percent out of Phoenix, and thirty-one percent out of SeaTac."

"You're kidding," Shelly said. She leaned against the divider, feeling as if her sails had just been deprived of their wind. "This isn't right. I transferred here to get a better schedule. This is a junior schedule."

The woman checked the paper again. "You're listed as junior status."

Shelly looked up at the ceiling and shook her head. "Why didn't they tell me this before I accepted the transfer?"

"I don't know," the woman said. "I suppose they assumed most flight attendants understood the system."

Shelly couldn't tell if the woman's comment was a subtle criticism of her ability to understand the complicated hierarchy of this particular airline's ever-changing flight attendant status, or if the supervisor was trying to express sympathy for her situation.

"You're not the only one," the woman said. "We had a transfer from Phoenix yesterday who was on the reserve list, too. She was so upset she quit."

Shelly looked at the schedule. She wasn't mad enough to quit. She needed the job. No other alternatives seemed open to her.

"So what's going to happen?" Shelly asked. "Do they anticipate flights picking up once we hit the holiday season?"

"It's anyone's guess at this point. Your years with the airline are in your favor. Although I should tell you that in Seattle, five years isn't much toward seniority."

"So I've heard." Shelly remembered jokes they used to make in L.A. about the flight attendants in Seattle going to work in wheelchairs because so many of them had twenty or more years' seniority. Seattle was where most of the West Coast flight attendants planned to retire. Therefore it had become the base of choice several decades ago. Apparently the tradition lived on.

"This is really awful news. I just moved here yesterday. If I'd known, I would have stayed in L.A. This is completely unfair."

The woman nodded. "They should have told you."

25

Shelly let out a huff. "Well . . ." She forced a smile. "I guess I have a few phone calls to make." She held up the schedule and shook her head. "This is incredible."

The woman nodded in sympathy. "Welcome to SeaTac," she said as Shelly walked away.

3

Shelly fumed all the way home in the bumper-to-bumper traffic. "This is so unfair! I can't believe it. Maybe I can still get back on in L.A. or at another airport. I can't stay here. I'll go crazy sitting around Mom and Dad's just waiting for the phone to ring. I came here for some stability in my schedule, not to live on-call all over again. Something has to change."

She kept her flight schedule crisis to herself that night and phoned an old friend to see if she wanted to go to the movies. Wendy wasn't home, so Shelly left a message on her voice mail and tried Meredith. Her sister's lyrical voice answered on her machine. "Hi there! I'm so glad you called. I'll buzz you back as soon as I can."

Shelly didn't wait for the beep to end before she hung up. She had no message to leave. Obviously Meredith's life was too full to fit in more. Shelly didn't try to call anyone else until the next morning when Mom and Dad were out of the house.

After three hours of calls to Sunlit Airline's Los Angeles office and four of their other destinations, she gave up. She was stuck. No transfers were being considered, and rumor had it the San Jose Airport would discontinue all Sunlit flights by the end of the year.

Shelly, a woman who had never known depression, now came face-to-face with the monster and felt its fiery breath searing her soul. Everything had always gone her way. School work had come easily, and she had had an abundance of friends. Then she had been accepted into flight attendant school when she moved to Los Angeles and had quickly found a position with a small airline that was bought out a year later by Sunlit. For five years she had been on the go with flights full of interesting passengers and a social life full of friends.

In one short week the usually full flow of her life had been choked down to a pitiful trickle. She thought she was going to curl up and die.

Baking was Shelly's comfort. If she ever felt that things were out of control, she could whip up a batch of oatmeal chocolate chip cookies or her favorite cinnamon sweet snickerdoodles, and everything would be fine again. So, with determination, she now headed for her mom's kitchen and began her emotionally renewing exercise of baking.

Four hours and twelve-dozen cookies later, Shelly snapped the switch on the dishwasher, leaving the kitchen cleaner than she had found it. The pantry was filled with her cookie creations. She felt only a little better. And she had very little appetite for the cookies once they were baked.

Evening was coming. Another warm, gorgeous, Seattle summer evening. Mom and Dad would be home soon, but Shelly didn't want to be there when they arrived. It would be too easy to break down and tell them how her life was being slowly strangled to death.

Shelly slipped out the front door, locked it, and walked down the front steps to her Firebird parked along the curb. She was already thinking about selling her car to get out of its high monthly payments. She could buy a used car to bring down her expenses.

What really irked Shelly as she started the car and pulled away from the curb was that, after working for five years, she had little to show for it. She didn't even own this car. All of her salary had been swallowed up by high rent in Pasadena and living expenses. She had some money in an IRA and a little bit in a savings account, but that was it. She owned nothing and had very little to fall back on.

All the way to the mall she thought about how she shouldn't go shopping when she was depressed. Why put herself through that kind of temptation when she didn't have the money and didn't need anything? But she convinced herself that no harm could come from just looking. Besides, it wasn't the lure of buying something that led her to the mall. It was her need to be out doing something. She needed to be around people and to hear the noise. It had been far too quiet at the house all day.

Parking close to J. C. Penney's entrance, Shelly locked her car and headed into the mall with a sudden desire for Chinese food. The first place she went was the food court to buy some mandarin orange chicken at the Chinese fast-food bar. Settling down at a table in the middle of the food court, Shelly drank in the sights and sounds of all the people. This was the tonic she needed. She realized she needed people and activity to feel balanced.

Enjoying every bite of the chicken, Shelly forced herself to think about looking for another job. She had avoided that idea all afternoon during her baking fest, but the obvious had pushed so far to the front of her mind that she couldn't ignore it any longer.

Perhaps she could hire on with another airline. The question was how much of her seniority would transfer over. Possibly none. Would she have to start at the bottom again and be right where she was now, taking any and all flights offered to her? What was it she loved about flying any-how? She certainly hadn't traveled on her own as much as she had thought she would. It had to be the people. She loved people.

Now, what job would allow her to get her daily fill of being around people? As she examined the list in her mind, only a few possibilities rose to the top. A job at the mall was one op-tion. Or she could sign on with a temporary agency and do secretarial work. There was always the day-care center at church, or sales of some kind. She dismissed all the ideas and consoled herself with the possibility that things might change at the airline.

The next morning she felt even more hopeful when the air-line called and needed her for the day. She flew to Portland and back and then was let go because the next two flights were canceled. That's when something inside her snapped. She left the airport certain she couldn't endure this kind of limbo living. Instead of driving home, she went to Meredith's apartment.

Meredith looked surprised to see Shelly.

"Do you have anything to eat?" Shelly asked, walking past her sister and heading for the kitchen. "Whoa! What a mess!"

"I'm packing," Meredith said defensively, closing the door and picking her way through the maze of boxes. She fol-lowed Shelly into the kitchen. "Help yourself. There's not much to choose from."

"Mind if I have this?" Shelly pulled a frozen microwave dinner from the freezer and tore open the box.

"Go ahead." Meredith cleared a space on the counter and pulled herself up. "So, what's going on?"

Shelly read the back of the box, then tossed the frozen beef and noodles into the microwave and pushed the buttons. "Nothing. Absolutely nothing." She returned to the refrigerator and poured herself a glass of some kind of pink beverage. "What is this?"

"Pink lemonade."

Taking a cautious sip, Shelly leaned against the counter and swallowed hard. It wasn't the lemonade that made her face begin to pucker. It was the tears she was trying so hard to swallow.

"Too strong?" Meredith guessed. "Try adding some water."

Shelly added the water even though she knew the lemonade was fine.

"Why did you say nothing was happening? Aren't you supposed to be working?" Meredith asked. "Or don't you want to talk about it?"

"I don't know," Shelly answered flatly.

Meredith paused. She tucked her blond hair behind her ears and made another attempt at conversation. "You don't know what's going on, or you don't know if you want to talk about it?"

"Both."

"Then do you want to help me pack?" Meredith hopped down and pointed to the open boxes and stacks of packing paper that filled the living room. "I could use some help."

Shelly followed her sister into the jungle of disorganization and silently went about taking the pictures off the walls and wrapping them. They worked without a word until the timer went off on the microwave. Then, as if that were the starting bell for Shelly to spill her guts, she took off running with her words.

"I'm totally lost, Meredith. I've never felt like this before. I don't know what I'm supposed to do. I don't think I want to be a flight attendant anymore. They put me on reserve. Can you believe that? I have no schedule. I'm at the mercy of sick people and people who want to go on vacation. It's crazy! I refuse to sit around Mom and Dad's all day. I'm so depressed. What am I going to do?"

Meredith sat down on the arm of the couch. She looked shocked, and Shelly could imagine why. Meredith had never seen Shelly like this before. She had never seen herself like this.

"I'd start crying now," Shelly said, leaning against the wall that had just been emptied of all its pictures, "except my tears are so deep inside me they won't come up."

"You've been through a lot of changes," Meredith offered. "Maybe you're in some kind of shock. I didn't know about the airline schedule. Do Mom and Dad know?"

"Not yet."

"Here," Meredith moved some boxes off her couch. "Sit down. We can figure this out. It's just a big change in your life, that's all. You can handle this. You'll get a regular schedule soon."

Shelly numbly sat on the couch and shook her head. "I think the airline is going under." She had always been the confident big sister with Meredith. Never had she fallen apart like this and let her sister be the ministering angel of mercy.

"Are they going to be bought out?"

"I don't know. It's just a gut feeling I have. I really don't know what will happen, and I sure don't know what I should do."

"What's God telling you in your heart?" Meredith asked softly.

Shelly's mind went blank. "I don't know."

Shelly had always felt close to God the way she felt close to her dad. He was there, and she could access him if she needed him, but if she could figure things out herself, why bother either her father or God? She had prayed about this, of course, asking God to fix everything, and it had felt strange. She had never been at such a loss before.

"This is probably a dumb question," Meredith said, "but did you check with other airlines or see about being transferred?"

Shelly explained all her efforts.

Meredith crossed and uncrossed her bare legs. "I can see how you would feel stuck."

"Stuck," Shelly repeated. "That's what I am. Stuck. I've never been stuck before."

"Except in the mud," Meredith said, releasing her tinkling laughter over the memory. "Remember when you and I went out to the tree house that one Sunday after church? We got our good shoes stuck in the mud, and then Jonathan came and pulled them out with that big stick. We had to walk home in our stocking feet. It started to rain, and our best dresses were soaked. Do you remember?"

Shelly remembered. It brought little comfort, though. They got in trouble for ruining their clothes and going to the forest without telling anyone.

"I remember," Shelly said flatly.

"Oh, I can tell that little memory isn't one of your favorites," Meri said, settling herself on the couch and getting down to business. "Come on, let's figure out what you're going to do. If you can't stay with the airline, you need another job, right?"

"It's beginning to look that way."

"What do you want to do?"

"I don't know. That's the problem. I've hit a brick wall, Meri. I don't know what I want anymore. Everything in my life seems to have changed overnight. I wish my problems were as easy to solve as getting stuck in the mud."

"Do you wish anything else?"

"Like what?"

"Like," Meredith cautiously picked her words as if she were picking apples at the grocery store, "do you wish anything else had been different when you were living at home?"

"What are you getting at?" Shelly never could stand the roundabout games Meredith played when she had something on her mind.

Meri looked at Shelly. "There's something I think you should know."

"What?"

"The week after you moved to Los Angeles, Jonathan and I went out to dinner."

Shelly felt a tiny stab at the thought of Jonathan going out with her sister. "What does that have to do with anything?" Shelly remembered the way Meredith had tried to talk to her about Jonathan once before. Meri had called Shelly a week after she left for L.A., but Shelly hadn't thought her little, six-teen-year-old sister could tell her anything that would change her decision to leave home.

"I've never really told you what Jonathan said to me that night." Meredith looked intently at Shelly.

"That was five years ago. What does that have to do with losing my job?" Shelly heard the tension in her own voice and realized she was about to lose control.

Meri looked down at her hands and then back up at her sister. "Jonathan told me what happened between you two. He used the same words you just used. A brick wall. That's what he felt happened to him. That he hit a brick wall." She paused and looked concerned. Meredith resembled their mother at that moment, and Shelly didn't like it one bit. "Have you ever talked that whole situation through with anyone?"

Shelly found herself unable to answer. A huge lump clogged her throat. Tears brimmed on her eyelids. Where was all this emotion coming from? She was sure it must be the stress of moving and the job problems.

"I know you've never wanted to talk about it with me," Meredith said slowly. "And that's fine if you don't want to, but if you do, I think I understand better now than I did when I was so young. I'll listen if you want to work it through."

"There's nothing to talk through. That was a long time ago. I didn't come here to analyze my past," Shelly said, trying to ignore the lump in her throat. "I'm worried about my future."

Meredith nodded with sympathy. "It's just when you said brick wall, it took me back to Jonathan. Sometimes to find the key that will unlock the future, we have to see what keys we buried in the past."

The pressure building inside Shelly hit the bursting point. Tears raced down her cheeks. Her breathing turned into aching sobs. For the first time ever, she let herself cry over Jonathan.

4

"My hormones must be way off," Shelly finally managed to say in an effort to explain her emotional outburst.

"That's okay," Meredith said. "You're normal." She went for a box of Kleenex and a glass of water. Clearing a spot on the end table next to her futon couch, Meredith offered her sister the drink.

"Okay," Shelly said, clearing her throat. "This is obviously deeper than I had imagined. I suppose we could talk about it, although I don't know what good it will do. It was so long ago. It shouldn't matter this much."

"Apparently it does," Meri said softly.

"I guess it does. I don't regret my decision." Shelly wiped her dripping nose. "When I look back, I still think it was the only choice I could have made. Jonathan should have understood that. He was so strong about it being all or nothing. We were both so immature." Shelly took a drink of water. "What did he tell you?"

Meredith tilted her head and gave Shelly a compassionate look. "Jonathan's heart was broken. I don't know if you ever really understood that. He loved you. He knew you well enough to know you wouldn't change your mind. As he said, you were a brick wall, and you weren't going to move."

Shelly closed her eyes and leaned her head back. "How can anyone know what love is at eighteen?"

"Jonathan was pretty sure he knew," Meredith said.

Just then the phone rang. Meredith ignored it. On the third ring the answering machine picked it up in the kitchen. They could hear the caller's voice. "Hey, it's Byron. Just wanted you to know I'm running a little late. I'll be over in twenty minutes to help you pack. Call me if you want me to bring some food."

Meredith sprang from her seat and grabbed the phone. "Hi, I'm here. Would you mind coming over a bit later?" Meri listened for a few minutes and then said, "Just a sec. I'm going to change phones." She motioned to Shelly to hang up the extension in the kitchen as Meredith moved to the bedroom.

Shelly hung up for her sister. She had done that dozens of times before. Meri liked her privacy when she was on the phone. Shelly guessed that was about the only thing the youngest of four sisters could demand that the others would respect.

Returning to her spot on the couch, Shelly took another sip of water. She closed her eyes and heard her sister's words once more. *Jonathan was pretty sure he knew.*

Deep inside, a memory begged to be brought to the forefront of Shelly's thoughts. Too weary to ward it off, she let the memory come.

She was sixteen again, and she and Jonathan were sailing with his uncle off the San Juan Islands. The summer day had been clear and warm when they started, with white clouds skittering overhead. By two o'clock a high, thin layer of gray clouds covered the sky. Jonathan's uncle called them "doom and gloom" clouds. The wind kicked up as the boat moved back toward the harbor. The three sailors tacked their way furiously back and forth, trying to get the wind to cooperate with them rather than send them back to sea.

Shelly secured herself and held tightly to the rope Jonathan's uncle handed her. The water splashed over the side of the small craft, rising like a fountain and raining itself down on Shelly. She shivered but held the rope with all her strength. The thrill of the adventure ran all the way to her toes. She wasn't a bit frightened. Ever since she had overcome her fear of heights by climbing up into Jonathan's tree house, she had been drawn to daring escapades. When the carnival came to town, she was the one who wanted to ride the roller coaster one more time. This confrontation with nature made her skin tingle.

Shelly distinctly remembered the moment Jonathan's uncle said, "Now!" She let go of the rope, and the sail unfurled, catching the wind and turning the sailboat. All that power was harnessed and then unleashed. Shelly flashed her smile at Jonathan, and their eyes met.

His light brown hair caught the wind, too, and was blown back, fully exposing his stormy, gray eyes and his ignited smile.

In that moment, Jonathan transformed before Shelly's eyes. She didn't know what it was, but he looked different to her. Vastly different. And her heart responded to that change. Under those "gloom and doom" clouds, three weeks before their seventeenth birthdays, Michelle Annalee Graham realized for the first time that she was in love with Jonathan Charles Renfield.

It took Jonathan a little longer to realize the same. Shelly was pretty sure she knew when it was, though. About five months later, they were in his garage. Jonathan was under his car, an old Jeep Cherokee, trying to prove his manliness by changing the oil. Shelly had come over to collect a CD he had borrowed from her. She walked into his garage wearing a dress because her family was leaving in a few minutes for Meredith's flute recital. Jonathan asked her to hand him a socket wrench. She made a random choice of the tools before her and slapped it into his grease-streaked hand.

An instant later, Jonathan rolled out and said, "Hey! You got it right this . . ." The words stopped, but his mouth stayed open. He stared at Shelly.

"What's wrong with you?" she teased. The dress was nothing like her eighth-grade graduation outfit, but it was blue and it was short. Her hair was out of its usual ponytail, and the curls on the ends calmly rested just below her shoulders. She had put on makeup and borrowed some of Megan's earrings.

"So?" Shelly prodded Jonathan. "Are you going to give me my CD or not?"

"I . . . I'll bring it over later," he fumbled. "Where are you going?"

"Out," Shelly answered, deciding to make the most of the moment.

"With who?"

"With *whom*, silly. Wouldn't you like to know," she teased. Turning on her heels, she called over her shoulder, "Make sure you bring that CD back by tomorrow at the very latest. You can send it on the zip if it's not raining, but I want it by tomorrow."

Late bloomers, Shelly thought as Meri returned to the living room, apologizing for taking so long on the phone. *That's what Jonathan and I were. Late bloomers. All our friends were dating and going together, but I was seventeen before I gave up my tomboy ways. Jonathan held on to his naiveté longer than any guy I knew. He was too kind-hearted for his own good.*

Meri sat down, and the phone rang again. "I can't believe

39

this. I'll be right back." She disappeared into the bedroom again, and Shelly returned to her daydream.

Within five minutes after her family had returned from Meri's flute recital that evening, the doorbell rang. It was nine-fifteen on a school night. There stood Jonathan, showered, with his hair combed back, and wearing clean clothes. He held out the CD to Shelly and said, "Here you go."

"Thanks," she answered.

"Are you doing anything?"

Shelly remembered the way he looked. Nervousness was not a trait she had seen in him before. It only made her fall more in love with him.

They went for a walk around the block. In her heels, Shelly matched his height. Jonathan was wearing after-shave. The February night was chilly. Their hands found each other easily, and instantly Shelly felt warm inside and out. Neither of them spoke. There was no need for words, not when they already knew each other by heart. Shelly had never felt happier.

After they walked around the block, Jonathan delivered Shelly back to her door and said, "Would you like to go out Friday night?"

She nodded and gave him her radiant smile. "To the movies?" she asked. It was their common Friday-night activity already.

"No, I'd like to take you out to dinner. Someplace nice."

Meredith bustled through the trail of boxes and back to the couch. "I'm sorry. Let's get back to what you were saying." She looked at Shelly's face and said, "You look a little better. Are you okay?"

Shelly nodded. She knew a trace of a smile was on her lips. She couldn't help it. Falling in love for the first time — the only time — brought up sweet emotions. If she could only stop the memory there, she would be fine. It was what followed that ruined everything.

"You were saying you two couldn't really have been in love at eighteen." Meredith tucked her legs under her and looked at Shelly.

"Is that what I was saying? I forgot."

"Well, try to remember," Meri urged. "I think this must be pretty important to cause such a strong emotional response."

Shelly shook her head. The fiery emotions had subsided. "Maybe it was a sort of love. But, Meri, we were just kids. And I . . . well, . . . I . . . ."

"You wanted to see the world," Meri added for her.

Shelly lowered her head. "Yeah, I did."

"But you loved him, didn't you?"

Shelly looked up and met her sister's gaze. She had never explained her relationship with Jonathan in those words to Meri or anyone else in her family. Looking back, she knew it must have been obvious to everyone who saw them together.

Meredith wrinkled her small nose slightly and leaned forward. "There's no shame in loving somebody. It might help you to admit it."

"Yes," Shelly whispered, feeling the tears coming back. "I loved him."

"It's probably none of my business," Meredith said, "but just because I'm your pesky little sis and I have the right to be annoying, I have one more question. You still love him, don't you?"

Shelly's mind went blank. How could she answer that? She knew that, deep down, over all these years, there had been only one love in her heart. Jonathan. Only Jonathan. She had dated lots during her time in Los Angeles, but none of the guys ever came close in comparison. She had loved only one man. In a rare moment of reflection about a year ago, she had struggled with the possibility that he may be the only man she would ever love so deeply. She might fall in love again, and even marry and spend the rest of her life with some terrific man. But Jonathan would always be in a corner of her heart. Her first true love.

"I don't know," she answered Meredith.

"What's to analyze?" Meredith asked. "When you love someone, you know. If you don't, you don't."

If Shelly had had the emotional energy, she might have challenged her sister's simplistic comment. What did Meredith know of love? She had dated more guys than she could list. Shelly even remembered when Meredith had first claimed she was in love. Meri was eleven years old. He was a movie star. Even though their parents forbade the Graham girls to buy Hollywood star magazines, Meredith borrowed copies from her friends at school and paid them for tear-out posters of her "true love."

No, Meredith knew nothing of what Shelly meant when she spoke of heart-knit-to-heart kind of love. Meri couldn't possibly understand what Jonathan and Shelly had, or why their relationship had to be all or nothing — and, therefore, had become nothing.

"I know you mean well," Shelly said. "But this isn't getting me anywhere. Right now my problems revolve around my job. Where am I going to work? Where am I going to live? What changes do I need to make, and what are my choices? I don't see how dredging up all these memories of Jonathan and trying to get me to define what I once felt for him are going to help me at all right now."

"You're probably right," Meredith said, pulling back. "It's just that when you said you felt like you had hit a brick wall, it reminded me of Jonathan and how torn up he was when you left. Don't you ever wonder where he is?"

"Sometimes."

"We could probably track down his parents to find out," Meredith suggested. "Where did they move to?"

"The Bahamas," Shelly said.

"It might be worth a try. For curiosity's sake, if nothing else."

"What would be the point?" Shelly asked quickly.

They sat silently for a moment. Meredith seemed to be reviewing her options. She chose not to challenge her sister again.

"Well, I should help you start packing," Shelly said, releasing her tension in a big breath. "We're not going to solve my problems sitting here when neither of us has the answers. We might as well solve your packing problems. At least you have a place to go and a job waiting for you."

Shelly didn't mean for the last line to carry a bite the way it did. She was happy for Meri and immediately caught herself by saying, "I'm sorry. I didn't mean for it to sound like that. I'm glad everything is working out for you."

The phone rang again. Meri excused herself to answer it, and Shelly busied herself wrapping pictures.

"She's right here," Meredith said, holding the phone out to Shelly. "It's Mom."

"Oh, good," Mom said when Shelly picked up the phone. "I wondered where you were. You received a phone call here from the airline. I didn't know if you needed to call them back right away, but they said something about calling by five."

"Thanks. I'll call them. Did they leave a number?" Shelly wrote the number down on the side of a packing box with a wide marking pen she found on the counter. "Thanks, Mom."

Shelly dialed the number and waited. A recording came on

asking her to wait. When a human voice answered, Shelly explained that she had been asked to call. Everything about the Seattle system was different from LAX's. When she called in there, she knew the people by first name, and they knew who she was. This stressed voice spoke with her only long enough to ask if she could work a red-eye flight to Philadelphia that night.

Her spirits instantly picked up when she agreed and promised to be there in forty-five minutes.

"Things might be working themselves out," Shelly said after she hung up. "I have a flight. I need to leave, though. Sorry I couldn't help more."

"That's fine. Byron said he would come if I needed him."

"Are you and Byron getting serious?" Shelly asked as she looked for her keys.

"Byron and me? Are you kidding? He's a lug. A sweet lug, but a lug. He went out with Trina from work, but she gave him the cold shoulder. Now he's crying on my shoulder. That's what the long conversation was about. I told him I wasn't interested in dating him, but he said he still wanted to help me move. I think he needs to be needed."

"Don't we all," Shelly muttered, moving around the packing paper on the kitchen counter. "Have you seen my keys?"

"No. Don't forget your microwave dinner. Do you still want it?"

Shelly opened the microwave and checked under the cardboard lid. The noodles had turned to mush, and the beef had a gray tinge to it. "No, and I don't recommend that you eat it either."

"Here are your keys," Meri said, lifting up the key chain from the top of a packing box by the front door. "What would you do without me?"

Shelly granted her little sister the smile of approval

Meredith seemed to be hoping for. "I don't know. What would I do without you?"

"Call me when you get back," Meri said as Shelly left the apartment.

Shelly drove through a fast-food taco place before entering the freeway. With each bite of her burrito, she assured herself things were looking up. They had called her to work tonight. Maybe she would actually end up with more hours on reserves.

In the back of her mind, Shelly heard the word *Bahamas*.

"That's silly," she muttered aloud. "I would never call the Renfields to ask about Jonathan. Never."

5

The passengers on the red-eye were placid, and the flight went without a hitch. The plane was nearly full, which was somewhat unusual but a good sign for the airline. Most of the passengers were families on summer vacations.

Dirk, the flight attendant whom Shelly shared the shift with, was overly cheerful and seemed a little too eager to welcome her on his usual flight. Shelly ignored his attempts at flirting and went about her job. She liked being on the longer flight. It was good to feel busy.

Not until about halfway through the return trip did she start to feel tired. She had stayed on the ground at the hotel the required eighteen hours and had managed to catch almost six hours of sleep, but now she was feeling rundown.

While the movie played, Shelly sat in the pull-down seat nearest the porthole in the back door. They were flying above the clouds, somewhere over Idaho, she guessed. She leaned over and contentedly gazed at the endless field of white fluff that spread out before them. This was the part of flying she loved most — the clouds. Always changing. So peaceful and beautiful. They reminded her of a meadow of freshly fallen snow. Only in a meadow, someone could walk through and leave footprints in the perfect snow. No one could walk through the clouds. No human could mar their perfection.

She remembered the first time she had decided she loved clouds. She had been with Jonathan in the tree house. They must have been close to twelve years old. Her poetic side was just beginning to sprout its wings. She was perched on the strong branch that jutted out of the top of the tree house, and Jonathan was busy with a hammer repairing the boards that had warped during the spring rains. Shelly had been watching the clouds perform their lazy May dance through the bright green leaves. "They're like a field of cotton stuffing," she said. "And no one can make them come or go."

"Are you going to help me or not?" Jonathan said.

Shelly ignored him and lingered on the branch, feeding her newly born poetic self by trying to describe the clouds in as many ways as she could.

That night, Shelly's older sisters had sat her down and given her a lecture about playing in the woods with Jonathan. They said if Mom and Dad didn't see the danger in it, they certainly did. At twelve, Shelly was too old to act like a tomboy. She needed to know that being alone with Jonathan was only giving him an invitation to kiss her.

The thought shocked Shelly. Kissing Jonathan would be like kissing her brother. Why would she do that? He wouldn't think of kissing her, either. She was sure of it.

As it was, nearly four years after the lecture Shelly began to think seriously about kissing a guy. She didn't know when Jonathan started to think about kissing her. It might have been when they were twelve. Or when they were seventeen and went for their hand-holding walk around the block. But he didn't act on it until he was eighteen.

"Shelly?" Dirk reached over and shook her shoulder. "Are you ready?"

"Oh, sorry. I must have dozed off. Sure. Is the beverage

cart ready, or do you want me to finish loading it?"

"It's all set."

Shelly rose and followed Dirk down the aisle, still trying to adjust her thoughts to catch up to the task at hand. "Something to drink for you?" she asked the passengers in the first row. Shelly began the familiar motions of pouring beverages and delivering them to the passengers with a smile. From then on everything was routine.

The flight landed at eleven-thirty in the morning, right on time. Shelly drove to her parents' home in light traffic, which was a nice change. She couldn't wait to take a hot bath and sleep.

Mom had left a note on her bed. "Call the church immediately." Shelly complied, and when the secretary answered, she said, "Oh, Shelly, your parents have been so worried about you. Are you okay?"

"Yes, why?"

"Your father's right here." The secretary put him on the phone.

"Hi, Daddy."

"Where have you been?"

"I got a call to take a red-eye to Philadelphia a couple of days ago. I just got back."

He was silent for a moment. "Your mother and I didn't know where you were."

"I work," Shelly said cautiously. "This is how my schedule goes sometimes. Mom knew I received a call from the airline. She called me at Meri's a couple of days ago."

"Meri's been gone, too," Dad said. "Or not answering her phone. We were concerned, that's all."

Shelly felt her life being pinched. It was bad enough to be home, trying to overlap her routine and habits with her parents', but for her parents to check on her like this was frustrating. For five years she had come and gone as she pleased at all hours of the day. Living at home with Mom and Dad was not going to work.

"I'll check on Meri," Shelly said. "Don't worry. I'm sure she's fine. She's been busy packing."

"As long as you're okay, that's all that matters. I'll let your mother know."

"Yes, I'm fine. Thanks, Dad." Shelly hung up and gave Meredith a call at work.

"Mom and Dad were worried about us," Shelly said when her sister came on the line. "Can you believe that? Are they like this all the time?"

"It goes in spurts," Meredith said. "Sometimes for a couple of weeks I don't hear from them. Then, all of a sudden, they decide they have to know exactly where I am and what I'm doing. I knew Mom called yesterday, or was it the day before? Anyway, with packing and finishing up everything at work, I haven't been returning my calls."

"When is your last day at work?"

"Tomorrow."

"Are you excited about your new job?"

"I feel like Cinderella," Meri said. "This is a huge leap for me. And getting into the lake cottage at the same time — I feel as if I'm dreaming."

"Meri," Shelly said cautiously. She hadn't planned out her words yet, but the thought had hedged its way into her mind when she first heard Meri was moving into the Tulip Cottage. "How would you feel about a roommate?"

There was a pause.

"You don't have to answer right away. Just think about it. I would hardly be there; so I don't think I'd be in your way or anything."

Shelly wished she hadn't mentioned the possibility. She

felt strange asking her sister for a favor. Meri had always been the one who asked Shelly to bail her out.

"I can't believe you're asking me," Meri said. "I kept wanting to suggest that you move in with me, but I thought you would think I was trying to run your life or something."

"Why would you think that?"

"You've never needed anything from me. It felt strange being the one in the position to give you something. Remember last May when I was going to send you that cookbook I found at The Elliott Bay Book Company? It was called *A World of Favorite Cookie Recipes*, and I was so excited about it because I knew how much you loved to bake."

Shelly vaguely remembered.

"I called you all jazzed about it," Meredith said. "And you said you already had it."

"So?" Shelly couldn't figure out where this was leading.

"So, you always have everything. When we were growing up, you had all the right clothes. You had all the right ideas. You had all the answers to everything. I'm not trying to be mean, but you don't need anyone or anything. I decided when I called you and you said you already had the cookie book that that was the last time I was going to try to give you anything. I know you don't intend to, but, Shelly, you push people away."

Shelly didn't know what to say.

"Don't get mad."

"I'm not mad," Shelly said. "I'm trying to figure out what you're telling me."

"Maybe I'm saying it too powerfully. I think I'm the one with the hormone rush today. Or maybe it's all this stress. Anyway, all I'm trying to say is, I want into your life. I'd love to have you live with me at the lake. I'm just asking that you want me to be in your life, too." Meredith drew in a deep

breath, then kept talking before Shelly had a chance to respond. "I felt things were really improving between you and
me the other day. Do you realize that was the first time we
have ever talked seriously about Jonathan?"

"Is this a yes?" Shelly asked. She wasn't comfortable with
this sudden evaluation from her sister. She had always
thought they had a terrific relationship and had never seen
herself as holding back.

"Yes," Meredith said firmly. "Yes, I want you to move in
with me, and yes, I want you to keep letting me into your life.
Is it a deal?"

"It's a deal. When do you move?"

"This weekend. You scheduled to fly then?"

"No, not yet. If I don't get called, I'll move in with you on
Saturday."

"Good." Meredith let out a sigh. It was a happy sigh.
"This is going to be great. I have the rent covered the first few
months, so why don't you plan to start paying your half when
we hit November."

"You sure that would work out?"

"Yes. I wasn't planning on sharing the rent. I have the
bucks this time. Maybe you'll end up carrying me for a couple
of months another time."

"Thanks, Meredith. I really appreciate this."

"Are you kidding? I'm the one who's excited. You don't
know how long I've hoped we could be sisters again like this."

After Shelly hung up, she headed for the bath she had been
promising herself. Soaking up to her chin, she thought over
her sister's words. What did Meri mean about hoping they
could be sisters again?

Shelly realized her crazy, come-and-go schedule had made
it hard for her to keep track of things over the past five years.
She had missed more than one family member's birthday be-

cause of her flight schedule. Sometimes she didn't even know what day it was. Her move to Seattle was supposed to bring some stability. And maybe it would, eventually.

The move to Whidbey Island would do her good, and she felt certain the hour commute by ferry wouldn't bother her. It was a small price to pay for the luxury of living in such natural beauty.

It was funny, but Jonathan had always said he wanted to live on one of the islands. At a camp. Shelly smiled to herself. *How strange that my life is turning out to be a fulfillment of Jonathan's dreams. I'm going to live on an island, right next to a camp. I never would have guessed it.*

As the steaming water ministered to her tired frame, Shelly allowed herself the luxury of sinking deeper than ever into her thoughts of Jonathan. *Why have I been so obsessed with him lately? It's not as if I've never thought about him since I left. But he always seemed so removed, so permanently gone from my life. Here, he's real. Ever present. Jonathan Renfield is so tightly woven into the fabric of my past that I can't have a future here without constantly being confronted with his memory. It's probably a good thing I'm moving out of this house and starting fresh on Whidbey. I have only one memory of Jonathan from that island, and that memory . . .*

Shelly could feel the battle break out inside her heart. One side defended her right to never recall that night, the other side charged into her emotions, waving the glittering memories and shouting at Shelly, "Remember! Let yourself remember!"

She gave in.

Pressing the hot-water faucet with her toes, Shelly invited more warm water into her chilling tub. With the flow of bath water came the tandem flow of her long-stopped-up memories of that starlit night on Whidbey Island.

Exactly one week after they both graduated from high school, they had summer jobs. They had been officially dating ever since the night of Meredith's flute recital and their hand-holding walk around the block. That was February; this was the middle of June. They hadn't fought once. They held hands every time they were together. Everyone thought they were "cute." When they kissed, it was as if the world around them turned into a spring garden, and the fragrance of that garden lingered on their lips long after the kiss ended.

Shelly closed her eyes and remembered Jonathan's kisses. Oh, man, could he kiss. Even their very first kiss had been tender, sweet, and not at all awkward. He didn't first kiss her in the tree house, as her older sisters had warned. It was at the front door after their first official date to the movies. Unlike their videotaped kiss as toddlers, this kiss was right on target.

The kiss took Shelly's breath for a moment and then returned it. Only it wasn't the breath she had breathed all her life. Jonathan's kiss had filled her lungs with a fresh hope. For weeks afterward, she found herself daydreaming about Jonathan, drawing in deep draughts of air and holding her breath, remembering the sensation of their first kiss.

In Shelly's estimation, it was in every way the perfect first kiss. It was the first kiss for both of them, and because they knew it, they treasured the gift even more. And like fine treasure, they gave their kisses to each other sparingly, neither of them willing to hurry the other. Their love, this pristine first love, was far more than "cute." To Shelly it was sacred. Perhaps that's why it had frightened her so and caused her to do what she did.

6

Adjusting herself in the just-right bathwater, Shelly turned her memory to the June night on Whidbey Island when everything changed in her relationship with Jonathan.

He had told her he had a surprise date planned, something he had been working on for quite some time. Shelly left work at a Hallmark gift shop at four that afternoon. Jonathan said he would pick her up. He arrived in his friend's truck, with a tarp covering something in the back. He refused to answer questions as they drove toward the harbor and got in line for the ferry to Whidbey Island. They sat in the cab of the truck with the engine off, in the line of bumper-to-bumper cars, waiting for the next ferry.

Shelly gave up trying to figure out Jonathan's scheme and began to tell him her big news. That morning's mail had brought the letter she had been waiting for. She had been accepted at flight attendant school and had her choice of start dates. She had talked about this for a long time, so Jonathan seemed only slightly surprised that she had heard back. Even when she told him that the flight school was in Los Angeles, he didn't seem ruffled.

"It's only for six weeks," Shelly told him. "I'm already thinking that most of the money I'm making at my summer job will end up going for my phone bill. I thought we could set a regular time each day, and that way we'll stay caught up on everything with each other. It won't even seem like I'm gone. It'll go fast."

Jonathan had only smiled that unsinkable smile of his and nodded at her suggestions. She talked about which session might be best: August or October. The next session started in four days, and that, of course, was too soon. Jonathan listened but said little.

Finally he let the words he seemed to be holding inside tumble from his upturned lips. "Life is a mystery. We never know what lies ahead in our path."

At the time Shelly had thought it strange. A quirky poetic thought that seemed to fit where Jonathan's head had been lately. As much as he loved the outdoors and talked about going to school to study forestry, a new side of Jonathan was emerging, a melancholy side. Sometimes he would put his arm around Shelly when they sat together at the movies or at home, and he would quietly hum in her ear. He had even bought a CD of classical love songs. She liked it. She liked their young love. She liked having Jonathan in her life. Shelly knew he would always be there for her.

Whenever she had tried to picture where the path was leading, she had seen Jonathan going off to college at Humboldt. Her senior picture in a brass frame would sit on his desk, and he would smile at her every time he passed by. They would talk long hours on the phone whenever she landed long enough to call. She would tell him all about the exciting places she had been and the things she had seen. Jonathan would listen. He always liked to listen to her. Then he would coax her to come home to Seattle for Christmas, and they would walk together on those long, dark, wintry nights.

It had seemed logical and likely to Shelly that their hearts would travel together down a long, straight, unbumpy road for many, many years while each of them explored their interests and lived out their dreams. They would always know the other would be there.

Shelly remembered how the ferry line had moved forward, and they had nudged the borrowed truck into the belly of the craft. Her eyes were full of stardust that evening as they climbed up to the deck and braced themselves against the wind off the amber waters. The bold Seattle skyline shrunk as the ferry carried them to Whidbey Island. Clouds gathered overhead like cancan dancers ready to fan their wide, frilly skirts the moment the spotlight from the setting sun hit them.

Shelly and Jonathan drove off with the weary residents who were eager to be home. Jonathan knew right where he was going, which was typical of him. The truck stopped at a public park. He got out, undid the tarp, and pulled out their two bicycles.

"But I'm wearing a skirt," Shelly moaned.

Jonathan smiled and handed her a grocery bag carefully folded at the top. Inside were a pair of her jeans, a deep green sweater, a pair of socks, and her tennis shoes. "Your mom packed it for me," Jonathan explained.

Shelly changed in the restroom and emerged looking like a model for an Eddie Bauer catalog. Off they rode, Jonathan leading the way as if he had this all planned out. The trail led them through a grove of marvelous, sturdy evergreens, past cottages, and up a very steep hill. At the top they stopped to rest by a video-rental store, and Jonathan urged Shelly to keep pedaling two more blocks. There stood their destination, a charming restaurant called "Rondi's," complete with an outdoor patio trimmed with tiny twinkling white lights. They found a table and caught their breath.

Jonathan smiled all through their gourmet dinner. Fresh

salmon, Shelly remembered, with an almond glaze. For dessert they shared a slab of angel-food cake drizzled with fresh raspberry sauce. The raspberries, they were told, were from Rondi's garden.

Every detail from that night returned to Shelly as she soaked in the tub. She hadn't thought of any of this for years. The way their knees touched under the small table; the way Jonathan's usually stormy, gray eyes had shone golden in the light of their table candle; the way he had put down his fork and cleared his throat.

"Michelle," he said. It was the only time she remembered his ever using her given name. "I've given this a lot of thought. I've talked to my parents, and I've talked to your dad."

Her heart had begun to pound then. She remembered the way Jonathan calmly reached across the table and enveloped her small hand with his.

"I love you," he whispered, looking deep into her eyes. "I've always loved you." With his free hand he reached inside the pocket of his jeans and held out, in the palm of his hand, a delicate diamond ring. "Will you marry me?"

Shelly remembered all too well the sensation that followed. All the breath had been sucked from her lungs. Not as it had when he first kissed her. That time the breath returned sweeter, fresher. This time she had to gasp for air, pulling it from the shrinking atmosphere all by herself. Jonathan could not give this breath back to her.

"What are you saying?" she had finally managed.

"I want to marry you. This summer. If my final acceptance comes through for Humboldt, we'll move there in the fall. I've already checked into their student housing. If you work full-time and if we accept the loan my parents have offered us, we should do just fine."

"What — what about my flight school?"

"That will always be there," Jonathan said. "You can enroll anytime. You even said so today. Maybe you can go next summer or after I get my degree. I'm thinking of the long term here, Shel. I know we can make it together. I can't go away to school without you. I don't want to wait four years to marry you. Don't you see? This is the best way for us."

Shelly's mind had clouded over so that she felt like a ship lost at sea. She had no idea which way to turn to find safe harbor. "Our parents agreed to this?"

Jonathan nodded eagerly. "Your dad was a little surprised, but he understands my reasons for not wanting to wait. My parents love you. You know that. They're all for it. That's why they offered us a loan."

Shelly pushed back in her chair so their knees no longer touched. She slowly extracted her hand from his. Her head was bent, her eyes staring at the dainty ring still offered in his palm.

"Shel?"

It took her a long time to find the words. "No," she finally managed in a hoarse whisper. "I can't. I just can't."

She watched as Jonathan's strong fingers slowly closed on the ring like an oyster protecting its pearl. She couldn't look at his face.

Neither of them spoke for a painful stretch of time. Shelly felt like apologizing. She wanted to cry but had no tears that would show themselves in this semipublic setting.

Jonathan paid the bill, unlocked their bikes, and led the way down the steep hill, past the placid cottages and through the somber forest of evergreens that watched them with boughs bent in the twilight.

Once the bikes were secure in the bed of the truck, they drove to the harbor, still shrouded in silence. Right before they were signaled to drive up the plank into the ferry, Shelly let loose. Everything inside her gushed out.

"Why didn't you discuss this with me before talking to our parents and buying a ring and everything? Doesn't my opinion matter? And what about my dreams? You know how long I've wanted to go to flight attendant school. How can you treat that as if it were nothing, and put your dreams and aspirations ahead of mine? Haven't we always been friends who shared everything with each other? Why did all that change? Suddenly you have to make all the decisions, and you have to have it all figured out, and you don't even think about consulting me! How can you say you love me? You don't even respect my opinion enough to ask for it!"

When Shelly stopped to catch her breath, the tears were streaming from her eyes. The boat was in motion, crossing the water, but instead of getting out of the truck and going up on top, the two of them remained fixed in the cab with the windows rolled up tight.

Jonathan jumped in the moment she paused and let loose with his own bottled-up hurt. "Where did you think our relationship was leading? You can't tell me you never thought about getting married right away. I know you must have. That's all I've thought about for weeks. Months, maybe. I planned everything. Everything! All you had to do was say yes! Why do you have to be so stubborn and insist on having everything your way?"

It was the worst fight the two of them had ever had. If there had been something for Shelly to throw at Jonathan in the cab of that truck, she would have thrown it. All she had were her words, and she heaved them at him until it seemed there was no breath left inside of her.

The ferry docked. They drove home with the silence hanging like a noose around their necks. One false move and they would be choked. Jonathan parked in front of his house. He turned off the engine and faced Shelly. She let his stormy gaze rain its misery all over her. It didn't matter. Everything was ruined. She was so mad at Jonathan Charles Renfield she could have slugged him.

His voice came to her across the openness on the bench seat that separated them. It was not a tame voice. "You know I'll always love you," he said.

Shelly didn't answer with words. Instead, she did something she had never expected to do. In one movement she went from her side of the cab to Jonathan's, and for the first time ever, she initiated a kiss. Not an innocent, gentle kiss like the ones they had strewn like wildflowers through their young love. This was a forceful, angry kiss, as if she were greedy to get back from him the perfect, simple love he had destroyed with his proposal. She kissed him hard.

He put his arms around her and tried to hold her, but Shelly pulled away with all her might. She caught only a glimpse of his face as she kicked open the passenger door and fled, but his look haunted her for months. It was as if she had cut loose his emotional moorings and sent him drifting out to sea without a sail.

What tortured Shelly the most as she sat in the now-tepid bathwater and let her tears cascade down her cheeks, was the shame she felt. She left home two days after that emotionally destructive night because there was an immediate opening at the flight school. She had started fresh in Los Angeles, as if Jonathan had never existed. The only thing that haunted her was her impulsive, aggressive kiss. Never would she have guessed she had that kind of fire inside her or the audacity to assault her best friend with such a misuse of her passion.

She had asked forgiveness from God a hundred times. She had never asked anything of Jonathan. They hadn't spoken since.

The only communication she had had with Jonathan in the last five years was a letter he had written her that fall. The return address was Boulder, Colorado. Apparently Humboldt hadn't worked out. She had read the letter only once, very quickly, then stuffed it back in the envelope and buried it in the bottom of her box of mismatched sheets of stationery. She had never taken it out again, and she had never written to him.

Shelly pulled herself from the tub and placed her dripping wet foot on the fluffy yellow bathroom rug. Drying off quickly and wrapping up in her robe, Shelly went down to the garage and scanned the stack of boxes until she found the one she was looking for. She carried it up to her bedroom. Sitting cross-legged on the rug where the filtered light streamed in, bringing a chorus line of tiny, dancing dust fairies, Shelly tore off the packing tape and opened the box marked "Desk Stuff."

7

The old box of mismatched stationery was halfway down on the right side. Shelly pulled it out and dumped its contents onto the floor. The last bit of paper that fluttered out was the envelope from Jonathan.

Shelly slowly ran her finger across his name and return address. She remembered how nervous she had felt the day the letter arrived. She had had some friends over and hoped none of them noticed the way her face flushed when she brought in the mail and saw the letter from Jonathan. Excusing herself from her friends for a moment, Shelly had gone into her bedroom, closed the door, and with shaking fingers, opened the envelope.

Now, on this quiet Seattle afternoon, Shelly once again went through the motions of pulling the single sheet of crisp onion-skin paper from the envelope.

Dear Shelly,

Your parents tell me you are doing well and enjoying your new position with the airlines. I'm glad you're getting to do what you always wanted to. This letter is only to wish you the best always.

I found this poem by Michael Drayton while doing research for my English lit. class. I had to send it to you. He wrote it more than four hundred years ago, but when I read it, I thought it could have been written four months ago.

Please know that I will always consider you my very best friend.

Jonathan

Shelly blinked back the tears and read the poem again that he had so carefully copied at the bottom of the page.

The Parting
Since there's no help, come let us kiss and part —
Nay, I have done, you get no more of me,
And I am glad, yea, glad with all my heart,
That thus so cleanly I myself can free.
Shake hands forever, cancel all our vows,
And when we meet at any time again,
Be it not seen in either of our brows
That we one jot of former love retain.
Now at the last gasp of Love's latest breath,
When, his pulse failing, Passion speechless lies,
When Faith is kneeling by his bed of death,
And Innocence is closing up his eyes
— Now if thou wouldst; when all have given him over;
From death to life thou might'st him yet recover.

Shelly's response to reading the poem this time was vastly different from what it had been that evening long ago in her California bedroom. That first time, she had taken great offense at the words. She imagined Jonathan was having the last dig by saying through the long-dead poet that he was done with her and glad it was over. She had read between the lines that if they should ever meet again, he would act as if there had never been any love between them. The deepest sting of his letter had come when he said he considered her his best friend.

That was the day Shelly cut her memories in half and stored them deep in the treasure chest of her heart. The love she had for Jonathan, the innocent, pure, and true first love, went on the bottom of the trunk. It was as if she had pressed it down as flat as she could and loaded the rest of the trunk with the carefree childhood memories of growing up with Jonathan, the memories that carried no remorse. Then, when it became painful to look even at those, Shelly closed the lid and tucked the treasure box far away from her everyday life.

Now she realized that everything had changed when she came home to Seattle less than a week ago. That first day in her room, all the light memories on top had floated out the minute she opened that invisible trunk. Now, only days later, she finally allowed herself to free the very bottom layer. And in her examination of those painful love remembrances came the urge to read the letter for the second time in five years.

From this reading came new understanding. "Now if thou wouldst; when all have given him over; From death to life thou might'st him yet recover," she read again aloud.

Was he trying to say it still wasn't too late? Folding the letter and letting it drop to her lap, Shelly looked up at the ceiling and whispered, "Is it possible, God? Was I too stubborn or too hurt to see this before?"

The silent, painted clouds didn't answer.

"Is Meredith right? Have I pushed people away from me? Has my urge for independence blinded me to others?"

The possibility was too sharply painful for her. She repelled it. All that entered her heart was the clear and life-giving thought that perhaps somewhere Jonathan still waited for her.

It was a fanciful thought, she knew, one that she kept to herself during the next week and a half while she moved into the Tulip Cottage. Right after moving in, she flew two days and stayed over in Denver to sleep between flights. It seemed a subtle torture to be so near Boulder, where Jonathan had lived when he wrote the letter, but not to have the time to drive there. Not that she knew what she would do if she did go there. See the university Jonathan attended? Maybe. Or drive by the address from the letter and picture what window he had looked out of as he wrote to her.

There was always the slightest chance that Jonathan still lived in Boulder. On a whim, Shelly scanned the Denver phone book in her hotel room. No Jonathan Renfield was listed. She called information for Boulder. It had no Renfields listed. Jonathan could be anywhere. He could be in Seattle, for all she knew. The only way to track him down would be to find his parents in the Bahamas and give them a call.

Shelly thought about asking her mom if she had the Renfields' address on her Christmas list. But Mom would want to know why Shelly asked. Mom wouldn't come right out and quiz Shelly, but Shelly knew the looks and that those looks would torture her for many months.

Those same looks had tortured her the first time her parents visited her in Pasadena. Shelly had explained very little to them about why she had turned down Jonathan's proposal. She said she didn't feel ready to get married, and since she and Jonathan were so close, it had to be an all-or-nothing relationship. There wasn't room for a casual friendship. Her parents seemed satisfied with her explanation.

If she brought up Jonathan now, they would definitely

want more information. As much as her dad loved Jonathan, he would probably want to help her locate him and push them together again.

Shelly wasn't ready for that. She wasn't sure what she was ready for, but whatever it was, she had to think it through carefully. Jonathan could be married, for all she knew. Although she probably would have heard if he were. That kind of news always managed to get to her mom through the congregation.

While flying home from Denver, Shelly had a plane change and layover in San Francisco. She stopped in a bookstore inside the airport and found a book that fed her current interest. It was entitled *A Collection of England's Best Poetry*. The piece by Michael Drayton was on the first page.

It felt good to land at SeaTac and drive home to the little Tulip Cottage that Indian-summer evening. Shelly and Meredith had made quick work of the move in and had been glad to see how large each of the bedrooms was. They agreed that the third bedroom, located in the loft, should be Meredith's office. Mom gave them the old patio furniture, which they painted a fresh white and set up on the front porch. Shelly had a unique dining-room table she had made herself from a stumplike slab of wood and a custom-cut circle of glass. Meredith gladly turned her old, pressed-wood table into a potting table, which they set up in the tiny mudroom off the back of the house.

As Shelly's Firebird rumbled down the short, gravel drive that led to their enchanted cottage, she noticed her parents' Buick parked out front. It was almost seven on a Thursday evening. Shelly thought maybe Dad had finally come over to help them figure out the electrical wiring in the living room. The ceiling fan insisted on twirling anytime a switch was flipped on — even the garbage-disposal switch.

Parking her car and pulling her small, black, wheeled bag from the trunk, Shelly entered the house with a cheerful smile.

"Anybody home?" she called out.

Both her parents and Meredith were seated at the table with a steaming bowl of pasta before them.

"You're home!" Meredith said. "I thought you had a flight."

"I did. Two of them. I'm back."

"I never could keep track of your schedule," Meredith said.

"You really should call," Mom urged gently.

"Have a seat," Dad said, getting up and offering Shelly his chair.

"That's okay. I'll grab a plate and set myself up over here by Mom. So, what are you guys up to?"

"We were eager to see your new place," Mom said. "Meredith didn't know your schedule, so we went ahead and made plans to come on a night that was free for us. We didn't know when you would be home."

"Well, here I am!" She sat down and helped herself to the pasta. Shelly had learned long ago the fine art of deflecting her mom's gentle digs. "What do you think? Pretty cute place, isn't it?"

"Wonderful," Dad said.

"You've both done a fine job fixing it up," Mom said. "Is it mostly Meredith's furniture and things? You didn't seem to bring very much back with you from Pasadena. Except this table."

"It's a combination of both of our things," Meredith said. She reached over and grabbed Shelly by the wrist. "You'll never guess what! I have some fantastic news."

"Can't be the job of your dreams; you already have that.

67

Can't be the house of my dreams because we both already have that. What's left?" Shelly slipped out of her dark brown flight jacket and noticed her dad's smile. He must already know the good news.

"I'm going to Frankfurt next month!"

"Germany?"

"Of course Germany. The publisher is sending me to the International Book Fair in Frankfurt to scout out new products. Isn't that great?"

"Terrific!" She tried to sound delighted for her sister, but it was hard. Shelly was the one who had always dreamed of exploring the ends of the earth, and yet somehow that had never happened. Either she would get time off from work and have no one to go with her, or she would have a friend going some place fun, but Shelly couldn't arrange her work schedule so she could go along.

"There's more," Meredith said.

Shelly wasn't sure how much more good news she was up for tonight. "Remember Jana, my old roommate from my freshman year? She and her husband live in Heidelberg. They oversee some kind of youth mission there. I called her today, and she invited us to come early and stay a couple of days with them in Heidelberg."

"Us?"

"Yes, us. You want to go, don't you? I mean, isn't that the advantage of working for an airline? You can fly free?"

"Well, almost free. When is this?"

"In two weeks. The book fair starts the first Wednesday in October so I thought we could leave on the Thursday before and have the weekend through Tuesday with Jana. She says Heidelberg is beautiful this time of year. There's lots to do there, too."

"You know," Mom said, "you girls could rent a car and

find the town my side of the family is from. I've never been there, but I understand it's right outside of Heidelberg. I'll have Mother write down the information for you."

Shelly's mind was spinning with all the details of how to pull this trip off in only two weeks. The last thing she was worried about was spending a day looking for her ancestor's grave site.

"Do you have a passport?" Shelly asked Meredith.

"Yes, of course."

"Then I guess we're all set!" Shelly smiled broadly at her sister and then at her mom and dad. "This is going to be fun. It could be the biggest plus of being on the reserves list. Now I don't have to find someone to trade hours with when I want to take vacation time."

"Your mother and I are glad to see you two taking advantage of these opportunities when they come along. It sounds as if your new publishing company has already put a lot of faith in you, Meredith. We're glad to see that," Dad said.

"I think I'm going to like working for them very much. I fly back to Chicago for meetings four days next week. I'll only be home a few days before we take off for Germany." Meredith pushed her half-empty dinner plate away and leaned back. Her lilting laugh filled the room. "I still haven't told you the most interesting thing I found out today."

They waited.

"You're not going to believe this. Especially you, Shelly."

"What?" she asked impatiently.

Meredith drew them all in with her giggle and sweeping glance. Her eyes sparkled with her secret news. "I know where Jonathan Renfield is."

8

Shelly swallowed hard, trying with all her might to hide the way her heart had just leapt into her throat. She didn't dare speak lest her words or even her tone of voice give away her thoughts.

"Did he call you?" Mom asked.

"Where's he living?" Dad asked.

"I haven't heard from Gayle and Ted since two Christmases ago. I think they moved again. Is Jonathan with them in the Bahamas?"

"No," Meredith said, cutting into her parents' speculations. "He's in Belgium."

Shelly's heart flew from her throat to her ears, where it pounded so loudly she was sure the others would turn to stare at her. *Jonathan is in Belgium? How far is Belgium from Germany?*

"Belgium!" Mom stated. "Whatever is he doing there? I thought he was going to become a forest ranger."

"He's a youth director with the mission that Jana and her husband oversee. When I called, she said she had been thinking of me because a few weeks ago they were visiting Jonathan in Belgium and it came up that he was originally from Seattle. She told him her old Bible-college roomie was from Seattle and did he happen to know the Graham family, and there you have it. Small world, huh?" Meredith's eyes were on Shelly.

"A youth leader," Dad repeated. "For a mission, no less. My hat goes off to him. It has to be a challenge working with teens in a different culture."

"Actually," Meredith said, "this organization works with American kids who are living on the military bases all over Europe. It's a gigantic mission field since the teens are kind of stuck over there with their families. The mission has huge turnouts whenever they run a camp or a special event that combines all the groups from the military bases around Europe. Jonathan apparently runs the youth club for the teens on a military base in Belgium. He's been there for more than a year."

Shelly felt her pulse returning to her neck, where it must have made her veins throb noticeably. *Jonathan has been in Belgium for more than a year working with high school students. I never would have guessed it.*

Shelly's parents went on to discuss Jonathan's parents and what good neighbors they had been. Her parents mentioned how they were planning to visit Jonathan's folks someday in the Bahamas. Maybe next spring would be a good time to do that.

"When you're in Germany," Dad said, "be sure to look up Jonathan. Even if it's only by phone." He looked directly at Shelly. "Okay? Promise me?"

She nodded.

"Tell him we would love to hear from him."

"And tell him to give you his parents' address. I don't want to lose track of them," Mom said.

Shelly nodded again.

"We may even, ah . . ." Meredith paused. "We may even get to ah . . . get in on an Octoberfest somewhere while we're over there."

"That could be interesting," Dad said.

Shelly felt that everyone was waiting for her to say something. Their quick, sideways glances were painfully obvious.

"I'm looking forward to using some of my accumulated vacation time," Shelly said, trying to keep her tone and words even. She had plunged her hands beneath the table to hide their trembling. The camouflage effort was wasted under the glass tabletop. She knew Meredith had noticed. Perhaps that's what had prompted her sister to change her sentence to the topic of the Octoberfest and to move it off of Jonathan. Shelly appreciated that and told Meri so late that night, after their mom and dad had left.

The two sisters went for their nightly walk around the lake carrying flashlights and wearing matching white sweatshirts that Meredith had bought for them after their first trek around the lake in dark clothes. About twenty yards from the back of their cottage, where the trail wound under the cedar trees and led straight to the lake, Meredith began the discussion. "I hope you don't mind my telling about Jonathan in front of Mom and Dad. It's so amazing that his name would come up, especially after you and I had talked about him just a little while ago. I was going to say there's a good chance we'll see him, but I decided not to say that in front of Mom and Dad."

"Thanks. I appreciate it." Shelly thought for a moment and then said, "Meri, I have to tell you something. Remember how you said I needed to find some key to unlock my past?"

"Yes."

"I've thought about that, and you may have something there. I've been thinking a lot about Jonathan, and maybe . . . I don't know. Maybe something is there that I wasn't willing to see before."

"Like maybe you're still in love with him?" Meredith ventured.

Shelly released a spontaneous, nervous laugh. "I don't know. It's been so long. What we knew as love was so naive and incomplete. I don't know what I think. All I know is that I've been thinking about him. A lot."

"Do you want to see him?"

"I think so. I mean, yes, I want to see him. I don't know if he wants to see me."

"Oh, he'll want to see you," Meredith said. She shone her flashlight out on the lake where a startled duck took flight, causing the lunar reflection to ripple. Ahead of them, the fat butterball of a harvest moon slumped over the treetops, drunk on its own moonshine.

"Look at that," Shelly said in a hushed voice, her chin tilted up toward the full, amber orb. "Is that the most gorgeous moon you have ever seen?"

"It's incredible," Meredith agreed with a sigh.

"It's so beautiful here."

"I know," Meri whispered back. The glow from the moon reflected off the water and gave Meredith's light blond hair an almost iridescent shine. "This is the best thing I ever could have done," Meredith said. "It's the best thing both of us could have done — to move here, I mean."

"You're right. Thanks for letting me move in with you."

"Are you kidding? This is a treat for me." Meredith stopped walking and touched Shelly on the arm. "I really appreciate your letting me into your life like this. I always wanted to be your best friend when we were growing up."

"I always thought we were good friends while we were growing up," Shelly said, slightly defensive. "You and I got along with each other most of the time, which is more than I can say about how either of us fared with Molly and Megan."

"But I wasn't your best friend. Jonathan was."

"Yeah," Shelly said slowly and dreamily, her mood matching the fairy-tale world around them. "I guess he was."

They kept walking, this time with their arms linked.

"We probably look like two little old spinsters," Shelly said after some time.

Meredith played along, patting her sister's arm. "We may look that way, dearie, but I have a very strong feeling that after our little trip to Germany, you'll come home with a nice big diamond on your finger and an eviction notice for me."

Shelly laughed. "That would never happen," she said. "Jonathan and I wouldn't make you move out. We would find our own place. As a matter of fact, we would probably build our own place. Right over there." She shone her flashlight on the broad meadow owned by the neighboring camp.

"Sounds like something Jonathan would do," Meredith agreed. "He always did want to build a log cabin or something, didn't he?"

"Yes," Shelly said softly. She remembered the summer night she and Jonathan had begged their parents to let the two of them sleep out in the tree house. Their parents finally agreed only after Jonathan's dad offered to spend the night with them. Shelly and Jonathan were both eleven. It was a miserable night. Mr. Renfield snored like a bear, and an owl kept echoing his every snore. Shelly's sleeping bag wasn't warm enough so she shivered till her teeth chattered.

"This is pretty amazing, isn't it?" Meredith said.

"What? The lake?"

"Yes, the lake and the moon and all of God's creation. But what I was thinking about was how amazing the last couple of weeks have been. Your moving back here, my getting a new job that sends me to Germany, and my friend Jana knowing Jonathan."

"Is Jana going to tell Jonathan we're coming?"

"No, I don't think so. First of all, I didn't know for sure if you could take the time off, and second, I didn't feel it was my place to tell her that you had once been his girlfriend. All Jana knows is that we used to be neighbors and that I'm coming. She may mention that to Jonathan, or she might not."

"That's good," Shelly said.

"Well, it's good if you want to avoid seeing him, but if you want to see him, you might call him to make sure he's going to be around. I have a very strong suspicion that you do in fact want to see him."

"I do," Shelly admitted.

"Should I get his number from Jana? I could call her to-morrow."

"No," Shelly said cautiously. "Why don't you give me Jana's number and let me call her? I want to think this through. It has been five years, you know. And I do have some apologizing to do before he might be willing to talk to me."

"It's up to you. I refuse to play the role of the pushy, matchmaking sister. It seems God has arranged all these con-nections fine so far without my help. All I ask is that you fill me in on the good stuff."

"Agreed," Shelly said. "That is, if there's any good stuff to fill you in on."

"Oh, I'm sure there will be!"

For days Shelly debated whether or not she should call Jana. There were only a few hours each day when it was con-venient to call Jana with the nine-hour time difference.

Shelly never did make the call. She wondered if she had done the right thing as she stared out the plane window on their flight bound for Frankfurt. Meredith mercifully hadn't bugged her about it, partly because Meredith had been in

Chicago and then had frantically prepared for the trip. She
and Shelly had had very little time to talk. Shelly had been
called to report for three long flights and one half-day com-
muter flight, so the weeks had gone by fast for her as well.

Now it was too late to call. They were in the air. On their
way. Whatever was going to happen was going to happen.

Outside, the sky was a seamless blue without a cloud. Far,
far below them lay the thick, brown earth, marked in perfect
patchwork squares of autumn fields plowed under.

Heartland, Shelly thought. *Kansas. Maybe Iowa. No, we're
too far north. Maybe it's Manitoba. How dry it looks. So precisely
measured and divided. And so lonely. I know that feeling. I think I
did the same thing to my heart, plowed it all under and left it in its
tidy little sections.*

Shelly glanced at her sister, who was wearing a headset
and watching the movie from the middle seat. Shifting her
position, Shelly returned her attention to the view out the
window.

She had never realized how compact the seat space was. A
passenger couldn't cross her legs if the person in front of her
had reclined the seat. And the meal tray barely fit on the tray
table if the seat was reclined. Buttering a roll without elbow-
ing one's neighbor was also a challenge. Shelly felt claustro-
phobic, which gave her a whole new appreciation for what it
was like to be a passenger.

The endless view out the window was her only source of
calm. Blue, blue skies kept her content for many miles, as her
imagination spun and wove and then unraveled a dozen sce-
narios of what it would be like to see Jonathan again.

She finally admitted to herself hours later that she was
scared to face him. She was a scaredy-cat, just like he had
called her years ago when she was so leery of climbing the
steps up to the tree house. But also just like that childhood

experience, Shelly knew she had to overcome her fear of seeing Jonathan.

Look at you! You're not afraid of heights anymore. You fly for a living. You've sat here for hours looking out this window. You can get over this fear of Jonathan Renfield.

Shelly continued to coach herself as the cabin lights came on and the drowsy passengers awakened. She knew she would have to take each step as it came. Maybe it would be convenient to rent a car and drive to Belgium, and maybe it wouldn't. Maybe when they arrived at Jana's she would have news that would help determine Shelly's next step. Maybe Jana had told Jonathan that Meredith was coming, and he had decided to come to Heidelberg to see her. When he arrived, he would be pleasantly surprised to see Shelly. At least she hoped he would consider it a pleasant surprise.

What if he had turned bitter toward her over the years? No, not Jonathan. He was nothing but tenderness and kindness.

Gazing below as the shadowy clouds of night cleared, Shelly watched a city stir with the morning. All the lights that had been turned on to protect homes during the night were being turned off. Shelly felt herself turning off her own security lights and letting the adventure of this new day light her path.

9

The last part of their journey seemed the longest. They encountered delays at the Frankfurt airport in the baggage-claim area. Security required that all baggage be checked to the claim tickets, and uniformed guards with the aid of dogs were randomly checking luggage. The intensity of the security made Shelly aware of the ever-present danger of bombings and terrorist activity. For the first time she felt nervous about being in a foreign country.

Strangely, Meredith seemed more confident and decisive than Shelly. She was the one who remembered they needed to exchange some money before trying to find the train station. Shelly felt physically and emotionally exhausted. All the exercise her mind and heart had done on the flight was showing up now when she really needed to be clear-headed.

Once their passports were stamped, their luggage cleared, their money exchanged, and they had found their seats on the train to Heidelberg, Shelly laid her head back and fell asleep. All too soon, Meredith shook her and said, "We're here. Get your stuff."

They had both packed light, on Shelly's insistence, and it paid off now when they had to grab their belongings and hop off the train. Pulling their wheeled bags behind them and wearing their warm jackets, Shelly and Meredith headed down the platform toward the main entrance. Meredith led the way as if she had been there before. Of course neither of them had.

"Jana's going to meet us at the curb out front. She said it was easier for her to do that than to park and come in. We're a few minutes late, but she should be there."

For an instant, Shelly wondered if by any remote possibility Jonathan might be with Jana. Shelly became self-conscious of her appearance. Her hair was much longer than Jonathan had ever seen it. At the moment, she had it pulled back in a ponytail holder. When she was working, she usually wore it in a twisted French roll, but it wouldn't be easy to locate her bobby pins now to try to fix it. She had worn no makeup on the flight since twelve hours was a long time for makeup to stay fresh. Besides, she wasn't working this flight so she didn't feel the need to try to look fresh and friendly to all the passengers.

Another thing that had changed in the past five years was her weight. Shelly had been more consistent in working out. She weighed five pounds more than she had in high school, but it was well distributed. Her figure had changed, too, she thought. A little more on top, a little rounder on the bottom. The tomboy was gone from her frame. Would Jonathan notice the way her shape had graced itself into a woman?

"Do you think we should stop and go to the restroom before we meet her?" Shelly asked.

"Do you need to go?"

"Well, not really, I guess. I can wait." Shelly hoped her sister couldn't read her thoughts and figure out why Shelly wanted to make the stop.

They stepped into the brisk air of the Heidelberg morning, and someone immediately called out, "Meri! Over here!

Meredith!" A woman hung her head from the open passenger window of a blue minivan and waved at them.

"There she is. Perfect," Meredith said. "Come on."

Jana and her husband, Mike, greeted them both enthusiastically and helped them into the van with the luggage.

"That's all you have?" Jana said. "I'm impressed." She was taller than Shelly and Meredith and wore funky, wire-rimmed glasses. Her dark hair was short, with a point at the back of her neck, a sort of backward widow's peak. Mike wore bizarre glasses, too, with large, colored wire frames. He was a large man, older than his wife, and had the build of someone who had played football in college and then stopped working out.

"We have to run a few quick errands," Jana said. "I hope you don't mind."

"Not at all. How are you two?" Meredith patted both of them on the back as Mike pulled out of the parking lot. "It's so good to see you."

"We're doing pretty good," Jana said.

"We're way too busy," Mike said. "We have our quarterly staff meeting starting tomorrow morning, so we apologize ahead of time if we don't get to spend a whole lot of time with you. Heidelberg is such a fun city you won't need a tour guide."

"I told you about the staff meeting, didn't I?" Jana said, turning around and smiling at them. "We live downtown near the university. It's a compact, typical European flat, but we do have a guest room. We'll give you a key; so you're welcome to come and go as you wish."

Meredith was asking questions about the famous Heidelberg Castle and about obtaining tickets for a tour-boat ride. All Shelly could think of were Mike's words, "quarterly staff meeting." Jonathan was staff. Maybe she wouldn't have to figure out a way to get to Belgium. Maybe Jonathan would come here. Maybe he was already here.

"Is there anything we can do to help you guys with your staff meeting?" Shelly asked. "Is it going to be held at your home?"

"No, we have a meeting room at a church," Jana said. "It's a two-day meeting. We'll have two other guests on our living room floor tomorrow night, but no, there's nothing you can do. You're welcome to meet us for dinner, if you would like."

Shelly's mind was reeling. How could she ask about Jonathan without letting out a wild shriek? What if he was one of the staff people who would be sleeping on the living room floor? Couldn't Meredith see her agony? Why couldn't she come right out and ask about Jonathan for Shelly?

"We could stay at a hotel," Meredith said, "if you need your guest room."

"Are you kidding? No way would I want you to spend the kind of money they demand for a decent room in this town. You put your bid in first. You're my guest. I don't want you to stay anywhere else."

"Really," Mike added. "She's been looking forward to this, Meredith. I'm counting on you to give her a good bit of refreshment. After our staff meeting you still have a few days, don't you?"

"I don't have to be in Frankfurt until Wednesday at nine in the morning," Meredith said. "Oh, look! That's the castle, isn't it? It looks just like the postcards you sent me. That was a pretty dumb thing to say. Of course it looks like the postcards." Meredith laughed contagiously.

"It's the jet lag," Mike offered. "It's hitting you already."

Meredith kept laughing as she looked out the window. The castle on the hill did indeed look enchanting. Even though it was far away, it was impressive. The stone wall stood in bold defiance of the hundreds of years that had sharpened their worst days on its ledges. Tawny, brazen, and unshaken, the Heidelberg Castle crouched like a lion overlooking the city.

Shelly pulled her gaze away and formed another question for their host and hostess, "Are your staff coming in tonight?"

"Some are. Some will drive in early tomorrow morning. Depends on where they're coming from," Mike said.

"Is this a quarterly meeting for everyone who works for your organization?" Shelly asked.

"Almost everyone is coming," Jana said.

There was a pause as the car rumbled over a bump in the narrow road and came to a halt in front of what looked like an automotive-repair shop. Shelly inconspicuously poked her sister, hoping Meredith would take the hint and ask outright about Jonathan. Too entranced by their surroundings, Meredith peered out the side window and seemed unaffected by Shelly's misery or the poke.

"That reminds me," Jana said as Mike ran into the small shop. "Your old neighbor will be here for the meetings. I haven't mentioned to him that you guys are here. Meri told you, didn't she, that we found out we both know Jonathan?"

"She told me," Shelly said cautiously.

"He's coming?" Meredith said, suddenly catching on. "That's fantastic! He'll be so surprised to see us." Meredith pinched Shelly on the thigh, causing Shelly to jump a little. Meredith's golden laughter spilled all over them.

"What's so funny?" Jana asked.

"Oh, just the thought of seeing Jonathan again," Meri said, trying to regain her composure. Shelly could tell Meredith's laugh was full of happiness, the kind of laugh she had tucked away for Easter-egg hunts and Christmas mornings when they were kids. She was as excited about Shelly seeing Jonathan as Shelly was.

"It's been a long time," Meredith explained. "More than five years. I was just wondering if he had changed much."

"The only way that guy could have changed is if he was a royal terror as a kid, because now he's a dream. Believe me, he is one of the best youth leaders we have on staff. Mike is really close to him. I think he's a doll."

Hearing this person Shelly had met twenty minutes ago talk about her Jonathan so freely made her want to spill her guts about her deep and abiding, albeit only recently resurrected, love for Jonathan.

Fortunately, Meredith spoke up first. "When is he coming? Is he staying at your house? Shelly and I should think of some way to surprise him."

"I'm not sure when he's arriving. He's not staying at our place. We have two staff women coming. We thought it would be a little easier, since we already had you two, to sign up for two women. With only one bathroom, a couple of guys would have really complicated things."

"What could we do to surprise him?" Meredith asked, her mischievous eyes twinkling.

Shelly swallowed hard and smiled at her sister.

"Just show up at our staff meeting tomorrow morning at nine. That should shock him enough. The church is only a few blocks from our house. You have to go through the *Floh Markt,* but that makes it a fun walk. I'll show you when we get home."

"What's that? A German flea market?" Meredith asked.

"Exactly."

Mike came running back to the car with a long, black rubber loop in his hand. "Okay," he said, jumping into the driver's seat. "They had the fan belt I ordered for Barb's car. What's next on the list?"

"The post office, and that's it."

Shelly absorbed herself with thoughts of Jonathan while Mike and Jana finished their errands. The billboards they passed looked similar to ones at home, only these were in German. The stores all looked vaguely familiar in this newer part of town. She could almost believe they were driving in an American city by the looks of things. But she noticed slight variations from the American versions of billboards, streetlights, buses, and the shapes of the cars and trucks that passed them on the noticeably narrow streets.

This is what Shelly had dreamed of for a long time, the opportunity to explore a wonderful and amazing corner of the world.

Inside her, the tension over seeing Jonathan was building. He would be here tomorrow, and if all went according to plan, she would walk into a meeting room at nine o'clock in some little church in Heidelberg and freak the socks off her best friend. Shelly knew she was not going to sleep a wink until that moment. She imagined Jonathan going about his day, just like any other, planning to attend a staff meeting, just like any other. He had no idea his life was about to be radically shaken.

10

"Here we are," Jana said, unlocking large double doors, which were set like straight teeth, at the bottom of a tall, long building; a very old, tall, long building. Everything around them was old. Shelly couldn't begin to guess how ancient, but below her feet were cobblestones. The original stones, she was sure.

When she leaned back and looked down the street, she saw nothing but the continuous pale yellow face of this block-long, three-story building. Above were rows of identical windows in straight lines and above them, jutting out of the rust-colored tile roof, were sets of protruding dormer windows wearing their brown-shingled caps.

How many years had this building looked down on the peasants and privileged who passed by on this street? How long had it stood its ground and watched the seasons change?

"This is like a European movie," Meredith said as they walked inside and found themselves facing a grand, white, winding staircase.

Jana chuckled. Shelly winced. Sometimes her sister sounded like such a ditz. First saying the castle looked like a postcard and now proclaiming that this house looked like something from a movie.

"It's real," Mike said softly so his voice wouldn't echo off the high ceiling. "However, we occupy only this tiny corner apartment here."

Jana unlocked a nondescript door that Shelly would have guessed to be the door to the broom closet. It opened into a fairly spacious living area with high ceilings circled by elegant plaster carvings.

"Wow," Shelly said, looking up. "That's beautiful."

"Yes," Jana said. "The ceiling is one of the nicest features of our little nest." She took them on the grand tour. First they stepped into a kitchen that was the size of a walk-in closet, then two small bedrooms and a large bathroom that was all tile — tile floors, tile walls, tile ceilings, tile shower. And the tile was a bright blue, which was a bit overwhelming.

"Makes for easy cleanup," Jana quipped. "I haven't quite figured out how to hang any pictures in here, though."

"Are you two thirsty? Hungry? What can I get you?" Mike asked.

"I could go for some water," Shelly said.

"Sounds good," Meredith agreed.

Mike disappeared for only a moment into the compact kitchen and returned with two bottles of mineral water.

"Oh, I meant just water, water," Meredith said.

"We don't drink our tap water," Jana said. "Old plumbing, you know. Don't let the reddish brown color surprise you when you take a shower. Besides, you might as well get used to drinking the mineral water. Restaurants around here will charge you plenty and bring you what they call, 'Wasser mit Gas.'"

Shelly lifted her bottle to their informative tour guide and said, "This will be fine. *Danke.*"

"*Bitte,*" Jana replied. "I can see you two are going to be easy. I love it when Americans come to visit and they can just go with the flow rather than trying to change everything to make it familiar."

"I told you my sister was a lot like me," Meredith said.

Shelly hoped Jana and Mike would consider that a good thing.

"Please make yourselves completely at home," Jana said. "The clean towels are in the cupboard in the bathroom. Just don't be surprised if anything else tumbles out when you open the door. We're a bit tight on storage around here."

Meredith and Jana started to chat, and Mike went into their bedroom to make some phone calls. Shelly decided she would lie down, even though she knew better than to let her fatigued body think it was okay to fall asleep. If she didn't stay up all day, she would never be able to sleep that night and convince her system to switch over to the time change.

In the privacy of the guest room, with the door closed, Shelly pulled a small book from her bag. It was her journal from the past few weeks and would now serve as her travel diary. On the first page she had copied word-for-word the poem Jonathan had sent her so long ago. Three pages later she had copied a poem she had found in the book of English poetry she had bought in San Francisco.

She urged her bleary eyes to scan the poem by Robert Herrick entitled, "To the Virgins, To Make Much of Time."

> Gather ye rosebuds while ye may,
> Old Time is still a-flying;
> And this same flower that smiles today,
> Tomorrow will be dying.
> The glorious lamp of heaven, the Sun,
> The higher he's a-getting;
> The sooner will his race be run,
> And nearer he's to setting.

That age is best, which is the first,
When youth and blood are warmer;
But being spent, the worse, and worst
Times still succeed the former.
Then be not coy, but use your time,
And while ye may, go marry;
For having lost but once your prime,
You may forever tarry.

Shelly had taken the words of this old lyric seriously when she first read them. The fear that she may become an old maid had hit her hard. She needed to get Jonathan back, and when she did, she needed to never let him go. It helped her to read the poem again, now that she was so close to seeing him. She gathered a new determination and purpose from the ancient exhortation. No more being coy. She would seize the day. Capture the moment. Use her time.

It seemed her pathway was being made clear, wonderfully clear. Confident that her destiny was sealed, Shelly took the rest of the day in stride.

Jana and Mike urged them to explore the local shops. With some money stuffed in their pockets, Shelly and Meredith ventured out onto the cobblestone streets in the crisp, autumn air.

"Just look at that, will you?" Meredith said, snapping a photo of the austere Heidelberg Castle wall that loomed above them on a hill behind the town. "It's so huge."

"Look at those trees," Shelly said. If she had had a camera with her, she would have photographed the rows of trees that lined the hillside on which the castle stood. The deciduous beauties were fully adorned in their finest golds, oranges, yellows, and bronze. All the trees needed was one strong wind, and Shelly was sure they would be robbed of their glittering jewels, stripped bare and left to wait for the merciful white softness of winter's snow to clothe their bare arms.

"Take a picture of the trees," Shelly said.

"The trees?"

"Yes, look at them. They're gorgeous."

"Okay, but let's go into the courtyard over there, and you can stand by the fountain with the trees in the background."

Shelly adjusted the turned-up collar on her suede jacket and smiled her biggest smile. Tomorrow at this time she might be having her picture taken with Jonathan beside her. The thought made the back of her neck tingle. It would feel so good to have his arm around her once again. How could she have turned off all her thoughts and feelings for him so quickly when she left for Los Angeles? It scared her to realize how successfully she had buried her first love.

"First stop must be a pastry shop," Meredith said, tucking the camera back into the big pocket of her jacket. "I saw one down the street when we drove in this way. Come on." Meredith linked arms with Shelly and started to hoof it toward the main street.

Shelly laughed. "Boy, when it comes to pastry you are unstoppable!"

"Always," Meredith said.

They laughed together and enjoyed the sun's warmth on their faces. Shelly quickly realized that she didn't need to wear her jacket on this glorious afternoon. It almost seemed to be warmer outside than it was in Jana and Mike's apartment.

Meredith pushed open the door to the tiny bakery. A fabulous, warm, yeast-laced-with-cinnamon scent rushed to greet them.

"Okay, I'm hungry now," Shelly said. Her mouth started to water for her favorite snickerdoodles. The gleaming case of goodies boasted a wide variety of pastries, but no snickerdoodles. She selected a flat delicacy that looked like a long piece of dough wrapped round and round in the shape of a pinwheel and dusted with sugar. They both ordered coffee and stepped to the side of the shop to enjoy their feast. Three tall, round tables stood at the side of the shop next to the shelves stocked with chocolates, teas, and coffee mugs. No chairs. Shelly and Meredith followed the lead of the others in the shop and stood while they ate their baked goods and sipped their dark, robust coffee.

"You know what they need over here?" Shelly said, licking the sugar from her lips. "They need those flavored coffee creamers."

Meredith laughed. "That's really a kick in the pants when you think about it. They advertise them in the U.S. as international coffee creamers, but from the looks of things, international coffee is as dark as night and as strong as a mule."

Shelly smiled. "You're right. I wonder what other misconceptions of Europe you and I might have."

"I have no misconceptions about their baked goods. Whatever this was, it's a memorable experience."

Shelly laughed softly, aware that they were talking louder than anyone else in the shop and in English, no less. There was no mistaking who the American tourists were.

"Meri, only you would describe the consumption of a muffin as a memorable experience."

"Well, it was." She tipped her white ceramic mug to capture the last ounce of black coffee. Lowering her voice she added, "Next time I'm going to order tea, I think."

"I think we're spoiled by the Seattle coffee experience," Shelly said. "You know, I've had so many lattes and mochas in my day, I don't know what black coffee tastes like anymore."

Meredith lifted her cup. "Drink and remember."

Shelly preferred to finish her pastry rather than her coffee. She was swallowing the last bite when Meredith said, "So?"

"So, what?"

"I've been waiting for you to say something."

"About the pastry? It's wonderful."

"No, you goose!" Meredith tucked her blond hair behind her ears. "About Jonathan! Aren't you excited?"

"Of course I am." Shelly subconsciously followed her sister's example and looped her soft brown hair behind her ears, too. "I'm so excited I can hardly think straight."

"You seem calm to me. Even when we found out he was coming here, you acted sedate, as if you already knew."

Shelly shrugged. She slipped out of her warm jacket and hung it over her arm. "All I can say is that I feel at peace. Not at peace, more on center, if that makes sense. I'm ready to see him. The timing is perfect. Two months ago I wouldn't have felt like this. I needed to work through my memories all these weeks. I'm ready now for the relationship he wanted before. It's just perfect timing, that's all."

"God's timing, if you ask me. Really, think about all this."

"I have been."

"What are you going to say when you see him?" Meredith asked.

"I don't know. That's the only part that makes my stomach tie into a knot. I want to apologize for how I acted the night we broke up. But somehow I feel he's already forgiven me. I don't know if I should dredge that up the first thing or if I should just act natural and show him how glad I am to see him. Then, when it's appropriate, I can tell him I'm sorry."

"That sounds reasonable. You're probably going to see him in a roomful of people," Meredith surmised. "It might be embarrassing if the first thing you did was start apologizing to

91

him in front of everyone."

"You're probably right." Shelly felt a wonderful shiver zipping up her spine. "I'm going to see Jonathan! I still can't believe it. I keep wondering if he's changed. Jana said he was a doll."

"He always was," Meredith said with a sigh. "One of the last few heroes left on planet Earth. You know, I told him once that I never forgave his mother for having only one child. He needed a brother."

"You mean you needed a brother," Shelly said. "You had your pick of boyfriends all your life and still do. What you needed was a brother who would have roughed you up some and shaken that prissiness right out of you."

"Oh, so now the truth comes out. You think I'm prissy?"

"Just a little."

"Well, it just so happens you've turned a little prissy in your old age, too. Don't think I didn't notice that book of poems you left on the coffee table at home. Not to mention your long hair and that little thing you do now when you walk. You didn't do that when you were a kid."

"What little thing?"

Meredith stuck her chin up and swayed her shoulders as she demonstrated by sauntering over to the pastry counter and back. "That little thing. That's definitely a feminine touch you've picked up. My guess is it came from all those trips up and down the narrow airplane aisles. You traded in your cowgirl swing for a soft little sway."

"What of it," Shelly said, teasing her sister with a hand on her hip.

"Nothing. It's fine. It's girlie. It's you. It's just that Jonathan has never seen it. I think once he recovers from the shock of seeing you, he's going to be enraptured by how you look. You know, don't you, that you've never looked better?"

"It's all those vitamins I've been taking," Shelly quipped.

"Well, then leave the bottle out on the counter for me, Sis!"

"Like you need any beauty enhancement."

Meredith didn't have a comeback. She glanced out the door at the cobblestone street lined with fascinating shops and said, "What do you think? Should we stand here and continue this mutual admiration stuff, or should we go exploring?"

"Exploring," Shelly said, slipping on her coat. "Definitely exploring."

Into the perfect afternoon they ventured, browsing through gift shops and book shops until the sun cast long shadows down the alleyways. They returned to Mike and Jana's to find a note on the table saying they had to go out and Shelly and Jana were welcome to help themselves to anything they could find to eat.

While Meredith took a bath, Shelly made some improvised grilled-cheese sandwiches. The bread was small, hard rolls, cut in half, and the cheese was white with a strong, not-so-pleasant smell. A jar of applesauce was in the cupboard and bottles of mineral water were lined up on the floor against the cold wall beside the stove.

Jana had explained that their apartment came without a kitchen, and they had bought all these appliances and cabinets and assembled the kitchen themselves. It cost them thousands of dollars and was far from what Shelly would consider an efficient, modern kitchen. But everything worked, and she thought it was kind of fun "playing" cook in this little home. It made her wonder what Jonathan's living situation was like. Did he cook for himself on a narrow little stove like this?

Leaning against the sink, Shelly allowed her daydream to

drift on. What if she and Jonathan got married? Would they live in Belgium? Would she one day soon be puttering around in a little kitchen like this? What if he wanted to get married right away? Would she perhaps stay and not even return to Seattle? She felt no remorse at the thought of giving up her job, such as it was. Meredith could pack up and ship over the things that were most valuable to Shelly. She had so little; her life was already compact. It wouldn't be difficult to pick up with a brand-new life in Europe with Jonathan.

Tomorrow. I'll see him tomorrow. A smile as broad as the dawn spread across Shelly's sun-kissed cheeks.

11

Like all momentous days in history, this one dawned like any other. Shelly had slept only in snatches, but her dreams were sweet enough to lure her back into a few more hours of floating between two spheres. She showered before the others were up and spent an unusually long time trying to decide what to wear. She finally chose a straight, simple dress she had brought for special occasions. This was definitely a special occasion. Since it was so chilly, Shelly wore a turtleneck under the dress and wondered why she had never thought of wearing it that way at home. It almost looked better as a jumper than as a sleeveless shift.

Her hair reacted strangely to the water, or perhaps it was the foreign shampoo she borrowed. To tame the fly-away wisps around her face, Shelly scrounged through the bottom of her bag and came up with a scarf that she twisted in her hair like a headband to keep the feathery rebels off her face.

It wasn't until she began to apply her mascara that she became aware of how much her hands were trembling. She could barely contain herself. It was only seven-twenty. The next two hours until they met at the church would seem like two days. Two years. Two lifetimes. She had to get out of this closed-in apartment and collect her thoughts.

Slipping into the kitchen, Shelly found Jana in her robe

making coffee. A pan of boiling water gently tumbled four brown eggs.

"Good morning," Shelly said. "I hope I didn't wake you guys by getting into the shower so early."

"No. I'm glad you found everything okay. You look bright and ready for the day," Jana said. "Did you sleep well?"

"Pretty good. Meri's in the shower. I was thinking of going for a little morning walk. Do you have any suggestions?"

"You should go to the *Floh Markt*. It's a lot of fun, especially this early in the morning. When you go out the main door of our building, turn left and walk to the end of the block. Then turn left again for two more blocks. The outdoor market starts there on the right side of the street and goes on for almost three blocks. The first part is all vegetables and fruits, but keep going and you'll hit the flowers and other fun stuff."

"Sounds perfect," Shelly said.

"You might want to take this shopping sack with you," Jana said, reaching for a canvas bag with two long shoulder straps that was hanging on a peg behind the kitchen door. "Do you want some breakfast before you go?"

"I think I'll grab something there." Shelly looped the canvas bag over her shoulder. "This is going to be fun. Where should I meet you at nine?"

"At nine?"

"Yes, didn't you say your staff meeting is this morning at the church? I was going to stop by to say hi to Jonathan." Shelly tried to make it sound casual, yet all the while she was thinking, *Say hi, take his handsome face in my hands, kiss his lips . . . Oh, man! Don't get me started thinking about his lips!*

"Oh, that's right," Jana said. "You guys wanted to come over this morning. The church is easy to find. You can see it from the end of the *Floh Markt*. Go all the way to the last stall, and the church is across the street on the right."

"Perfect," Shelly said, checking her watch. "Tell Meri I was eager to go exploring and I'll see her at the church at nine."

"I'll tell her."

Just then the phone rang, and Jana shook her head. "It'll be like this the whole time the staff are in town."

" 'Bye," Shelly said with a smile and a wave. She stepped out of the apartment and then through the large double doors into the wide, wonderful world. Right on cue, some birds twittered in the tree across the way. She felt as if she had stepped into a fairy tale.

The early-morning light was kind to the old, yellow building, causing it to look like a fine duchess of regal standing. Any lady who could stand for so many years, unwavering on these worn gray, rust, and brown cobblestones, had to be a fine lady, indeed.

At the end of the road, a round woman wearing a white apron over her dark blue dress and a pair of black, overly sensible shoes, stood on her doorstep, shaking out a braided rug. *"Morgen,"* the woman said cheerfully as Shelly strolled past.

Shelly smiled and nodded. *"Guten Morgen,"* she said. She quickly tried to pull to the forefront of her memory all the mental files she had retained of her high school German. There wasn't a lot to draw from. Fortunately, that was all the neighbor woman said.

Continuing along the course Jana had described to her, Shelly was delighted to find that the streets were a merry maze all connected by the flecked cobblestone arteries. The rising sun was at her back as she turned the last corner. Her figure cast a long shadow. She felt every bit that tall.

Browsing through the fruit stands, Shelly found each vendor eager to strike up a conversation with her. *"Nein, Danke,"* became her standard answer accompanied with a bright smile. Not because she wasn't interested in buying their wares, but because she couldn't figure out what they were saying. She stopped at one stand and pointed to the bosc pears. *"Einen Dissen, bitte,"* she said, hoping she had just asked for one pear.

"Eine Kilo?" the vendor in the wool cap asked.

"Nein," Shelly said. She didn't want a whole kilo, only one pear.

"English?" the man asked, squinting his eyes as the sun poured over his deeply wrinkled face.

"Yes," Shelly said and nodded, trying to hide her embarrassment at not being able to speak German well enough.

"You wish one kilo?" he said with a deep accent.

"Nein!" Shelly spouted.

The man scratched his head. "You wish nine kilos?"

Shelly waved both her hands in front of the man as if her action could erase all her language goof-ups. "I only want one," she said slowly, holding up one finger.

"Ja, ja," the man said, nodding and reaching for the pears.

Shelly breathed a little easier and glanced around, hoping no one had been watching her little cultural faux pas. When she looked back, the vendor was speaking to her in rapid German and motioning for her to open her canvas shopping bag. He had weighed out one kilo of pears on his scale and was prepared to pour them into her bag. She was about to stop him and then decided it wasn't worth it. One pear, nine pears, five pears. It didn't matter. She opened her bag.

He rattled off the price, and she tried to figure out what he had said. Reaching into her pocket, she pulled out some money and held out to him one of the bills. With all her heart she wished she knew what she was doing. This guy could rip her off, and she would never know it. She could just see herself relating this story to Mike and Jana and having them tell her she had spent thirty-five dollars on five pears.

The man nodded, said, *"Ja, ja,"* a few more times. He handed her two bills and eight coins on a tiny tray that looked like a square coaster.

"Danke," Shelly said.

"You welcome," he said.

She grinned as she walked away. *How pathetic. I took two years of German, and I can't even buy myself a single pear. And he speaks English to boot!*

Rubbing one of the pears carefully on the side of the canvas bag, Shelly hoped it would have the same effect as rinsing it would. Then she took a bite. It was a wonderful pear, sweet and firm. Actually, it was the best pear she had ever eaten, simply because it was a German pear.

She made her way down the row as the crowd of early-morning shoppers thickened. Everyone carried a tote bag, Shelly noticed. And all the Germans seemed to be speaking so loudly. Or maybe it was the tone of their language that sounded gruff. More than once she turned to look at what had sounded like a threat or a command only to see two friends greeting each other warmly or a vendor greeting a customer.

The other thing Shelly became aware of was the way people looked at her. They stared. She checked her skirt more than once, ran her tongue over her teeth in case any pear skin had stuck between them. She even checked her scarf headband to make sure it wasn't sticking up. Nothing seemed out of place. Maybe it was a cultural thing. These people simply felt comfortable staring unashamedly at foreigners.

And that's how she felt, like a self-conscious foreigner who couldn't even order a pear for herself.

To lift her spirits, Shelly stopped at a flower stand. Under a striped umbrella, bunches of fresh flowers waited in big white buckets, showing off their upturned faces to the shoppers. Shelly decided to buy a bunch of bright yellow daisies for Jana and Mike as a thank-you gift. She lifted a bouquet from the bucket, and a large woman wearing a pink knit sweater over her dress and an apron over that, rose to her feet and began to speak rapidly in German. It sounded to Shelly as if the woman was scolding her.

"I'm sorry," Shelly said. "I just wanted to buy these."

"*Ja, sehr gut,*" the woman said, extending her pudgy hand. She rattled off some words that sounded like numbers to Shelly.

"Oh, yes. Here," Shelly said, fumbling for the money in her pocket. "Here you go." She handed the woman a bill.

The woman looked at it, then held it back out to Shelly and barked a few more words, shaking her head.

Stumped, Shelly asked, "You need more?"

The woman spoke again, this time louder.

Shelly pulled a few more bills from her pocket, and the woman snatched the small bill and put the larger one back in Shelly's hand.

"Oh," Shelly mumbled. "You didn't have change to break a fifty. Why didn't you say so?"

The flower vendor returned Shelly's change on the same kind of tiny tray the fruit vendor had used. Then the vendor spoke loudly again, pointing to something down by Shelly's foot. She looked down. She hadn't dropped anything. Was the woman criticizing her shoes? Then Shelly noticed the roll of plastic bags to wrap the wet flowers in. "Oh, yes. I see," Shelly said. "Thank you. I mean, *danke.*"

"*Bitte,*" the woman immediately replied.

Shelly wrapped her daisies and carefully tucked them into

her tote. With a last-ditch effort, she smiled warmly at the woman and then turned to move on, eager to be out of this embarrassing situation.

When she turned toward the flow of people, her eyes caught on a figure striding toward the flower stand. She couldn't move. She couldn't breathe. This tall, muscular man brushed his light brown hair off his forehead and wove his way through the crowd. He wore a denim work shirt that matched his stormy, gray eyes. His face was fuller than she remembered. His stature taller and more broad shouldered. And that handsome face was wearing a tight but determined smile.

Her Jonathan had turned into a man. Shelly drew on all her strength not to topple over. He came closer, scanning the buckets of flowers as he approached. Then he stopped less than two feet away from Shelly and greeted the flower vendor with a friendly, *"Morgen."*

The sound of his voice took all the breath she had left. Shelly faced him, staring at his profile as he examined a bouquet of irises. Her lips formed the word *Jonathan*, but no sound came from inside her. She felt like a ghost that he couldn't see.

Stretching out her quivering hand, Shelly touched her true love's shoulder ever so slightly. Jonathan turned. The instant he saw her face, all the color drained from his. He froze.

"Shelly?" It was barely a whisper.

Her voice suddenly returned and came rushing up through her throat to her lips. In a wild exclamation, she breathed out, "Jonathan."

12

With all the joy she had been storing up in her heart, Shelly flew into his arms, hugging him tightly. He felt solid, strong, and almost like a statue. Shelly pulled away and blinked the tears from her eyes. Jonathan was still frozen, unable to respond.

"I'm sorry," were the first words Shelly heard herself say. "I should have called you. Meredith and I just arrived yesterday. We're staying at Jana and Mike's. I found out you were going to be here, and I should have called instead of shocking you like this. I'm sorry."

"Shel?" Jonathan repeated, the color slowly returning to his face. She didn't know if he had heard any of her explanation. Why hadn't she remembered that Jonathan had never been one for surprises? He liked things orderly and planned out. She never should have surprised him like this. It would have been worse at the staff meeting in front of all his friends.

The woman at the flower stand called out something to them. Shelly ignored her. Her eyes were locked onto Jonathan's, and her heart was still pounding wildly. They stood there, each silently drinking in the sight of the other.

"Hi," Jonathan finally said when his voice returned.

"Hi," Shelly said with a giggle. "How are you? You look . . . you look great."

"So do you," he said.

"I'm so glad to see you," Shelly began.

The flower vendor spoke again. This time Jonathan reluctantly turned his head to respond. His eyes were the last part of him to turn away from Shelly. He said something to the woman at the stand, and she spoke back using large hand motions.

"What's she saying?" Shelly asked, moving closer to Jonathan.

His smile returned, and his gaze moved back to Shelly's face. "She says she has a special today on roses for, well, for people like us."

"She said *Liebespaar,* didn't she? I remember that word. Isn't it 'sweethearts'?"

Jonathan nodded and continued to take in a full view of Shelly.

The woman heckled him once again. Whatever she said made him laugh. He suddenly wrapped his right arm around Shelly's shoulder and drew her close.

"Meine gutten Freundin," Jonathan answered the woman. Then, for Shelly's benefit she was sure, he stated, "We're just good friends."

She stood and, with a tease in her voice, threw a handful of long-stemmed pink and red roses at their feet.

Shelly laughed at the gesture, even though she didn't know exactly what was going on. Jonathan released his warm grip on her shoulder and bent to pick up the mixed bouquet of roses, speaking his confident German phrases, saying something that made the woman laugh. He then handed her some money.

"Would you like to get some coffee?" Jonathan asked as he gently took Shelly by the elbow and steered her away from the flower woman. He held the bouquet of roses and didn't offer it to Shelly.

"Sure. I know you have your meeting at nine."

"That's okay. There's so much we need to talk about."

"You're right," Shelly said. "I . . . I . . . ." The words wouldn't come.

"Let's find a place to sit down," Jonathan suggested.

They were winding their way through the crowds, away from the church. Jonathan's touch on her elbow felt marvelous. That was the only way she could describe it. In years past she had resented it whenever he tried to lead her or direct her. Now she welcomed his confident and tender touch.

They had just reached the end of the row of fruit stands when Jana and Meredith appeared from around the corner and spotted them.

"Jonathan!" Meredith called out with a squeal. She came running to meet him and gave him a hug. "We were going to surprise you at the staff meeting," she said. "How did you find Shelly?"

"I . . . I . . ." Jonathan was now at a loss for words. "We just . . ."

"It was at the flower stand," Shelly said, enjoying all the romantic insinuations that came with that admission. "I turned around, and there he was. Oh, and these are for you, Jana. Thanks for letting us stay at your home."

"Thanks," Jana said, taking the bouquet of daisies from her.

"Were you surprised?" Meredith asked Jonathan eagerly.

"Surprised?" Jonathan put his hand over his heart. In the other hand he still held the roses. "I think I'm still in shock."

"We're on our way to the church," Jana said. "Were you guys coming to get us?"

"No, we were . . ." Jonathan fumbled again. "I mean, it's . . ." He looked at his watch.

"We were going to grab a cup of coffee," Shelly explained.

"We have coffee and pastry waiting for us at the church," Jana said. "Why don't you guys come with us? If you two start to catch up on old times now, Jonathan will never make it to the staff meeting."

"Ah . . ." He still seemed completely flustered.

"Mike's already there," Jana continued. "We should try to get there a little early. Come on. You three friends can catch up at dinner tonight."

It seemed they had no choice but to go along. Shelly thought it might be for the best. Jonathan seemed so rattled. A couple of hours to let the shock subside might be good. The evening could then be all theirs.

Shelly had made note of a charming restaurant the day before when she and Meredith had done some browsing. If Jonathan didn't have a suggestion for dinner, Shelly would take him there. They would sit at a small, round table once again, with their knees touching. In the glow of the candlelight she would be able to explain everything to him, and he would readily forgive her. Their love would finally be free to breathe again, and they could pick up where they had left off. Already she was wondering what it would be like to feel his lips pressed against hers. It had been so long.

They followed Jana through the crowds. Shelly wanted to reach over and take Jonathan's hand. But she knew Jonathan. He wouldn't want to show affection toward Shelly around Jana until it had been defined that Shelly was more than just an old neighbor.

All in good time.

They entered through the side door of the church and walked down a long hallway to a meeting room at the end. Meredith had been chattering all the way over and was now in her element, meeting new people and observing all the details of their surroundings.

Shelly was usually like that, too. However, only one detail interested her today. And she was standing next to him. It was then that she noticed he had on aftershave. Not his dad's spicy stuff he had worn that night they first walked around the block together hand in hand. This morning Jonathan smelled like a cedar tree after the rain. He smelled like Jonathan, he looked like Jonathan, and in every way he was Jonathan. Shelly could hardly believe this was happening.

"So, are you two going to see the sights?" Jonathan asked Shelly.

"That's the plan. As soon as I can get the little social butterfly out of here. Jana invited us to have dinner with the whole group, but if you want to meet separately or something . . ."

Tiny beads of perspiration broke out on Jonathan's forehead. Shelly imagined it was from the vigorous pace they had been walking.

"Look," he said, gently taking hold of her wrist, "we need to talk."

"I know," Shelly agreed. Even though they were in a room filled with staff workers, Shelly had a strong urge to place her hand on his cheek and run her thumb across his lips to silence them. She wanted him to know everything was going to be okay. But she held back, giving him only a smile.

He let go of her wrist and looked up at the ceiling. Shelly thought she saw tears. Jonathan was blinking back tears! Any love she had formerly felt for this man instantly multiplied and coursed through her being, forcing tears to her own eyes.

"I'll see you later," Shelly said, blinking quickly and hoping that by stepping away she would allow Jonathan the opportunity to collect his emotions before he had to sit through this all-day staff meeting. Her mind spun with plans for what they would do tonight. She wondered if he could slip out of the meeting a little early so they could go for a twilight stroll along the Neckar River.

"Shel," he said, as she turned to locate her sister.

"Yes?"

Jonathan didn't stop the two tears that escaped and rolled down his smooth shaven cheeks. He seemed to be waiting for her to say something. She raised her eyebrows and waited for a cue.

Before he could give any indication of what was brewing in his melancholy mind, someone entered the room and broke their concentration by calling out, "Johnny!"

At any other time, Shelly would have burst out laughing to hear someone call Jonathan "Johnny." He had never liked that name. He didn't even like "John." Ever since he found out that "John" and "Johnny" were sometimes used to mean a bathroom, he refused to let anyone call him anything other than Jonathan.

He swallowed hard. The tears evaporated, and as he turned away from Shelly, a short, spunky young woman with brown hair and brown eyes attached herself to his side and looped her arm around his middle. "I thought you were going to come over and meet me this morning," she said. "Did you get the flowers?"

"I put them over there on the table," he said, looking at the young woman and smiling.

Shelly thought she looked a little too old to be one of his high school students and a little too young to be a staff member. Her head barely came up to his shoulder.

"Elena," Jonathan said, "I'd like you to meet Shelly Graham. This is Elena Mills."

"Hi," Elena said brightly, turning her attention to Shelly for the first time. "Are you new?"

"No, just visiting," Shelly said, returning the same bright

smile that Elena was smiling at her.

"Okay, everyone!" Mike called from the front of the room. "Find a seat. Let's get started."

"Shelly and I grew up together," Jonathan explained, trying to look at Shelly but seeming to have difficulty keeping his eyes on her.

"Really? Cool. Seattle?"

Shelly nodded.

"This is perfect, isn't it, Johnny?" Elena turned back to Shelly. "You picked the perfect day to come visit."

"Come on, people," Mike said loudly. "Find a seat."

Jonathan didn't respond to Elena's comment.

"We better sit down," she said, glancing over at the table. "I'll quickly put the flowers in water. You save me a seat, okay, Johnny?"

"Nice meeting you," Shelly said.

"Oh, you can't go yet," Elena said, turning back around with a swish. "You have to stay. Just five minutes. It'll mean a lot to Johnny. Tell her she can't go." Elena turned her energy back to the bouquet.

Shelly's and Jonathan's eyes met one more time. It seemed he had the words right there, wadded up in his throat, but just couldn't say them. Shelly couldn't figure out what was going on. With a great effort, Jonathan tilted his head and said in a tone she had only heard him use once before, "Shelly, don't go." It didn't sound at all the way Elena's "don't go" had sounded. For a flash of a moment, Shelly remembered that same untamed voice. That was the voice Jonathan had used in the cab of the truck when he said, "You know I'll always love you." It seemed it had taken him five years to finish that sentence with, "Shelly, don't go."

But she had gone. She had gone far away and had been out of his life for many years. Not until this moment did Shelly begin to understand the pain she had caused her best friend when she left. She wanted to fall into his arms and tell him she was sorry. Everything inside her urged her to grab hold of him and say, "Jonathan, I'm back. I want you back."

She couldn't do it, not in this public place. Not now. It would be too embarrassing to both of them. No, their reunion could wait. Shelly could hold back this one, last time.

"We're going to start with an announcement," Mike said from the front.

Most of the staff were seated. Meredith was working her way around to the back door. Shelly and Jonathan were still standing next to each other by the back table where Elena was quickly arranging the flowers behind a beautiful tray of pastry.

"I received a call this morning that one of our staff members has an announcement to make." Mike pointed toward the back of the room where Shelly and Jonathan were standing. "Go ahead, Jonathan. You have the floor."

Every eye turned toward them. Jonathan gave Shelly one last, searching gaze. Again she raised her eyebrows as if to say, "What?"

Elena moved in between Shelly and Jonathan and linked her arm in his. Jonathan looked down at Elena's bright, smiling face. His smile seemed to return, as if he had just drawn the strength he needed from this young sprite.

"Go ahead," Elena said.

"Well," Jonathan stammered. "I guess, um . . ."

Elena laughed and turned to face the group. "I think we're both still a little shocked, so I'll tell you. Last night Jonathan and I decided to get married."

Shelly physically staggered backward. She caught herself on the end of the serving table as the staff let out a wild cheer for the newly engaged couple. Her sudden contact with the table shook the vase, causing it to topple and crash to the floor, scattering the bouquet and sending water and glass everywhere.

"Be careful," Meredith said. She grabbed a dish towel and immediately rushed in. "It's okay," she called out. "I've got it."

Shelly couldn't look at Jonathan. She could barely breathe. Moving as if in a dream, she cautiously made her way to the back of the table where Meredith was carefully picking up the shards of glass with the dish towel.

"It's okay," Meredith whispered to her. "It's okay. Take a deep breath, Shel. It's okay."

Bending down, Shelly took a shallow breath and then another. She blinked back the tears and gathered up the roses.

13

"She's still pretty wiped out," Shelly heard her sister telling Jana outside the guest bedroom door that evening. "I think she would rather stay here while you guys all go out to dinner. I was thinking of staying, too. This jet lag really catches you the second night, doesn't it?"

"Yeah, it can catch up with you. Will you be okay?" Jana said. "There's not a lot to eat here. Do you want us to bring back something for you?"

"No, we had a late lunch. We'll be fine. Thanks. You guys have fun."

Shelly heard the door to the apartment close and then the door to the guest room open. "You're a saint," she said to Meredith. Shelly was curled up in bed with blankets heaped over her. She had pulled on warm socks and crawled into bed at three-thirty that afternoon, when the shock of the day had taken its toll.

At first, she had tried to act as if Jonathan's engagement were nothing. When Meredith and she left the staff meeting at the church, Shelly insisted they go up to the castle as planned. With all her attention focused on the tour guide, she tried to take in the history of the lovely old bastion.

The bit of information that struck her interest was that this fortress, which the medieval world had thought was impenetrable, had in fact been plundered. Not by a cannonball or a raid from the outside. The destruction had come when a fire was set in one of the towers where all the ammunition was stored. With one loud bang, the tower split, and the indestructible bricks crumbled into a pile. That corner of the castle had never been restored.

Hanging back from the tour group, Shelly lingered at the front of the castle by the waist-high wall and gazed on the city below. Yesterday she had looked up at this fortress and thought it immovable. Today she stood within its influence and saw firsthand how even the surest of things in life can be destroyed in one explosive moment.

Below, Heidelberg stretched out on the banks of the Neckar River. Red-tile roofs clustered together hiding their inhabitants the way a hen protects her wee ones. Across the river a hill swelled above the buildings on the water's edge. The great green hump faced the castle in a silent stare down. On the hill's spine, splashes of gold, orange, and yellow were splattered against the green as if they were blobs from a painter's brush. No pattern or order existed in the arrangement of the buildings or the colors, but somehow it all blended to make a breathtaking picture.

In the center stood a grand church, which had donned its black spire cap and wore its black roof like a shawl flung over a russet-colored brick gown. Martin Luther had preached there, the guide had said. Unlike the buffeted castle, the church stood unscathed after all these years. Worship services were still held there.

"A mighty fortress is our God," Shelly remembered from her years of Sunday morning hymn singing. *"A bulwark never failing; our helper he, amid the flood of mortal ills prevailing."*

She couldn't remember the rest of the first verse and

moved on to the second, humming softly. *"Did we in our own strength confide, our striving would be losing, were not the right man on our side, the man of God's own choosing. Dost ask who that may be? Christ Jesus, it is he; Lord Sabaoth his name, from age to age the same, and he must win the battle."*

If she remembered right, Martin Luther was the one who wrote that hymn. Did he come up with the bulwark image after seeing this fortress? Or was it some other castle? Germany was full of them, according to the guide, and full of churches as well.

This was the homeland of her relatives on her mother's side. Shelly thought of the paper Mom had given her a few days before with the information from Shelly's grandmother as to where her ancestors were from. It might be kind of fun to search out the small town and church where her great-great-great-grandfather had once lived and preached.

The idea seemed especially good now that her coming days would not be filled with quiet dinners with Jonathan or strolls along the river. Shelly fought back the bitter taste that formed in her mouth as she allowed herself to make that admission.

It was time for a new plan and some new dreams. How foolish she had been to let her imagination take her to a dead end with Jonathan. She should have known better.

Meredith finished the guided tour and then came and stood silently beside Shelly. They admired the view, discussed the many austere statues, took some pictures, and then started back to Jana and Mike's on foot. They had taken a tour bus up the hill, but it didn't seem too threatening to try to walk down it. About halfway down the steep, winding road, they ducked into a small restaurant and ordered *Schnitzel.*

"It was the only thing on the menu I could pronounce,"

Meredith said after the waiter walked away. "I hope *Apfelsaft* is apple juice."

"I'm pretty sure it is," Shelly said. "If not, we'll make a new discovery." A cold snap followed her words. *Discovery* used to be a fun word. Today her discovery about Jonathan and Elena had destroyed that concept. She held at bay all the thoughts that wanted to pounce on her when her mind floated over to Jonathan.

The breaded veal arrived and turned out to be a nice, tender piece of meat. The *Apfelsaft* was warm but definitely apple juice. Not very exciting.

The two sisters talked about how cold it had turned since the clouds had moved in. Meredith kindly didn't say a word about Jonathan.

They walked home at least a mile, maybe more, in a drizzle. As soon as they reached the apartment, Shelly climbed into bed in an effort to warm up.

For an hour she had been trying to, but she still felt cold, cold from the inside out. Her screaming emotions wouldn't quiet down long enough for her exhausted body to sleep, which only made her more tired.

"How are you doing?" Meredith asked, sitting on the edge of the bed and giving Shelly's foot a squeeze.

"I'm freezing," Shelly said.

"Do you think you're coming down with something?"

"I don't know. I can't seem to warm up. I can't sleep."

"Why don't I see if I can make something hot to drink? Jana might have some cocoa or some tea."

Meredith padded out into the silent apartment. Shelly could hear her going through the cupboards. "I found a bag of loose tea. How does jasmine tea sound to you?"

"Fine," Shelly called back. Pulling herself up, she flipped on the light beside the bed and checked her travel alarm clock. The incandescent green numbers blared out "5:52." She drew the blanket up over her shoulders and sat with her back against the chilled wall with only a pillow to insulate her from it.

Her mom used to have a cure for a chill on a damp Seattle winter day. She used to say, "The best cure for a chill is a broom." She meant, of course, "Get up and do something useful, like sweeping the floor, and you'll warm up real fast."

"Do you want anything to eat?" Meredith asked, popping her head back into the room.

"No, I'm not hungry."

"The tea should be ready in a minute. Would you like me to rub your feet or anything?"

"No, that's okay."

"Do you want another pillow?"

"Meredith," Shelly snapped, "cut it out! I'm not your little first aid project. I'm cold. That's all."

"You're in shock," Meredith stated. "I think even you will have to admit I have been the perfect sister in this whole catastrophe. I've treated you and the situation with utmost honor, and I haven't made a peep about it." Her face was turning red. She folded her arms across her chest and stuck her chin out. "I guess I shouldn't care if you want to hold all your feelings in like some kind of freak. But, Shelly, get real! What you faced today rocked your world. Come on, talk about it. You have to get it out. You're going to make yourself sick if you don't."

"Thank you, Dr. Meredith," Shelly muttered.

"Go ahead. Get mad at me. I can take it. There's nobody here. Yell at me. Cry. Scream. Hit something." Meredith gestured wildly. "Do anything! Just don't lie there in denial."

"In denial?"

"Well, whatever it is you do with all your feelings. It's not natural to be so stoic."

A sharp whistle sounded from the kitchen.

Shelly's heart paused to listen for a moment. She thought it was Jonathan giving one of the whistles they had used as kids. For half a second, she thought he was calling her.

"I'll make the tea," Meredith said in response to the whistling tea kettle. "When I come back, you'd better tell me how you're going to process all this."

For the five minutes Meredith was gone, Shelly considered breaking down. It might feel good to cry. Or pound the wall and wail. The problem was, her remorse had been enveloped by her guilt. It was difficult to get through all the self-condemnation to properly mourn the loss of her first love.

When Meredith handed Shelly the mug of fragrant tea, her cold hands immediately welcomed the warmth. She was so cold, it stung when she wrapped her hands around the white ceramic cup. Holding it close and breathing in the inviting floral scent, Shelly said in a calm voice, "There's not much to say, Meri. It's all my fault. I set myself up."

Meredith adjusted herself cross-legged on the end of the bed and waited for Shelly to go on.

"Why in the world did I think Jonathan had been living the life of a monk, waiting for me to come to my senses and return to him? I never gave him any indication that I wanted to get back together. I show up, on the other side of the world, without warning, and I expect him to do what? Drop everything, including his fiancée, and take me in his arms?" Shelly cautiously sipped her hot tea.

"Meredith," she continued, "look at what I put that poor guy through today. I materialize out of thin air, I force myself into his world, and I expect that he's been building his own

116

little fantasy dream world about me like I've been building about him these past few weeks. He didn't give me any indication he was the slightest bit interested in me. We're just old friends. That's what he said to Ellen, or whatever her name is. 'We grew up together.' That's all he said."

Meredith tilted her head and looked at Shelly cautiously. After a pause she said, "You did notice, didn't you, that Elena looks an awful lot like you did when you were eighteen."

The comparison hadn't hit Shelly before. There was the bright smile, the shoulder-length brown hair. Elena had brown eyes, too.

"She's a lot shorter than I am, or than I was," Shelly stated.

"You were that short once," Meredith stated right back.

"Yeah, right. When I was eleven."

Meredith raised her eyebrows and didn't say anything.

"What? You think Jonathan has spent the last five years trying to find my clone?"

Meredith shrugged her shoulders. "It was just an observation. She's outgoing like you, too."

"So?"

"So, haven't you spent the last five years comparing every guy you dated with Jonathan?"

"Of course not," Shelly said. She immediately recognized it as a lie and quickly amended her statement. "Well, maybe a few of them."

Meredith sipped her tea and kept her scrutinizing gaze on her sister. "He was awestruck when he saw you, wasn't he?"

"He was surprised," Shelly said. "Shocked, like he said. It really wasn't fair of me to —"

"To what? Be shopping for flowers at the flea market the same time he was? It's Providence, Shel. Why do you keep making it sound as if you've done something wrong?"

"Because I think I have."

"What?"

"What do you mean, what?"

"What do you feel you've done wrong?" Meredith asked.

Shelly didn't answer for a few moments. "I don't know," she said with a shake of her head. "I feel guilty."

"Then figure out what it is that's dragging you down, confess it to God, seek his forgiveness, and move on."

Shelly sipped her tea and wiggled her toes. She was feeling a tiny bit warmer. "The facts remain the same no matter what kind of formula you suggest. Jonathan has found the girl he wants to spend the rest of his life with, and I, as his childhood friend, wish him well. Maybe the whole reason we came was so I could see them make their announcement firsthand. It eliminates all questions about the future. What's done is done. Now I can get on with my life. If I hadn't seen him and had only heard from Mom or someone that he had gotten married, I think it would have hit me harder than this did."

They sat in strained silence.

"It's better this way," Shelly said. "Jonathan deserves the right to go on with his life, too. He and I probably never would have been able to make it all the way to the altar. We were great as friends, but we probably would have fought continually if we ever did try to be serious about each other. It's better this way."

"Better for whom?" Meredith challenged.

"Better for everyone," Shelly said calmly.

Meredith shook her head. "I don't agree."

"You don't have to," Shelly said.

"I think you should pray about this. It's not like they're married yet and you're stepping in trying to bust up a holy union. They're engaged. Barely engaged. People break engagements all the time."

118

"You don't know Jonathan," Shelly said. "When he makes a promise, he seals it with his own blood. He would never break an engagement once it's announced the way it was today. He's too serious about stuff like this. He would rather spend the rest of his life married to the wrong person with his honor intact than hurt someone else to get his way."

"The last true knight," Meredith said. "Where's his white horse?"

"You don't think I'm right?"

"I think you have an exaggerated view of Jonathan. He's a flesh-and-blood man. If he's so big on truth, why don't you give him some? Tell him you're still in love with him, and see how his nobility handles that."

"You don't understand," Shelly said, shaking her head. "I could never do that to him. I've broken his heart once. You said so yourself. I could never elbow my way back into his life and force him to make a choice."

"Then we'll have to get Elena to break up with him," Meredith said, peaking over the rim of her coffee mug. Shelly shot her such a disgusted look that Meri quickly said, "I was only kidding! Lighten up."

Shelly leaned forward and with all the seriousness she possessed, she glared at her flippant sister. "I want you to promise me that you will never in your life tell Jonathan or anyone else what I've confided in you."

Meredith hesitated.

"Promise me," Shelly demanded.

"Okay, okay, I promise. I won't tell Jonathan or anyone else the things you've confided in me."

"I'm serious about this," Shelly said sternly.

"I can tell."

Shelly leaned back. Her face, hands, and feet felt fiery warm, having been ignited by the blaze that burned inside her.

14

The next morning Shelly and Meredith woke up and started to argue. They did it quietly, just like they used to at home when they were young. One look out their window had given Shelly enough of a weather report to know she preferred to spend this overcast, drizzly day inside or maybe ducking in and out of a library, museum, or even the street of shops they had barely begun to explore a few days ago.

Meredith, however, was determined to go on a boat ride. The brochure she had said the tour lasted four hours.

After getting so chilled the day before, Shelly had no desire to putter down a river under an umbrella, no matter how quaint the scenery.

The two sisters decided to go their separate ways. After making that decision, they opened their bedroom door, ready to be sweet and civil to each other and everyone else.

It didn't matter. Mike and Jana had left the apartment at seven that morning for a staff breakfast, and the two women who had slept in the living room the night before had gone with them. If it weren't for the two additional cosmetic bags in the blue-tiled bathroom and the gym bags tucked in the corner of the living room, Shelly would never have known someone else had stayed there the night before. Meredith showered first while Shelly lingered under the deliciously warm covers. Once Meredith was out the door, Shelly got ready herself.

It felt strange to be alone. The sensation was much harder than she had thought it would be. After dressing in her wool pants, turtleneck, and cardigan Shelly helped herself to one of her pears, which she had put in a bowl in the kitchen. Rolls were on the table along with a note from Jana saying they would be back after eight that night.

The daisies Shelly had bought the day before sat in a plastic glass at the end of the small kitchen table. They added a warm and cheery touch to the room. She was glad she had purchased them for Jana.

A catch in her throat caused her to stop and turn away from the daisies.

Don't do this, Shelly. This isn't about Jonathan. This is about daisies. That's all. Don't weep over nothing.

Shelly borrowed Jana's canvas shopping bag and tucked a scarf around the neck of her brown suede jacket. She was prepared for the chill of the day and the intrigue of what awaited her in this charming city.

A sharp wind met her the instant she stepped out the front doors. It whistled through the alleyways and chased her across the cobblestone square. This was autumn as she knew it in Seattle. All those years in balmy southern California had softened her up. She needed to be roughed up by the elements a little, just to know that, indeed, the season had changed.

Following the same steps she and Meredith had taken arm in arm only two days before, Shelly plunged her hands into her pockets and, with her head down, forged her way across the square. Out of curiosity, she stopped at the place Meredith had taken the picture of her with the autumn trees behind her. Today those same golden beauties, which had barely lifted a leaf to wave at Shelly before, were now quivering in the wind and tossing their leaves overboard the way a sailor heaves his cargo into the deep when the storm seems insurmountable.

I know how you feel, Shelly thought. Not that the maples, elms, and oaks could receive any comfort from her sympathetic thoughts. In a way, though, their actions, so simple and natural, were a comfort to her. If the trees could surrender all their glorious, shining gems, maybe she could toss away her dreams about Jonathan, too. The spring would come again. It always did. She knew it would take some time, but her life would eventually bud again with new plans, dreams, and hopes.

Taking long strides, she made her way down the leaf-strewn streets. She passed the bakery where she and Meredith had stopped before. On down the lane she went, past geometric fountains harpooned with gilded statues, past gift shops, past banks, and past stubby women wearing head scarves and riding bicycles. She loved the ambiance all around her.

Stopping in front of a store window, Shelly caught her breath. The name *"Geschenk-Schatulle"* hung in gold letters like a rainbow of promise over the detailed display of goods. Dolls, candles, china plates, a model train, and miniature angels made of hazelnut pods and wearing white feather skirts caught her eye. Shelly wondered how many years this shop had stood and how many eager children had pressed their noses to this glass, looking to see if the Christmas toys were on display yet.

She could smell it in the air. In this city, the past and the present met and found harmony.

She wished with all her heart that that had been her experience with Jonathan. True, she had come up with all the rational responses for her sister last night. And she had meant every word. But today the wind was blowing, and she was feeling awfully bare, stripped of her glory like the trees.

The day passed at an even pace. She shopped a while, buying mostly Christmas ornaments from a shop that specialized in German wood carvings. She purchased a T-shirt at the Hard Rock Cafe, even though she wasn't sure why. She didn't collect them, but certainly somebody she knew did.

She strolled past the university, which was founded in 1386, according to the bronze plaque on the wall. As an American, her mind was boggled to think that a century before Columbus even sailed to her side of the world, this university was drawing students to its humble doors.

Lunch was found at one of the many bakeries, where she bought a *Brezel,* a large pretzel made from bread dough. She watched the people go by and thought about what would happen if she saw Jonathan one more time. He and Elena might stop by Jana and Mike's before returning to Belgium together. Shelly assumed that's where they had met. She also assumed they were going back there together. Now she knew the reason Jonathan had kept saying they needed to talk. Being a gentleman, he wanted to tell her privately that he was engaged.

It would only stand to reason that he would try to say good-bye to Shelly in a gentlemanly fashion as well. The question was, how would she respond? It took all afternoon and many miles of cobblestone-walking to decide. She would let him go. There was no point in saying anything about what she had felt, thought, or wondered. Those bits of information would only torture him in his new life with Elena. He needed to be free of Shelly, just as Shelly needed to be free of him. The twisted cord of their shared lives needed to be unraveled far enough so they could both go on.

Arriving back at the apartment at almost six o'clock, Shelly unlocked the door with the key Jana had given her. No one else was home. A note from Mike said they had all gone to dinner, including Meredith. He gave directions in case Shelly wanted to join them. She was hungry, and Italian food sounded good. But Jonathan would most likely be there with Elena, and that would make things uncomfortable for Shelly. If she were to see Jonathan one more time, it would have to be because he came to see her.

She hung up her jacket and put on the kettle for a cup of hot tea. With a hunk of cheese as her dinner companion and another lovely German pear to enjoy, Shelly waited to see if she would have any evening visitors.

At almost eleven Mike, Jana, and Meredith arrived. They laughed softly in the hallway and then let loose right at the door. Shelly had gone to bed in her clothes and had fallen asleep reading a book. She rose and went into the living room, squinting in the bright light and trying her best to smile at the three of them, who were obviously having a great time.

"Did you have a good day?" Meredith asked.

"Wonderful," Shelly said. "And you?"

Meredith sneezed. "I had a great time! It was beautiful."

"Good. Well, I think I'll go to bed," Shelly said.

"We will, too, in a minute," Jana said.

"Guess what?" Meredith said. "Remember how you said you wanted to rent a car and go find Grandpa Rudi's grave?"

"Yes. It was only a thought. I wasn't saying we had to do that."

"Well, we're going to. Tomorrow. I rented the car and everything."

Shelly wished her sister would have talked this over with her, but after the argument they had had that morning about what the day's activity should be, Shelly decided not to argue over this one. "Great. What time do you want to get up?"

"It's Sunday," Meredith said. "We should go to church with these guys first and then head out around noon."

Again, Shelly saw no merit in arguing. "Okay. That's what we'll do tomorrow."

Sometime in the middle of the night, Meredith started to cough. She seemed to be coughing without waking herself up. Since Shelly was only a foot away from her sister in the compact room, she couldn't go back to sleep. Finally she got up and brought Meredith a bottle of water.

"Take a drink," she said, gently shaking Meredith's shoulder. Meri felt hot to Shelly's cold hand. "Are you okay?"

"My throat is sore," Meredith said. "Thanks for the water. Do you have any cold medicine with you?"

Shelly always carried a variety of antihistamines since it was miserable to fly with plugged-up ears or clogged sinuses. She brought her sister a couple of pills and asked if she wanted anything other than the bottled water to drink.

"No, thanks. I think I got a little too chilled on that boat ride. It was fun, but I didn't wear enough layers."

"You'll probably feel better in the morning," Shelly said. "Try to sleep."

Meredith didn't feel better in the morning. She asked for some salt water to gargle with and went back to bed. Shelly went back to bed, too. When Jana and Mike were ready to leave for church at nine, Shelly was still in bed.

"We'll be back around eleven," Jana said.

"Sorry I didn't plan better so I could have gone with you," Shelly said. She had wandered into the living room when she realized what time it was.

"Don't worry about it," Mike said. "We go to a local church that we really enjoy being part of, but most of our visitors don't feel comfortable with the high-church style of worship."

"Or that everything is in German," Jana added.

"I would have liked to have gone," Shelly said, pressing her cold, bare feet together. "I just goofed up on the time."

"That's okay. You're on vacation. Get your rest in while you can," Jana said. "Some devotional books are on the shelf in the living room if you want to have your own quiet time here. We'll see you in a couple of hours."

Jana and Mike slipped out the door. The apartment was quiet again. Scanning the shelves for the devotional books Jana mentioned, Shelly quickly lost interest when she thought of how she had grown up hearing morning devotions read from these books. The words of Spurgeon, Moody, Chambers, and other classic Christian writers had been delivered at the breakfast table every morning for years by her father's rumbling speaker's voice. She had heard it all. Not that it wasn't interesting and inspirational, but this morning Shelly didn't feel up for it.

Settling into a well-worn chair in the corner of the living room, Shelly tucked her feet under her and thought about Jonathan. It surprised her that he hadn't stopped by the night before to say good-bye. Not that it would have changed anything. Maybe he didn't want to see her again. Maybe this was his way of getting at her for the abrupt departure she had inflicted on him.

No, she couldn't believe that. Jonathan wasn't vindictive. Or at least he hadn't been. It was possible his heart had changed. Their encounter had been too brief to know. She had certainly changed over the years. Why did she think Jonathan's character had been unswerving?

I don't know him anymore. I don't have the right to assume anything of him, not even friendship.

Shelly let out a heavy sigh. The roller coaster of her emotions from the last two days appeared to be coming to a stop.

What has been is in the past. What is forms the present. What will be remains to be seen.

Satisfied with her philosophy, Shelly headed for the shower. It may not have been the kind of inspiration she would have received from one of the devotional books, but it was solid reasoning she could live with. The jostling of her emotions should not ruin her time in Germany, especially since she may never get here again. Whatever she wanted to see, she should go see.

Today, the plan was to travel to the town of Hilsbach, where her ancestors came from, and to find her great-great-great-grandfather's grave.

15

After a warm, luxurious shower, Shelly checked on Meredith. She was still sleeping soundly so Shelly didn't bother her. Since Meredith had mentioned the night before leaving at noon to search for their ancestor's grave, Shelly began to wonder if Meredith would feel well enough to go when she woke up. Should Shelly take the car herself, or was it signed out in Meredith's name only? Would Jana want to go, too? Where could they find a map to locate Hilsbach?

Shelly dressed and applied her makeup. Then she decided she would wake Meredith at eleven-thirty if she wasn't up already. As Shelly made her way into the kitchen to start the teakettle, she heard the door open and the sound of several voices. Jana and Mike were home, and they had company.

Shelly rounded the corner with a smile, ready to greet Mike and Jana. There stood Jonathan. Elena was right beside him.

"Hi," everyone seemed to say at once.

"How's Meredith feeling?" Jana asked, taking off her coat and hanging it on a peg on the wall.

"She's, ah . . . she's still in bed." Shelly kept her smile lit, but everything else in her had turned off. Her eyes stayed on Jana.

"Do you think she still wants to go with us?" Elena asked. Shelly couldn't force herself to look at Jonathan's fiancée.

"To go with us?" Shelly repeated, looking at Jana.

"Yeah," Elena said. "To go with us to find your grandmother's house or something."

"Just a minute," Shelly said. "I'll go check on her." With straight, deliberate steps, Shelly went into the guest room and closed the door behind her. "Meredith," she stated firmly, "wake up."

"Yeah?" Meredith turned over and blinked her eyes. "What's going on?"

"Why don't you tell me? Why are Jonathan and Elena standing out there in the living room?" Shelly tried to keep her voice low. "What did you say to them?"

Meredith forced herself to sit up. "What time is it?"

"Eleven. Why does that matter? Answer my question."

Meredith pushed her stringy blond hair off her face. "I really konked out. I didn't say anything wrong, Shelly. Don't jump to conclusions. I didn't think Elena would come."

"I could use a little more of an explanation than that," Shelly said, trying to control her temper. "What did you tell them?"

"Will you relax?" Meredith said. "Last night at dinner I told Jonathan that you and I were thinking of going to Hilsbach, and we needed to rent a car. He mentioned that we could use his car since he wasn't going back to Belgium until Monday, but I never agreed to that. I didn't think he and Elena would show up here."

"Not only did they show up here, but Elena asked if you were going with us. Sounds very much as if she plans to go."

"I'm sorry," Meredith said defensively. Shelly noticed that Meredith's eyes were red and her voice raspy. "I'll go talk to them. May I borrow your robe?" Meredith punctuated her sentence with a series of deep coughs.

"You don't have to," Shelly said, backing down. "I'm sure I'm making a bigger deal out of this than it is. You're not feeling well, are you?"

"I feel awful."

Shelly let out a sigh. "Stay in bed. Get better. I'll figure this out. Sorry I jumped all over you."

"Honest," Meredith said, covering her mouth as she coughed again, "I didn't say anything to Jonathan. You know I wouldn't. I promised."

"I know. Thanks." Shelly tried to regain her composure. She left the room, quietly closing the door, and faced the waiting group. Her years of working for the airline had taught her diplomacy. She could handle this situation. "I appreciate you guys coming over, but I'm afraid we'll have to cancel our plans. Meredith has come down with a cold. Thanks anyway."

"Don't you still want to go?" Jana asked. "Hilsbach is only about forty kilometers. You can be there and back in a few short hours."

"Oh, I don't know. It's . . ." Shelly hadn't expected any resistance to her backing out since Meredith was sick.

"You don't know when you're ever going to be back here again," Mike said.

"The sun broke through a little while ago," Jana added. "Could be a nice Sunday-afternoon drive. Besides, you and Jonathan haven't had time to catch up yet."

"I'm sure Jonathan and Elena have better things to do than to spend the afternoon with us," Shelly said smoothly. She thought it wouldn't be so bad to go to Hilsbach with Mike and Jana, but since it hadn't yet been defined who was going on this jaunt, she thought it best to start her own process of elimination.

"Oh," Jana said. "Mike and I weren't planning to go. We have a counseling situation with one of our staff members that will pretty much take all afternoon."

"You, Jonathan, and Elena should go," Mike urged. "Have some fun. To be honest with you, we kind of need you out of the house while we have this counseling meeting. It's okay for Meredith to stay, of course, since she's in bed, but our place isn't really big enough to have a private meeting."

"So we're going to go?" Elena said.

Shelly glanced at her and gave a sweeping glance at Jonathan, trying to read his expression. The smile was there. The eyes were looking down at the keys in his hand. She couldn't tell what he was thinking. It had been too long. Not a jot of their former mind reading remained.

There seemed to be no choice. "I guess we are." She checked her jeans, black turtleneck, and black ankle boots and decided she should be warm enough with her jacket and a scarf. Her hair was pulled up in a loose French twist, which she usually wore at work. It showed off her small gold hoop earrings. "I'll grab my jacket," Shelly said.

Hurrying back into the bedroom, she reached for her thin-strapped shoulder pouch that held her passport, driver's license, and money.

"Are you going?" Meredith asked and then blew her nose.

"I guess I am," Shelly said. "Mike and Jana pretty much let me know this is what I need to do."

"You'll be fine," Meredith said.

"Do you want me to bring you anything?" Shelly asked, reaching for her paisley scarf and her jacket.

"No, I think I'll be okay. Why don't you take my camera? It's on top of the desk." Meredith turned over and coughed again. As Shelly was about to leave, Meredith said, "I'll pray for you."

Shelly laughed. "Thanks, but I think it's a little too late for that."

Jonathan and Elena led the way to his car, which was parked down at the end of the next street because parking was such a problem in the old town. At least with the two of them walking ahead of her, Shelly could find her pace and catch her breath. The sun had gone behind the clouds and then reappeared for a moment. The air was cool, much cooler than it had been her first day here, and Shelly was glad for her warm jacket. She felt no emotions. She wasn't nervous, remorseful, or angry. Only cold.

Jonathan unlocked the car doors, and Elena climbed into the back seat stating, "You're our guest, Shelly. You ride in the front."

Shelly hesitated, then got in. It felt strange. She hadn't been in the front seat of a car with Jonathan since that night in his friend's truck. This was awkward.

"I have a map," Jonathan said, reaching down next to his seat and pulling it out. He handed it to Shelly. "Is the name of the town Hilsbach?"

"Yes. I have the information here." She pulled out the note from her grandmother and unfolded it. "It doesn't say much. Just 'C. C. Rudi, October 5, 1827, *Evangelische Kirche,* 1509, Hilsbach, Baden.' Then she left a space and wrote, 'Weiler, Ludwig Rudi, St. Annakapella.' Does any of that make sense to you?"

Jonathan kept looking straight ahead and drove down the street out of Heidelberg. "I'm not sure. Your grandfather is C. C. Rudi, right?"

"Great-great-great-grandfather. On my mom's side. I think he's the one who was the pastor in Hilsbach."

"At the *Evangelische Kirche,* no doubt," Jonathan said.

"What is that?" Shelly asked. It seemed easier to talk with a common goal to work on.

"The church. In most German towns there's the Catholic church and then the church that came about as a result of the Reformation. That's probably where your grandfather preached."

"I guess," Shelly said. "You know, this could all be a worthless goose chase. If you guys want to just drop me at a museum or something, I'd completely understand. You don't have to do this."

"It was my idea," Elena said from the back seat.

Shelly turned around and forced herself to make eye contact with Elena.

"Listen, Shelly," Elena said, leaning forward, "Johnny told me that you two were best friends when you were growing up. I think that's so cool. I also thought it might seem kind of uncomfortable for you to show up and have us announce our engagement and everything, since you didn't know before you got here."

Shelly didn't mean to, but she looked away, as if something out the window required her sudden attention. "I was the one who crashed your party," she said. "I mean, I should have let Jonathan know I was coming."

"I'm just glad you came," Elena said. "I wanted you and me to have a chance to get to know each other. To hear Johnny tell it, you two were inseparable the whole time you were growing up. Besides his parents, you're the closest thing he has to a relative."

Shelly pursed her lips.

"Since I haven't met anyone else in his family, I wanted to get to know you," Elena said. "I hope we haven't been too pushy about it."

"Actually," Jonathan said, adding to Elena's sentence, "I wanted to spend some time with you, too. I thought it might be good."

Shelly nodded slowly and tried to find all her professional, accommodating responses. "I appreciate both of you being so thoughtful. Thanks for giving up your Sunday afternoon to drive me around."

"So, tell me about yourself," Elena said. "Johnny says you're a flight attendant."

"Yes."

"It sounds exciting. What's it like?"

"I don't know. It's, ah . . . it's actually not as glamorous and exciting as you might think." Shelly wondered if Jonathan picked up any hidden meaning in her words. Would he perceive that her endeavor to go off and see the world hadn't panned out the way she had hoped?

"And you live in California? Is that right?"

"I did," Shelly said. It felt underhanded communicating information to Jonathan through Elena's questions. "I recently moved back to Seattle." She was ready to drop the big shocker that she lived in the Tulip Cottage on Whidbey Island, but somehow Shelly couldn't bring herself to slip that information to Jonathan. Perhaps Meredith had already told him anyway.

"Where are you from?" Shelly said, eager to turn the attention off herself.

"Akron. I grew up there. I came over this summer on an outreach trip with my church youth group, and then I decided to stay."

"How long have you been here?"

"Since the middle of June," Elena said.

Shelly did a quick count. *Four months? You've known this girl less than four months, Jonathan?*

"Is that when you two met?" Shelly felt a little peculiar asking. It was as if she were playing a game with Jonathan.

"Yes," Jonathan said firmly. "June 17. We met at the quarterly staff meeting."

If Shelly was reading his body language correctly, he wasn't comfortable with the brevity of their acquaintance.

"The minute I saw him, I was smitten," Elena said, reaching up and massaging Jonathan's neck. "Then I found out his name was Johnny, and I about flipped. My dad and my brother are both named Johnny. It was like a sign."

Shelly briefly considered rolling down her window to let the fresh air slap her in the face and keep her from bursting out laughing. *Three months? Your name was a sign? Jonathan, what has happened to you?*

Shelly was dying to ask Elena how old she was, but she didn't know how to do it subtly.

"Do you have a boyfriend?" Elena suddenly asked Shelly.

Why was I so concerned about being subtle?

Jonathan suddenly slammed on the brakes and barely missed ramming into a large truck that had swerved in front of them.

"That was close!" Elena said. "I tell you, people here drive crazy. Crazy and fast. Have you been on the *Autobahn* yet, Shelly?"

"No, not yet." Her heart was pounding, not only from the near accident but also from the way Jonathan had automatically reached out his right arm to protect her. He had done that once before when they were in high school driving his mom's car home from school. A dog had run into the road, and Jonathan had reacted with his human arm barrier to protect Shelly. That time she had yelled at him because in his quick reflex, he had tagged her jaw. This time he didn't touch her at all.

"You both okay?" Jonathan asked.

"Yes," Shelly said calmly.

"Not a scratch," Elena said. "So what were we talking about?"

Shelly made a wish that Elena wouldn't remember and bring up the question about a boyfriend again. It crossed her mind to lie and say yes, just so Jonathan would never suspect that she had been busy the past few weeks rekindling her long-lost feelings of love for him.

"I remember. I was going to ask you how you do your hair up like that. It's really pretty. I don't think mine is long enough. Do you just twist it, or do you have to pin it first?"

Jonathan remained silent the rest of the trip. Elena stayed on her friendly course of conversation, asking about Shelly's sisters and telling Shelly about her family. The longer they talked, the harder it was for Shelly to dislike Elena. She was young and a little blunt, but Meredith was right: Elena not only resembled the way Shelly had looked when she was in high school, but Elena also seemed to have some of Shelly's old mannerisms, especially the one habit Shelly had tried so hard to break and finally had — nail biting.

Jonathan had never said anything about Shelly's bad habit. It was possible he was used to it, having grown up watching her chew on her nails. But once they started to date, Shelly was the one who had decided to stop biting her nails. When they held hands, Jonathan would rub his thumb over her thumbnail. She had been sure it was a subconscious gesture, but it served as a subtle reminder that her cuticles were rough and her thumbnail was a jagged stub. She had wanted her hands to be smooth and beautiful for him, so she stopped biting her nails.

Elena nibbled away at hers all the way to Hilsbach. She also flipped her hair over her shoulder the way Shelly used to.

Molly had cured Shelly of that habit by teasing with the observation, "You look like a nervous person shooing invisible bugs away from your shoulders."

Watching Elena and listening to her, Shelly felt she was around one of her younger cousins. She never would have expected to feel the kind of camaraderie that she did.

"This is it," Jonathan said, pointing out the sign beside the road that marked the small town of Hilsbach, Baden. "Now where to?"

"I guess we find the church," Shelly said. "Or ask directions from someone. Do you feel like practicing your German?"

"I only know enough to get by," Jonathan said. "Elena is fluent."

"You are?" Shelly hadn't expected her face and her tone of voice to carry as much surprise as they did. "German is big in Akron, Ohio, is it?"

"It's big in my family. My grandmother lives with us, and her original language was German. I grew up hearing it, and then I took it in school."

Shelly didn't want to admit that she grew up hearing German from both her grandparents and also took it in school. Apparently very little of it had stuck.

"I think we can ask some people in here what we want to know," Jonathan pulled into the parking lot of a small, modern bakery. The sign in the window read *"Bäckerei."*

"It looks closed," Elena noticed. "That's right. It's Sunday afternoon."

"Stores still close in the smaller towns on Sundays," Jonathan explained. "I guess we're on our own. It's a pretty small town. Can't be too hard to find the church. Usually the Catholic church and the Protestant church are the only two in town, and they're close to each other." He drove down the street, and the houses began to look older. Within a block, they drove past a large church with a cemetery next to it.

"Bingo," Jonathan said.

Shelly closed her lips. It was strange. She had been about to say "bingo" herself. "That wasn't so hard, was it?" Jonathan said. He parked across the street and turned off the engine.

"Well," Shelly said, grabbing Meri's camera, "we shall see what we shall see."

"I don't believe it!" Elena said as she got out behind Shelly. "That's exactly what Johnny says all the time. You two really are like brother and sister."

Jonathan climbed out of his side of the car, and for the first time that day, he looked directly at Shelly. She let her eyes meet his. His dark, gray expression resembled "doom and gloom" clouds. She could only wonder what he read in hers.

16

The three of them walked across the vacant street in the little farming town and entered the graveyard. Shelly was amazed to see that it was more of a garden than a cemetery. The sites were all large plots with granite- and marble-carved headstones. Each of the plots was well tended. Many had fresh flowers placed on them or small bushes planted beside the headstones. Some were lined with pansies, which were still blooming even in the autumn chill.

"What name are we looking for?" Elena asked.

"Rudi," Shelly said. "C. C. Rudi. The only date I have is October 5, 1827. I don't know if that's when he was born or when he died."

"How bizarre," Elena exclaimed, zipping up her red jacket and sticking her hands in her pockets.

"What's bizarre?" Shelly asked, looking around.

"October fifth. That's today."

Shelly felt a shiver up her spine. She pulled the scarf from her coat pocket and wrapped it around her neck. "You're right," she said in a hushed voice. "It is."

"We should probably split up," Elena said, looking around at the large space they had to cover. "There are rows and rows to check, and I'm sure they're not alphabetical."

139

She giggled at her own joke.

Shelly didn't find it funny. Apparently Jonathan didn't either.

"I'll start to look around here," Elena said quickly.

"Okay," Jonathan agreed. "Then I'll go to the left, and you go right, Shelly Bean."

All three of them stopped. Shelly and Elena both looked at Jonathan. It was silent for a moment as the crimson crept up his face. Shelly wondered if it was her imagination, or was he having the same memory flashback?

They were kids, playing football in the school yard. Shelly was on Jonathan's team, and he was counting on her to make the final touchdown. She went left, and the quarterback threw the ball to her, but she couldn't quite wrap her hands around it. The ball pirouetted on her fingertips as she fumbled it. It was one of those twilight-zone moments when everything turns into slow motion. She had the ball for one fleeting second in her palm, and then it slipped out, and she crossed the goal line empty-handed.

"Shelly Bean," Elena repeated joyously. "That's a cute nickname."

It wasn't really a nickname. It was Jonathan's childhood name for her. No one ever called her that except Jonathan, and he had finally stopped in junior high when, for a stretch of about five months, Shelly was nearly four inches taller than Jonathan and she outweighed him by about ten pounds. She threatened to give him a bloody nose if he ever called her "Shelly Bean" again. He had taken the threat seriously and immediately stopped. She hadn't heard him use that term in more than ten years.

"Let's meet back here in about five minutes," Jonathan suggested, brushing over the nickname slip as if it hadn't happened. He took off to the left. Shelly went to the right.

Up and down the rows she reverently moved, checking the names and dates as she went. The grass beneath her feet was well manicured. She found a whole row of Müllers and one with a date of 1897. No Rudis anywhere.

She couldn't see Elena anymore. Jonathan was in the far corner with his head bent, examining grave markers.

"This is crazy," she said to herself. "What am I doing here?"

Starting to head down another row, she passed a wide old oak tree. She hadn't noticed the man standing there earlier. When he stepped from behind the tree and addressed her in German, she was startled. He had on simple, casual clothes and a felt hat. Nodding to her, he spoke to her in German again.

Shelly knew she had heard the phrase he used before. What did it mean? She broke down the familiar words, and the meaning came to her. "Who am I looking for?" she repeated to the man. He looked like the gardener. Maybe he knew some of the names from having tended this garden graveyard. *"Mein grosse, grosse, grosse Grossvater,"* Shelly told him, hoping he could understand her limited German. Then in English she explained. "My great-great-great-grandfather. His name was C. C. Rudi."

"Rudi!" The old man's eyes lit up. *"Ja,* Rudi," he began and then let go with a string of words that were impossible for Shelly to decipher. He reached over and shook her hand vigorously, his eyes still aglow. She couldn't understand a single syllable.

"Eine moment, *bitte,"* she said, holding up her hand in a gesture to get the man to stay put. "I'll be right back. Wait here. My friend, ah . . ." She tried to use her German again. *"Mein Freund sprechen Deutsche.* Wait."

She turned to run back and bring Jonathan to interpret for

her, but it was Elena who saw her and came hurrying over.

"Come with me," Shelly said excitedly. "There's a man who can tell me everything."

Elena plunged into the conversation with the man by greeting him formally, and then after her flow of perfect German sentences, the man shook his head earnestly and excitedly told his story again.

"Wow," Elena said.

"What?"

"Your ancestors are highly respected around here. Rudi was one of the founding families of the neighboring town called 'Weiler.' There's a castle there, the man says, and a monument to your ancestors."

"Seriously?"

"Do I look as if I could make all this up?" Elena said in her perky way.

Shelly kept herself from answering that question and realized again how much Elena sounded like Shelly five years ago. She suddenly wished she could go back and apologize to all her high school teachers for her case of terminal perkiness. She had never known how irritating it could be.

"He says we should go see the castle," Elena said.

"Would you ask him if he knows where my grandfather's grave is?"

Elena began her question and then stopped. "How do you say graveyard in German?" she asked Shelly.

"Can't help you there," Shelly said.

Turning back to the gardener, Elena acted out what she wanted to know. First she put her hands around her throat and strangled herself back and forth. Then she closed her eyes and stuck out her tongue, dropping her head to the side. With quick hand motions, Elena pantomimed the ground with a big grave marker.

"*Grab?*" the man asked carefully.

"Yes, of course," said Elena, tapping her forehead. "*Grab. Grave.*"

"Where's his grave? Can you show us?" Shelly jumped in.

The man began to speak in earnest. He pointed and tipped his head. Jonathan arrived and listened in.

"Can you understand him?" Jonathan asked Shelly.

"Not a word."

"There's a graveyard in the next town. Isn't that what he said?" he asked Elena.

"Yes. I don't quite understand what he's saying. Something about the way the graves are tended."

"Thank you very much," Shelly said, extending her hand to the old gentleman. "*Danke.*"

"*Bitte,*" he replied with a smile. He tipped his head once more, but he didn't take Shelly's offered hand.

Shelly turned to Jonathan and Elena. Elena had slipped her arm through Jonathan's and was sharing his coat pocket with his hand.

Seeing them snuggling like that made Shelly feel sick in the pit of her stomach. She tried to ignore it and said, "That's great news, isn't it? At least we know we're on the right trail. Wrong graveyard, but we're not far."

"What about the *Evangelische Kirche?*" Jonathan said. "Did you ask where that was? I found out this is the Catholic church."

"Oh, good point." Shelly turned back to ask the man, but he was gone. He must have bent behind a gravestone or slipped back behind one of the ancient trees.

"It can't be far," Jonathan said. "As a matter of fact," he looked up and craned his neck to see between the trees, "over there." He motioned behind Shelly. "I think that's another church spire. Should we walk or drive?"

"Walk," Shelly said.

"Drive," Elena said. "I'm cold."

"Then let's walk," Jonathan decided. "It'll warm us up."

Elena let out a little moan of complaint. It surprised Shelly. Jonathan loved to walk. So did Shelly. That had always been their favorite time together, ever since their first walk around the block. Shelly couldn't imagine Jonathan ending up with someone who didn't love to walk.

They had only covered two or so blocks through the old part of town when Elena pulled on Jonathan's arm, urging him to slow down. "I can't keep up with your long-legged strides, Johnny."

Shelly had thought they were going too slow as it was.

Jonathan slowed down and commented on the buildings they were passing. "That's probably the newest structure on this block," he said, motioning to a red-brick building with a large stone marker over the entryway with the words "*RATHAUS* 1893" carved into the smooth stone.

Shelly giggled at the sign. "Rat house," she repeated. "Is that where they send all the scoundrels?"

"No," Jonathan said patiently, "actually, the *Rathaus* is like the town meeting hall. All little German towns have one."

"Oh," Shelly said. She felt silly not knowing that. Turning a corner, they could see the spire in plain view as it stretched into the overcast sky behind a giant elm tree. On the other side of the elm tree stood a large, three-story building that seemed typical of the kind of old German construction they had seen today. The tile roof was the familiar orange tile with pop-out dormer windows set above two tiers of shuttered windows. It wouldn't have been such an unusual sight except that the building was painted the brightest lime green Shelly had ever seen. She had a T-shirt that color but never imagined it would work on a house. And such a large house. The shutters and door frames were painted a mustard yellow, and the flower boxes along the second-story windows bubbled over with deep red geraniums.

"Whoever lives there has a flair for color," Shelly said softly.

"Don't laugh," Jonathan said. "It could have once been the home of your relatives. It's old enough, and even though it's a little large for a parsonage and does look newer than a lot of these buildings, the *Pfarrer* usually lived right by the church."

"The *Pfarrer?*" Shelly repeated.

"That's German for pastor," Elena said. "It's a pretty church, isn't it?"

They could now see the clock tower beneath the black spire. The gold Roman numerals were set against a deep brown rim with sweeping, gold hands.

"Doesn't it give you the wonders?" Elena said as they stepped into the cobblestone courtyard that surrounded the church.

"The wonders?" Jonathan repeated.

"Yeah, to think your relatives once walked on this very ground. Doesn't that give you the wonders, Shelly?"

"It does. I only wish I knew more. I mean, was he the pastor at this church or was he born here and then pastored at the church in Weiler where he's buried?"

"We can knock on a few doors," Elena suggested. "Someone might be able to tell us where the current pastor lives, and we could ask him to check the church records."

"But it's Sunday," Shelly said, glancing up at the clock. The time was one-thirty-five. How well she remembered the routine around her house while growing up with a pastor. Dad would preach two services on Sunday morning and then

145

come home to a big lunch that Mom had ready. She was famous for her Sunday pot roast, which she stuck in the oven at two-hundred degrees at eight o'clock on Sunday mornings. By one-thirty the family had eaten heartily of the meat, potatoes, carrots, and Sunday pie, usually with ice cream. All they wanted to do was find a quiet corner and read the funny papers or take a nap. Shelly didn't feel right about disturbing the local pastor on a Sunday to bother him about dusty old church records. Especially not at one-thirty, when he was most likely stretching out for a nap.

"I'm content to see the church," Shelly said. "And maybe find the graveyard. Would you guys take my picture?" She held out Meredith's camera and moved into position in front of the church. A large arch had been created long ago from ginger- and marjoram-colored blocks of varying sizes and shapes. Across the entryway was an ornate iron gate locking out any who may try to harm the exquisite wooden church doors. However, they also locked out the occasional pilgrim, like Shelly, who showed up at off hours and wanted in.

"Smile," Elena said, focusing quickly and snapping the picture. "Could you take one of Johnny and me?" She held out the camera and smiled her winning smile.

"Sure," Shelly heard herself say.

Jonathan took his place in front of the iron gate. Elena flew to his side and curled up under his arm, wrapping her arm around his middle. Jonathan drew her close and gave her a little squeeze. Shelly focused the viewfinder. Jonathan was smiling. He had his arm around this girl, and he was smiling. As hard as it was for Shelly to admit, Jonathan appeared happy. She snapped the picture, refusing to let herself think about how she should have been the one standing beside him, receiving that squeeze, smiling and holding him tight.

She pulled the camera away and for a flash of a second,

white dots swirled before her eyes. Drawing in a deep breath, Shelly forced herself to smile at the couple.

Then she saw something she wasn't ready to see. Elena turned her face up toward Jonathan's. He leaned over and exchanged a sweet kiss with her. Elena whispered something to him, and he smiled.

Shelly felt as if the ground under her feet were beginning to shake. If she stayed where she was, it would certainly open up and swallow her.

"I'm going to walk around this other side," she said, looking down at the camera. "I'll meet you guys back at the car."

She turned her head and began to walk quickly before either of them could notice the tears stinging their way down to her quivering lips.

17

Shelly didn't cry long, and she didn't cry a lot of tears. She stopped by the old church wall that overlooked the town and the pleasant green farmlands beyond. Far to the right was a forested hill, and at the north end of that hill stood a castle. Not a grand, brazen castle like the one in Heidelberg, but a light gray structure with a single turret rising above the forest.

"God," Shelly whispered. Then she stopped. She had no idea what she wanted to say, or how she thought she should pray about all her mixed-up feelings. It seemed a long time since she had bothered God with any of her concerns. Her unspoken desire that Jonathan should not marry Elena was too selfish for her to pray. Jonathan apparently had found happiness. She was the one who needed the blessing. But how could she ask God for a blessing when it had been so long since she had done anything for him?

A soft wind swept in across the cobblestones and met the rumpled-up maple leaves, challenging them to a leaping contest. Around her feet the dying leaves hopped, as if they could prove by movement that they still had one last breath of life in them. They didn't fool Shelly. Tomorrow at this time, those same leaves would be strewn across this walkway in a hundred dried-out little shards. Some would have been flung over this wall where their tissue-thin skeletons would lie in the pathway, waiting for the imprint of some villager's boot.

Without having it all straight in her mind, Shelly sympathized with the leaves. There was no "last gasp of love's latest breath" left between Jonathan and her after all. The poets all lied. So did the spinners of fairy tales. Happy endings are not for everyone.

Shelly drew in a deep breath of the smoke-laced air from the old town below the wall. She told herself not to let it hurt. A real friend would be happy for Jonathan and his newfound love.

Bending over, Shelly picked up one of the curling leaves and pressed it between the paper with the information from her grandmother. That's when she noticed the rest of the information and realized that if these were clues to track down her ancestors, she had done pretty well. The church existed. Even the date, 1509, had appeared over the arched entryway above the iron gate. Only a bit of information remained unproved: Weiler, Ludwig Rudi, St. Annakapella. Shelly could guess that Ludwig Rudi was another relative, and the gardener had confirmed that they needed to go to the neighboring burg of Weiler. But she wasn't sure who St. Annakapella was.

The jaunt back to the car helped Shelly compose herself. She walked at her usual fast pace, and as she did, she thought about her sister's comment that Shelly had a little sway in the way she walked. She certainly hadn't tried to add anything to her walk. She had changed as she became older. Everyone did. Jonathan certainly had. If only some of the slight changes in his stature and personality had been disagreeable ones, she might have found it easier to say, "Boy, am I glad I didn't marry him!" Unfortunately, he seemed to have only become more perfect.

Mr. Perfect and his adoring fiancée were just hiking the

last street when Shelly caught up with them. Elena, with her short, thin legs, was a much slower walker than Jonathan. Shelly wondered if that would eventually be a problem for them. Even if it was, she doubted Jonathan would say anything. He never got mad.

"Which way to Weiler?" Shelly asked once they were all settled in the car. This time she had insisted on taking the back seat.

"I saw the sign for it back the way we came from Hilsbach," Jonathan said, turning the car around.

They noticed a family with two children on tricycles out for an afternoon stroll. Aside from the man in the cemetery, these were the first people they had seen in all of Hilsbach. The absence of residents had made the place a little too quiet for Shelly, but the people of this town obviously still honored the commandment to keep the Sabbath holy.

As the narrow road led them out of town, Shelly looked over her shoulder. It did, as Elena had said, give her the "wonders" to think of what this place had been like in 1509 and what kind of hearty ancestors she had who could build a wall from limestone blocks and harvest the fields. What incredible people they must have been, especially to have built the castle the traveling trio now saw coming into view as they wound up the hillside into Weiler.

"Let's check out the castle first," Elena suggested. "The graveyard might even be there."

They followed a slow Mercedes up the well-paved road to the castle. On either side of them lay terraced acres of grapevines. From the looks of the vines, they were at the end of their season, and all the usable fruit had been picked. A few stragglers clung to the withering branches.

The parking lot was large enough to hold hundreds of cars, but only five were parked there this Sabbath afternoon.

The three explorers got out and hiked up the asphalt path to the stone-hewn walls and tower. The trail turned to dirt, mud, and a little gravel dusted with autumn leaves. As they walked where once oxcarts had rumbled along and noblemen had pranced on groomed horses, Shelly stopped under one of the arches to examine the amazing wall of this fortress. The rocks were fitted together like a puzzle and worn smooth after centuries of work by heaven's natural cosmetologists — rain, wind, sun, sleet, and hail. Thick, green vines came over the top of the stone wall and tumbled down like Rapunzel's fabled tresses. Next to where Shelly stood at the base of the great tower, a smear of moss grew over the rock like a green five o'clock shadow on the face of a sleeping giant.

All around her was the scent of history. She touched the stone and found it as cold as she had imagined it would be. She gathered a flat, smooth pebble and tucked it in her pocket.

"This is what you love, isn't it?" Jonathan said. She hadn't seen him retrace his steps and come back to her.

"Oh, this? Yes," she said, "I love this."

Jonathan's smile was faint, somber, and astute. "This is what I've pictured you doing all these years. It wasn't enough for you to hear about places around the world. You needed to smell them and touch them, didn't you?"

His insight penetrated her, not because she hadn't ended up experiencing the world in the way he said, but because the Jonathan she once knew hadn't understood that.

"Actually, the thing is, during all these years, I . . ." Shelly was cut off by Elena coming back down the road and calling to them. She didn't know how to tell Jonathan that this was the first bit of Europe she had been to.

"Are you guys coming, or should I go ahead?" Elena called out.

Shelly looked at her feet and said, "Never mind." She stuck her hands in her coat pockets and held her little flat stone tightly. "We should get going."

Jonathan didn't say anything. She was having a hard time reading him. He had developed new expressions and shifted his jaw in a way that mystified her. What did it mean? She didn't know.

Silently they walked up the dirt road, each of them matching the other's long-legged strides in perfect rhythm. They both had to slow when Elena joined them. Up the road they went until they entered the castle courtyard. To Shelly's surprise, next to the ancient cistern was a stage, complete with flying banners and enough folding chairs to accommodate an oompah band. It seemed so out of place with the rest of the grounds.

"I think that's a restaurant," Elena said, pointing to a door that seemed to lead into the castle area.

A few other people were shuffling around, but there was no sight of a visitor's information sign. Shelly realized that they were off the beaten trail, and it was unlikely many people would come here desiring a tour. The place seemed to be more of a local park or community hangout than a tourist attraction. Of course, with her limited experience with castles, Shelly found it hard to believe that anyone could be nonchalant about having a castle in the backyard. But then, that's how people used to react when she lived thirty miles from Disneyland and told them she had only been there once.

"Are you hungry?" Jonathan asked Elena.

"Might be fun to check it out," she said.

They tried the door and found it open, which surprised Shelly since everything else had been closed on Sunday. A life-sized, authentic suit of armor stood guard just inside the door. Shelly stopped and gazed at it in amazement. She wanted to touch it. Next to the armor was a velvet cushioned bench, apparently for waiting customers. Real swords pointed upward with their flat sides forming the back of the bench and offering support to the customer's back.

"That's convenient," Shelly said. "Lean back, and you can get your hair cut while you wait to be seated."

Elena burst out laughing. Jonathan smiled appreciatively. Shelly was surprised she could think up anything bordering on wit. She was supposed to be nervous and uncomfortable around Jonathan and Elena. She was also supposed to despise this woman who had stolen her only true love. But somehow the events of the past few days were all mashed together and not at all cut and dried.

A woman behind the bar to the right of the entryway called out to them in German. Elena went over to chat with her. Jonathan and Shelly followed.

"They don't open until six for dinner," Elena said. "If we want something from the bar, she'll get it for us."

"Nothing for me, thanks," Shelly said. "But could you ask her if she knows anything about a Saint Annakapella?"

The woman began to respond before Elena could ask her in German. She motioned toward the door and nodded at them with a friendly smile.

"There's a *Spielplatz* down the way," Elena began her translation. "You know a, what do we call it? Playground. That's it. Down on the other side of the castle grounds is a playground and a trail that leads to the chapel. A 'Kapelle' is a chapel. This one is called St. Anna Chapel."

"One of many," Jonathan added for Shelly's benefit. "There are a lot of St. Anna churches because they're named after St. Anna's Church in Augsburg. St. Anna's was one of Martin Luther's last hideouts."

Shelly vaguely remembered hearing about Augsburg in

her early church-history lessons. She knew a little about Martin Luther, the priest who turned the religious world of his time against him because he taught that we are saved by God's grace only and not because of anything we do to deserve it. She hadn't known St. Anna's had been his last hideout. Perhaps that was the church from which he had written, "A Mighty Fortress Is Our God."

These details had held little interest to a nine-year-old sitting in a cold folding chair in the corner of the church basement and watching Mrs. Wentchel put figures up on a flannel board. But now it all came alive for Shelly.

She wasn't hungry or thirsty. All she wanted to do was see the chapel at the end of the trail past the playground. "If you guys want to stay," Shelly suggested, "I'll go on down to the chapel and meet you back here in a bit."

"Sounds good to me," Elena said.

Shelly turned to go before Jonathan responded. She left the restaurant and strode through the courtyard and down the trail to the playground. Several children were swinging and squealing as they slid down the slide. The mothers sat on a long bench under two tall trees. As Shelly approached, she thought how the two trees seemed to have a comical contest going, each trying to see who could be the first to drop a leaf dead center on the head of one of the mothers. As Shelly strode past them, she thought the tree on the right might be winning.

At the end of the playground, as the woman at the bar had said, a trail led into a thickly wooded area. Shelly entered the woods. Everything seemed suddenly hushed; even the laughter of the children on the playground. The trail was a thick carpet of amber leaves, and the fragrance was intoxicating to Shelly. She stopped and drew it in, trying to identify it. Moss and wood bark mixed with something else. A spicy-sweet, earthy scent. Oh, it was wonderful.

Did my ancestors ever walk through these woods? I can picture it being exactly like this, unchanged, for centuries. Did secret lovers meet here and whisper their eternal pledges of devotion to each other? Did priests or pastors meet them at the chapel at the end of the trail and bless their covert marriages?

Above her, Shelly could hear some birds engaged in a squabble. Somewhere, out of her view, a little bird was giving another bird "what for." That seemed to set off a reaction in the neighboring penthouses as a chorus of chittering and chirping enveloped her.

She chuckled to herself and kept looking around in the changing shadows for evidence of where the feuding was coming from. On the tree closest to her right, a squirrel darted across one branch and leaped to the next tree with an acorn in his mouth. As she watched him go, a small feather began to float toward her, seemingly out of thin air. Shelly caught the treasure before it touched the ground and examined it closely. She almost expected to see blood on the tip as evidence of the fight that raged in the treetops. There was no blood. The chittering died down. Shelly tucked the feather in her pocket next to the smooth stone and smiled to herself.

She had taken only a few more steps down the trail when she heard something that made her stop short. It was a whistle. One long, one short, one long, with the short a note higher.

Meet me at the tree house, Shelly's brain interpreted for her. She slowly turned to watch Jonathan stride down the trail toward her.

He was alone.

18

"It's been a long time since I've heard that one," Shelly said as Jonathan approached. She felt nervous but decided to make light of the situation.

"Do you remember what that one was?" He was now beside her, and they automatically fell into step, continuing down the trail.

"Come to the tree house?" Shelly asked.

"Are you asking me or telling me?" Jonathan challenged.

Shelly laughed aloud. That had been one of his favorite sayings as a kid. His dad used to use it all the time, too.

"I'm telling you," Shelly stated confidently. "Come to the tree house."

"You're right," Jonathan said. "I'm surprised you remember."

Something in Shelly's core tightened up like a fist. She wanted to punch him with her words. *You would be surprised to know all the stuff I remember, Jonathan Renfield! I remember everything. Everything! You don't know how long I stifled it all. Now I have it all back, and it's of no use because I don't have you.*

All she said to him was, "I remember."

They walked in silence. The trail ended abruptly, and they entered a flat, grassy area where a stately chapel stood. The square building was made of blue-gray stones and was held together with a brown mortar that had blended itself so well with the stones over the years that it was difficult to see the edges. A simple wooden door stood under a stone archway shaped like the head of a bullet. Beside the door stood two life-sized statues on ornately sculpted pedestals. Shelly had no idea who the statues were of.

"It's locked," Jonathan said after trying the door. No one was around. The chapel was surrounded by sweet grass and a beautiful view of the valley below where the village snuggled down under a blanket of thick gray clouds.

"I don't see a graveyard," Shelly said.

"No."

"I thought there might be something here. Too bad it's locked."

"Yeah," Jonathan agreed.

"I guess the graveyard is probably in the town. That looks like a church spire over there on the left."

"Could be," Jonathan said.

An uncomfortable silence held them together on the cold, gray chapel steps. They were looking all around but not at each other. Shelly touched the side of one of the statues. The unidentified frozen man offered no assistance.

"We should probably go back. Elena will be wondering what happened to us," Shelly said.

"I'm going to ask you a question," Jonathan said, not moving an inch. "Did you ever receive a letter from me?"

"Yes." Shelly cautiously met his gaze.

His eyebrows lifted slightly. "You did?"

Shelly nodded.

His brows seemed to cave in, and his eyes squinted. "Then why didn't you write back?"

Shelly didn't know what to say.

Jonathan turned from her and marched out onto the grass. He spun around and looked at her with fire in his expression. "I think I deserve an explanation!" he yelled at her.

She was so surprised to see this side of him that she had no response.

"You never gave me a chance, Shelly. You just freaked out and ran away. What was I supposed to do? I gave you your space. I waited. I tried to understand. How could you throw away our friendship just like that?"

"I was afraid," Shelly answered.

"Afraid of what?" Jonathan came closer.

"Of marriage. Of commitment. Of not being able to do what I wanted to do."

"Ah, there it is," Jonathan said, pointing at her when she made her last statement. "You were afraid of giving up your dreams, but didn't you see? I was trying to find a way for us both to have our dreams and each other, too. But you weren't even willing to talk it through. The truth was, you didn't want me."

Shelly fought back the tears and shook her head. "That's not true. We were young, Jonathan. We didn't know what we were doing."

His nostrils flared as he took in a deep breath and tried to calm down. "I agree. We were. But we could have worked it out. We could have corresponded or told each other we would go our separate directions for a year and then see if we still felt the same way. You cut me off. What was I supposed to do?"

Shelly's ears felt cold. Her nose was about to drip from the tears she was holding back. She felt miserable inside and out. "You could have come to me," she said quietly.

"In Pasadena?"

Shelly nodded.

Jonathan stared at her and then let out a laugh of disbelief and shook his head. "What did you want me to do? Come riding in on a white horse and take you back? Shelly, you don't get it. No prince is going to rescue a runaway. That would be like kidnapping you from yourself. You didn't want to be found. If you did, you would have responded."

"How was I supposed to respond?" Shelly's voice rose. "You wanted all or nothing. I had no choice but to take nothing. Your plan was all about you, your life, and your college education."

"And I was wrong," Jonathan said calmly.

The fire drained from Shelly's lips. After a silence she said, "I was wrong, too. I should have talked things through with you rather than leaving the way I did. I'm sorry, Jonathan." The tears began to well in her eyes. "When I came to Europe, I wanted to see you to tell you I was sorry. Please forgive me."

"I'm sorry, too, Shel. You don't know how long I've waited to be able to say that to you. Will you forgive me?"

"Yes," Shelly said, blinking back the tears. "Of course I forgive you. Will you forgive me?"

A tear coursed down Jonathan's cheek. "Yes, I forgive you. I meant what I said in my letter. You'll always be my best friend."

Shelly opened her arms, inviting Jonathan to embrace her. He held back. She could see his chest heaving as he harnessed his emotions. His lips remained slightly parted, but no words came out. With his stormy gray eyes he searched her face for understanding.

Shelly slowly drew her arms in and tried to silence her own pounding heart. Jonathan couldn't let himself go to her. Not here, where they were all alone with their emotions racing, not with their history, their familiarity with each other's kisses.

He took a cautious step toward her. "Shel . . ."

"It's okay," she said, coaxing a smile to her lips. "You don't have to say anything."

He ran his fingers through his fawn brown hair and shifted his weight nervously from his right foot to his left. He looked just the way he had when he had stood at the front door and told Shelly's mom that his new puppy, Bob, had dug in her garden and ruined her flowers. Jonathan had produced from behind his back a fistful of drooping zinnias, snapdragons, and marigolds — Mom's trampled flowers — as his peace offering.

This time he had nothing behind his back to offer. He couldn't even give Shelly back her trampled heart.

"Jonathan, I want you to know that I like Elena. I'm sincerely happy for you. For both of you. And I wish you both the very best."

He stared at her. Shelly couldn't read him. It was the same look he had given her the other day right before he and Elena announced their engagement. She felt he was waiting for her to say something, but she didn't know what it was.

If the situation were different, Shelly would have pursued that thought until she found out what he wanted. She would have opened her heart to him and told him everything she had been thinking and feeling and how she wanted him back. But now she couldn't put that kind of burden on him. Jonathan was engaged to another woman. As his best friend, Shelly would honor that relationship. She wouldn't download her emotional baggage on him. What was past, had happened. What was now, had to be.

He continued to wait for her to say something. She wanted to ask if he and Elena had set a date yet, to find out why Elena didn't have a ring. She wanted to know if they were going to stay in Belgium or move back to the States. She wondered what he had told Elena about Shelly. It seemed all he had told

Elena was that he and Shelly were childhood companions, and he had left out the part about their being in love with each other as teens. She mostly wanted to ask Jonathan if he loved Elena.

But all she asked was, "May I have your parents' new address? My folks wanted me to ask. In case I saw you. I didn't want to forget."

Jonathan looked as if he was about to say something, but his lips finally closed, and he nodded. Turning to head back up the trail, Jonathan fell into a quick stride, and Shelly walked beside him. As they entered the woods, she felt a sharp pain in her chest. It was the kind of pain she used to get on cold winter days in Seattle if she ran and then tried to draw a deep breath.

She knew what it was. She didn't want to admit it, though. And she knew why this pain was happening here in these woods. She was walking beside the only man she had ever truly loved, and the two of them were in the most romantic, enchanting place she had ever been in her life. The woods begged for secrets to be whispered under the sympathetic eaves, for lovers to promise themselves to each other and to seal their pledge with a kiss. Here Shelly and Jonathan walked; yet they harbored no hope of any vows or of any more kisses between them. Ever.

Yes, she knew where this pain came from, all right. This sensation came to anyone who had such a full treasure chest in her heart and then locked it up for good and heaved it into the depths of nothingness.

They emerged from the woods and marched past the playground, where the carefree children still spun each other on the merry-go-round and laughed happily.

Enjoy it, dear hearts, Shelly silently exhorted the young ones. *Enjoy your moment of innocence. One day it will be gone.*

19

"I told Elena we would meet her at the car," Jonathan said in words that were unevenly spaced. Had the woods jolted his soul as well?

"Do you want to walk down the back side of the castle or go around the way we first came up?" Shelly asked.

"This is fine."

They continued down the wide trail away from the castle wall. Just before the parking lot, facing the valley, they saw a ten-foot-tall memorial surrounded by a short iron fence. Inside the fence grew a dozen rosebushes, guarding the simple yet regal-looking monument.

"What do you suppose this is?" Shelly asked, stepping off the trail to have a look. Jonathan followed her. He was the first to find the carved names.

"Look. The one at the top: Ludwig Rudi. He's listed as one of the founding fathers of this town."

Shelly felt a swell of pride in her heritage. "Would you mind taking a picture for my mom?"

Jonathan snapped her photo, and when he handed her camera back, his fingers brushed softly across her hand. They felt warm on her chilly flesh. Shelly decided right then that the farther she stayed away from Jonathan the better. The two of them could not pretend they didn't still feel something for each other.

Shelly reasoned that Jonathan wouldn't have proposed to Elena unless he loved her. And he wouldn't break a commitment once he had made it.

They needed to be away from each other if his relationship with Elena was going to work. As much as Shelly hated the idea, she knew that the sooner she extracted herself from Jonathan's life, the sooner he could get on with it. And wasn't that the true test of love? Being willing to give up something for the other? Shelly knew right then that she loved Jonathan so much she was willing to give him his future, void of any complications from her.

Elena was waiting inside the car, curled up in the back seat taking a nap. She perked up when they arrived and asked Shelly if they had found the grave.

"No. We think we saw a church spire down in the valley. Do you mind if we look for a graveyard near the church?"

"Of course not. You don't mind that I came to the car, do you?"

"No," Shelly said.

Elena motioned to her. "You have a little smear of something right there under your eye." Shelly pulled down the visor and checked the mirror. Her eyes were a puffy, red mess. The smear was mascara that had most likely run when she had started to cry. Shelly dabbed it away. It felt strange to be told by her former boyfriend's fiancée that she had smeared makeup, which had happened when she cried over that boyfriend.

Yes, the sooner I extract myself from this crazy triangle, the better. There are other fish in the sea, as they always say. Maybe some wonderful man is right around the corner waiting for me, but I couldn't meet him until I had closure on this relationship.

She kept pumping herself with logical explanations of why this was happening to her as they drove through the quiet town and made a circle around the church. There were no graveyards.

"Entschuldigung ich, bitte," Elena said, rolling down her window and calling out to a man walking down the street. He stopped, and she proceeded to ask him where the graveyard was. He answered, and she thanked him. Shelly found it hard not to admire Elena's spunk and ability with the language.

"Two kilometers down this road," Elena reported as she rolled up her window. "Be sure to take lots of pictures. Your grandmother will cry when she sees them."

"Yes," Shelly agreed. "I'm sure she will."

When they arrived, they all got out and walked into the graveyard. The first headstone they saw read "Rudi."

"Look," Elena said, "another one is over here. And one is over here. This little cul de sac looks like a whole family of Rudis. No wonder that guy at the Hilsbach graveyard was so excited when you told him you were a Rudi. It looks as if the Rudis once ran this town."

Shelly strolled up and down the rows. She was distantly related to all of them. The thought amazed her and sent shivers down her spine at the same time. They were all gone. She was their offspring. In a sense they had entrusted her to carry on. But carry on what? A career?

Suddenly her life felt shallow. Even if she lived to be a hundred, her life was almost a quarter of the way gone. What had she done with it? There rose within her an urge to accomplish something, to create some kind of heritage she could pass on. For the first time she felt an urgency to have children. She wanted to live on in them, the way her rows of relatives somehow lived on in her.

"I don't see a C. C. Rudi yet," Jonathan said, continuing

up and down the rows in his quest. "Do you have any idea what his first name was or his parents' names?"

"No, I don't." Shelly continued to look, too. But it didn't matter so much that she find the grave now. It seemed she had already found something in this hunt. She understood, or at least thought she understood, a little better the beautiful gift of her Christian heritage, and she had arrived at a clearer picture of what she wanted out of life. She wanted to be married, to raise a family, and to bring them up, as her mother used to say, "in the nurture and admonition of the Lord."

The painful part of making such a discovery was that less than an hour earlier she had purposed to emotionally release herself from the only man with whom she had ever wanted to undertake such an endeavor.

All the logic, emotions, and self-discovery gave Shelly a headache. She was hungrier than she had realized and didn't think she could handle any more exploring.

"Can you take a couple of pictures for me?" she asked.

Elena reached for Shelly's camera and directed her to the most attractive of the Rudi-family graves. Pink geraniums bloomed atop the grave mound. The marker was done in black marble with white highlighting behind the letters. Next to the names, "Lina and Alfred Rudi," was an impressive carving of Christ dressed as a shepherd, carrying a staff, and knocking on a closed door.

"Thanks," Shelly said after Elena snapped the picture. "My mom and grandma will both be very happy." Shelly put out her hand, palm up, and as she did so she felt a raindrop hit her hand.

"Looks like we found this just in time," Elena said. "The heavens are about ready to dump on us. Are either of you as starving as I am? Let's find someplace to eat."

They hurried to the car and drove away as the rain began

to seriously come down. Jonathan drove almost to Heidel-berg before they found a tavern that was open. It was a smoky, loud, brawl-just-waiting-to-happen kind of eatery, but Jonathan assured Shelly that this was the best they would be able to find on a Sunday evening in this part of Germany.

The waiter recommended the special of the evening when Elena asked what was good. She closed her menu and took his advice. Shelly couldn't read much of the menu anyway, so she ordered the same, as did Jonathan.

They weren't disappointed. A two-inch-thick slab of raw meat was delivered to each of them on a sizzling flat rock bed-ded on a wooden paddle board. Two sauces were provided in metal dividers. The idea was to slice the meat as it cooked on the hot stone.

Shelly was a little leery, but the first portion that looked cooked came right off with her knife. It was like cutting but-ter. The meat cooled quickly, and when she took a bite, it seemed to melt in her mouth. She was so hungry she ate al-most all of it before trying the last few bites with the accompa-nying sauces. The sauces only made it better.

"This is unbelievable," she said, searing the last bit of beef. "What do they feed their cattle?"

"This isn't beef," Jonathan said. "You're eating venison. And judging by the color, this fellow may have been on the hoof this morning."

"Try these potatoes," Elena said, offering Shelly the large bowl of whipped potatoes. "They taste really good if you warm them on the platter."

Shelly ate until she couldn't take another bite. This was the first time since she had been in Germany that she had eaten her usual amount.

She had always had a quick metabolism and was teased about how much she could eat. As she thought about it, she realized that she hadn't had much of an appetite since she had moved back to Seattle. Maybe this was a sign that her emotional struggles of the past few months might be coming to an end.

"Do you have a boyfriend, Shelly?" Elena asked on their drive home. "Or did I already ask you that?"

"You did," was all Shelly said.

"The reason I ask is because I know this guy that I think you would really like. He's a little younger than you, I think. But he's nice. His name is Tony. He's just about your height probably," Elena said. "I come up to his nose, if that helps you judge. Anyway, he works at an auto body shop in Akron, but he wants to work on airplane jet engines. That's why I thought you two might be interested in each other. Plus he likes brunettes."

"Flight attendants and jet-engine mechanics don't often overlap in their job descriptions," Jonathan said. He said it nicely, but Shelly realized he thought Elena's logic was off.

"I know, but he's a really nice guy, and I just think Shelly would like him. I'm sure he would like her."

Shelly was sitting in the back seat biting the inside of her mouth to keep from laughing. This was crazy. Her old boyfriend's fiancée was trying to set her up with a mechanic in Ohio. Meredith would get a good laugh out of this one.

When they arrived back at Mike and Jana's, it was dark. Shelly thanked Jonathan and Elena from the back seat of the car and told them they didn't have to drive around to find a parking place, they could just drop her off.

Elena reached over the seat when they said good-bye and gave Shelly's arm a squeeze. "I'm so glad I got to meet you. I know Jonathan thinks highly of you. I can see why. I wish you lived here. It would be great to get to know you better."

Shelly absorbed Elena's words with the affection with

which they were being offered. Of course Elena liked her. She didn't know that Shelly had once been inside of Jonathan's heart the way Elena apparently was now. Jonathan had chosen not to show her any of his past scars. Shelly could only assume that when Elena had entered his heart, she had found no shrines to past loves that she had to knock down, which meant that Jonathan had swept his life clean of Shelly. Either that or Elena didn't yet have full access to his heart.

"I'm glad we got to spend this time together, too," Shelly said sincerely. "You know, don't you, that you're marrying the last true hero on this planet?"

Elena beamed her appreciation at Shelly and then showered her warm approval on Jonathan.

"At least, that's what my sister tells me," Shelly added as she opened the door. She knew the remark had a twist, but she couldn't resist getting in a final tease. Then, because she was full of red meat and feeling a bit aggressive, she said, " 'Bye, Johnny."

Before she closed the car door, Shelly caught his final comment, which also carried a snap. "Feel free to write sometime," he said.

She opened the tall, double wooden doors without looking back. When she entered Mike and Jana's apartment, Shelly felt overwhelmed. She wanted to throw herself on the bed and sob over Jonathan's driving away and out of her life forever. She hadn't expected to feel this strong reaction and found it hard to keep her smile from quivering when Jana asked how the day had gone.

"Wonderful," Shelly stated. "How's Meredith feeling?"

"Better, I think. She went back to bed, and she might be asleep already. But she was up for a few hours this afternoon, and we had a good time finally catching up. Are you hungry?"

"Not at all. I'm ready to hit the sack. I could use a bath,

though, if that's okay. We ate at a smoky place, and I can't stand the way I smell right now."

"Go ahead. Make yourself comfy. I told Meri if she felt better tomorrow I'd take her to my favorite place for breakfast. Do you have plans, or would you like to go with us?"

"I'd love to go. I have no plans, no plans at all." As Shelly headed for the bathtub, she added silently, *No plans at all for the rest of my life.*

20

Shelly's statement that she had no plans for the rest of her life didn't turn out to be completely accurate. She stayed in Germany only two more days and flew home when Meredith went on to her convention in Frankfurt. Shelly didn't think she could absorb any more stimulation than she had experienced in the last few days.

The decision to return when she did proved to be a good one financially because she was able to pick up another flight attendant's schedule. During the rest of October, she worked the eighty-five hours allotted to full-time flight attendants for Sunlit Airlines.

During her downtime, Shelly painted her bedroom furniture, weatherized the front porch, and planted tulip bulbs. Busyness was her best friend. Meredith's new job kept her on the go, and they ended up communicating mostly by notes on the refrigerator door. It made Shelly glad that she and Meri had had the chance to spend those few days together in Heidelberg. In every way, Shelly was determined to start another chapter in her life. She was done with Jonathan.

She did okay until Christmas. Christmas at the Graham house had always been a festive occasion. Shelly's grandparents on both sides were still living, and they came to Seattle for Christmas week. The oldest Graham daughter, Megan, and her husband and two daughters came for the week also. Mom and Dad's house was a hub of yuletide activity.

Shelly was able to join in on only a fraction of the fun. She had four flights right before Christmas and wore her beeper through the Christmas Eve candlelight service as well as all Christmas day. Fortunately, no calls came. But being on call was starting to unnerve her. It made it difficult to relax, knowing that at any moment she could be buzzed.

On Christmas day, after the dishes from their big meal had all been washed and everyone had found a comfortable chair to flop into, Shelly sat down with her grandmother Rudi at the kitchen table. Grandma had been eager to see Shelly's photos from Germany but said she wouldn't look at them unless Shelly gave a comment on each one. They spent hours together at the kitchen table with mugs of cocoa and a plate of cookies. Her grandmother had never been to Germany, so she wanted to know every detail.

When they came to the picture of Jonathan standing in front of the church with his arm around Elena, Shelly felt a stab of remorse. It was the first she had let herself feel in months.

"This is Jonathan, isn't it?" Grandma asked.

"Yes, that's Jonathan. And that's Elena. His fiancée or maybe his wife. I don't know when they were planning to get married."

Grandma Rudi peered at Shelly through her glasses with a peculiar expression. "I didn't know your Jonathan was getting married."

"He's not my Jonathan," Shelly said quickly. "We're still good friends. But he's not my Jonathan."

Grandma clucked her tongue. "Of course he's your Jonathan. He was always your Jonathan, and you were always his

Shelly Bean. It will always be so."

Shelly swallowed her regret. "Not this time, I'm afraid. I'm nobody's Shelly Bean."

Grandma reached her wrinkled hand over and patted Shelly's cool, clammy hand. "This is sad news to me, dear one."

"It's not so sad. I don't want to look at it that way."

"But, my dear, you have made so many deposits into this relationship for so many years. How can you not feel robbed?"

An impulsive tear slipped down Shelly's cheek. "I don't know," she whispered. "I just have to go on."

With her thin eyebrows drawn together over the frames of her glasses, Grandma Rudi looked compassionately at Shelly. Slowly shaking her head Grandma said, "Two things in life should never be taken for granted. One is a godly heritage. The other is true friends."

Shelly blinked hard and tried to force her tears back with a smile. "I don't take either of those gifts lightly," she said in a hoarse voice. Pulling out the next picture from the stack, she covered up Jonathan's perpetually smiling face.

"This one is from the cemetery. Dozens of Rudis are buried there, but we couldn't find a marker for C. C. Rudi," Shelly said.

"Of course you couldn't," Grandma said matter-of-factly. "He's buried in Texas."

"In Texas!"

"Yes, didn't you know that? Carl Christian Rudi was the first one from our family to immigrate to the U.S. He was a circuit preacher in Texas for many years."

"I searched all over for his grave. I thought he was buried in Hilsbach or Weiler," Shelly said. "All the information I had was this." She pulled out the slip of paper with the pertinent details Grandma had jotted down before the trip. When Shelly unfolded the sheet, a perfectly pressed leaf fluttered to the table. Its amber brilliance had faded, but it remained intact.

Grandma Rudi reached across the table and, with a slightly trembling touch, picked up the maple leaf by its dry, spindly stem. "From Germany?" she asked.

"Yes."

Shelly remembered how she had kidnapped the frail leaf at the church wall and had kept it from being swept away by the wind.

"It's from the church," Shelly said, "the one with the date 1509 over the archway. This one." She turned back to the photo of Jonathan and Elena. "I picked up this little orphan leaf by the stone wall that surrounds the church grounds."

At the time it had reminded Shelly of the "last gasp of Love's latest breath." This evening it gave her the "wonders," as Elena would say. It was amazing to her that the leaf was still so finely preserved.

"Would you like it?" Shelly asked as Grandma held the frail skeleton up to the light.

"I would."

"I wish I'd brought you back something better," Shelly said. "I should have bought you some kind of special souvenir from Germany."

"This is the best gift you could give me," Grandma said. "This was once living in the homeland of my ancestors. You preserved it perfectly. Your visit to the church and the cemetery paid a great honor to my family. Thank you, dear."

"I only wish I'd had a better idea of what I was looking for when I was there. These clues were pretty vague."

Shelly's grandma looked at the list. "This is all I had from my mother's Bible. I believe the significance of the church in

Hilsbach was that Carl Christian Rudi was christened there."

"What about St. Annakapella?"

"I don't know. I think he was married in the States."

"It's a beautiful little chapel with a gorgeous view of the valley. You have to walk through the woods to get to it," Shelly said, smiling at the memory. "I'll never forget how I felt when I walked through the hushed woods. It was as if I had entered a private domain, and yet I was welcomed by all the woodland creatures. And the fragrance! Oh, the scent of those trees — I'll always remember it."

Grandma Rudi smiled. "Then you have your answer. All you ever need to know about St. Annakapella is that you were drawn closer to God through his creation on your journey to it. It doesn't matter what it meant to someone from our family's past. It has meaning to you now. Write it down so your children will know."

Shelly felt the corners of her heart squeeze in. *My children! What if I never have children? Then what will it matter a hundred years from now that I walked in a distant woods with the only man I've ever loved, but all we shared was the breathing in and out of the same air?*

The visit with her grandmother ignited in Shelly a fear that life was going to pass her by. Everyone was going to get married and leave her in the dust. In the days that followed Christmas, her mind kept repeating the first line of the poem Jonathan had sent her so long ago: "Since there's no help."

She added her own twist to it. *Since there's no hope.*

As the after-Christmas depression set in, Shelly felt even more abandoned. She longed for busyness to keep her mind occupied, but it kept running in the same circle of hopelessness. Shelly was emotionally fatigued.

Through it all, she learned that her fear of never marrying

was only fed by encountering women who were married or engaged. She learned it was better to hang out with women who weren't getting married. Women like Meredith.

21

"I'm serious," Shelly said one chilly January night as she and Meredith were sitting by the fire in their cozy cabin. "If you fall in love, I don't want to hear about it. If you decide to get married, don't tell me."

"Did you get another wedding announcement from one of your high school friends?" Meredith asked. She was sitting on the floor with a shish-kebab skewer and a bag of marshmallows. "How many do you want? Two okay?"

"Sure. Two is good for starters. And no, I didn't get another invitation. I'm not looking for wedding invitations in the mail."

"That's not what I think," Meredith said in a teasing voice. "I think you're waiting for the invitation from Jonathan and Elena, and every day it doesn't arrive you wonder all over again if they're still engaged."

"That's not what I was thinking," Shelly said. Meredith's surmise was only half true. She did wonder every now and then if Jonathan and Elena were still together. But she didn't think about it every single day.

The airline's business had picked up over the holidays, and Shelly had worked a full schedule in both November and December. Her bank account was in the pink again, which meant it was a shade above red. Because of her hectic flying schedule during November and December, Shelly hadn't found much time to relax, let alone to feel sorry for herself or to ponder the state of Jonathan and Elena's relationship.

However, now that January had brought a slower schedule, Shelly was afraid the loneliness and restlessness would drive her crazy.

"I think I need a hobby or something," she said. "I don't have enough to do, and I'm certain I won't be working many hours until the summer. Do you want to take a tole-painting class with me?"

"What would we tole paint?" Meredith asked, carefully turning the marshmallows in the fireplace.

"I don't know. What about ballroom dancing? Didn't you always want to learn to dance?"

"Where are you coming up with these?" Meri asked.

"The community college adult electives classes. We received a catalog in the mail today for next semester's classes."

"Here," Meri said, holding out the skewer. "Take the top two. Careful."

Shelly extracted the gooey wads of toasted sugar and popped one in her mouth.

Meredith put her marshmallows back in the fire. "Did I tell you I saw Mr. Hadley today at the mailbox? He said the camp needs a new dining room hostess, and if we know anyone, we should tell him."

"Exactly what is a dining room hostess?" Shelly asked, licking her sticky lips.

"Did you ever meet Emma Jane? She was the hostess for years. She would coordinate the setup for the different groups that came in and make sure everything ran smoothly at mealtime. I think she ended up doing a lot of their welcoming, too. When the conferees arrived, she would check them in and give them maps and keys to their cabins."

"Sounds like a fun job," Shelly said.

"Why don't you do it?"

"Me?"

"Sure. Just until they can hire someone. Especially if your flight schedule for the spring is going to be as sparse as you say." Meredith pulled her browned marshmallows from the fire and looked at them with approval. "Perfect."

"I hate to admit this, but that's not such a bad idea. I can walk to work, wear whatever I want, and eat camp food."

Meredith laughed. "You've forgotten the biggest bonus. I almost considered taking the position for this reason."

"What's that?"

"Their weekend single men's retreats!" Meredith lifted her skewer triumphantly. "You take the job, tell me when some fine specimens of God's creation are checking in, and I'll come over to set tables or something."

In spite of all the joking, Shelly ended up taking the job. Jack Hadley said he understood about her sporadic schedule, and the camp was just glad to have her for whatever hours she could spare. His wife said she would fill in during the times Shelly had to fly.

The first two weeks the camp had two outdoor education groups come in back to back. The first week one hundred-twenty sixth-graders descended on the camp from the public school. They spent four days and three nights at the conference center. During the day they were taught science lessons regarding the trees and wildlife in the area. At night, they were the wildlife in the area. For the second group, the counselors kept tighter control of the kids, and the nights were much more peaceful.

Shelly's duties were easy enough for her to finish in a few hours each day. She checked with the cook on the meals and gave him the number of campers to expect. She saw to setting the tables before each meal and made sure everything was cleared at the end of the meals.

During those two weeks, Shelly flew once. She streamlined and mastered the workload in the dining room and then asked Jack Hadley if she could take on a few other projects around the conference center. He was thrilled and gave her an open invitation to jump in to coordinate the hospitality area.

Shelly found that she was in her element. She designed a tea-and-coffee cart that could be set up at the back of the meeting rooms for the adult conferences. It met with immediate success at the first couples' weekend conference. Jack called her into his office Monday morning. A middle-aged, balding man, he always wore knit vests. Shelly suspected his wife knitted them for him.

"I realize this may be way out of line," Jack said, "but I want to at least ask. Would you consider coming on staff with us full-time? We could give you a combined job description that covered all the areas in which your talents lie. I was thinking of something like Hospitality and Facility Coordinator."

Shelly hadn't expected his offer and pulled back. She knew conference centers were not known for their abundance of funds for employees. Sometimes workers even had to raise their own support to work on staff. Since finances had been tight as it was with the airline position in flux, to join the staff of a camp was a scary thought.

"I've penciled out a benefits package for you," Jack said. "We can discuss this, of course, and make whatever adjustments might be possible. All I ask is that you give it some prayer, and let's meet next Monday at the same time. How does that sound?"

"Okay," Shelly agreed, taking the paper from him. She considered telling him right then and there that her answer would have to be no. While she loved helping out part-time, she had never intended this to be her occupation. "I'll give it some thought," she said instead.

"Fine." Jack got up and saw her to the door of his cramped office. "We'll talk next Monday."

Shelly couldn't help but think he could use his space much more efficiently if he put in floor-to-ceiling bookshelves on the long south wall. A four-drawer filing cabinet instead of the short two-drawer would make more sense and would help clear the counter of all those stacks of files.

What am I doing? I'm already trying to coordinate the facilities! I'd better get out of here.

Shelly finished up her paperwork for the kitchen staff and went home. Meredith was busy working in her loft office so Shelly quietly settled in their one comfortable living room chair and took a closer look at the papers from Jack. The salary offer was lower than the amount she would receive for working eighty-five hours a month for the airline. She had expected that. Other benefits were being offered, though, that she hadn't expected.

The Tulip Cottage was owned by someone on the camp's board of directors. If Shelly joined the staff full-time, the cottage's rent would be waived. That would save both Meredith and her a big chunk each month. Medical and dental coverage was included in the package, and meals were always available to her in the dining hall. To anyone else, that last point might not have been much of a perk, but ever since Shelly had become more active, her voracious appetite had returned, and she was eating constantly. The free meals could actually save her more than a hundred dollars a month.

The offer wasn't looking so ridiculous after all. She would

know when she was going to work every day, which had been the biggest drain on her at the airline. She would do what she loved, and she would be around lots of people. Besides, it wasn't likely she would be scheduled for a full eighty-five hours of flight time until summer. Her total hours for January had been seventeen.

Folding the paper and looking out the window into the forest, Shelly wondered if this might be exactly what she needed. She could hear Meredith on the phone with her publishing house in Chicago discussing a project for a series of three children's books about a couple of squirrels who lived under a hydrangea bush. Meredith sounded quite enthusiastic about the proposal she had received and was saying she wanted to see the author before offering the contract. Apparently it fit within her travel plans and budget, because she ended the conversation by saying, "Terrific! I'll make the plans and let you know what happens. Talk to you later. 'Bye."

Meredith came downstairs wearing wool socks, her fluffy slippers, and a thick chenille robe over her pajamas. A purple headband held back her short, straight blond hair.

"Dressed for success, I see," Shelly teased.

"I love my job," Meredith said, wadding up some newspaper and stuffing it into the fireplace. "Is it me, or is it cold in here?"

"It's cold." Shelly still had on her thick jacket from when she had walked over from the camp. "Snow is predicted for tonight. Wouldn't that be great? We haven't had much snow this winter."

"We'd better chop some kindling then," Meredith said.

"I'll do it. I have some time. The group doesn't arrive at camp until dinner. And guess what!"

Meredith stacked the wood inside the fireplace and lit a

181

match to the newspaper. "I give up. What?"

"Jack offered me a full-time position at Camp Autumn Brook. He even said they would customize it. And get this: If I went full-time, our rent would be zilch."

"You're kidding!" Meredith fanned the flickering sparks and tried to coax the fire to get going. "That would be fantastic. If that happened, I would cover all the utilities because I'm the one using the electricity around here. I was thinking of that the other day. You shouldn't have to split the cost since it's my computer and fax machine that are using up all the electricity. Last month your portion of the phone bill was under ten dollars."

"Pathetic, isn't it. I have no friends to call."

"Oh, stop it," Meredith said. "The truth is you've been too busy to call your friends." She turned her backside to the fire and tried to warm her hands. "So are you going to take the position?"

"I'm thinking about it. I might be able to stay on reserve a few more months and work full-time at the camp, too."

"I don't know how you could swing that, but more power to you if you can. Do you want something to drink?" Meredith padded into the kitchen and put a kettle of water on the stove. Picking up a basket from the counter, Meri came back into the living room. "Did you make this up?"

"Yes. I was trying to figure out what would work best at the camp."

The basket was filled with an assortment of tea bags and packets of hot cocoa, hot apple cider, and instant coffee. The look was colorful and appealing.

"I didn't like the way they put out the boxes of generic tea and big canisters of cocoa at the break times," Shelly explained. "I picked up twelve of those baskets in town on clearance at the hardware store. I also found a distributor who will

182

supply us with the individual packages of hot beverages at the same cost we were paying for the industrial-sized generic stuff. The only catch was that we had to buy five big coffee-makers from them, too, which was no problem because we needed them."

"Sounds like you scored some points there," Meredith said, filing through the packets. "This is fun. Kind of like a little treasure hunt."

"I also found a couple of steel carts in the storehouse, and I fixed them up, covered them with lace tablecloths, and set them up in the back of the two main meeting rooms so people could take coffee breaks in there."

"I thought last week you said the linens were ancient."

"They are," Shelly said. "I decided to work with what was available and go with the old-fashioned look. I bleached all the stained white tablecloths, and then I soaked them in tea to make them look like antiques. Now the unraveling places look charming rather than ratty."

Meredith laughed. "You are a nut! No wonder they love you. How do you think up all these things?"

"I don't know. I guess I think if people are paying to get away for a few days, they like to feel a little pampered. I think of them as the first class passengers on the plane. When first class boards, we hang up coats, help store carry-ons, and bring everyone something to drink. They're offered their choice of reading material, and anytime they want something more to drink, it's available."

The teakettle whistled. "Do you want something?" Meredith asked.

"Is there any Constant Comment tea in the basket?" Shelly asked.

"Yep."

"That's what I want. With a little honey." As soon as

Shelly said that, an idea occurred to her. She needed to add an accoutrement tray to the coffee carts. It wasn't in the camp budget, but maybe she could run to town and buy some cartons of flavored coffee creamers and a squeezable honey bottle. She would use her money and try it with tonight's group as an experiment before pitching the idea to Jack. The camp was expecting a group of 125 women tonight, who would stay until Wednesday. Shelly tried to estimate how many cartons of creamer she would need to buy.

"Here you go," Meredith said, handing her a mug. "I brought you a spoon because the honey all sank to the bottom."

"Thanks. This is great." Shelly outlined her idea to her sister, and Meredith laughed some more. It was her sweet, affectionate laugh, the one that enveloped others in her gentle spirit.

"No wonder they want you to work for them full-time, Shelly. This could actually be your calling in life. Who would have guessed? The wanderlust girl finds contentment in her own backyard. It's not an original plot, but it's always a favorite."

"You sound as if you're evaluating my life the way you critique your manuscripts. This isn't pretend. It's a huge decision."

"Oh, I know," Meredith said, curling up close to the fire. "I didn't mean for it to sound flippant. I honestly think you would love to work at the camp. It's evident they're crazy about you."

Shelly sipped her tea and let Meredith's comment sink in. That's what she had been longing for. Whether she knew how to express it or not, Shelly Graham desired with all her heart that someone, somewhere in this world would be crazy about her. She wanted someone to think she was wonderful. Was

184

that what she had secretly wished for all this time? Someone to pursue her?

She never would have guessed it would be Camp Autumn Brook's proposal that would light this fire within her. A place, rather than a person? She had a lot of thinking to do.

22

With a burst of inspiration, Shelly spent the afternoon going all out to prepare the facilities for the women's group that was scheduled to arrive at five. She instructed the kitchen staff to set the tables with linen for dinner. Usually they created a nice meal for the last night, but Shelly convinced them that first impressions were everything; so the first night should be the most impressive.

Shelly pulled out all the fancy hurricane candleholders and inserted fresh candles in them. She brought in an armful of cut evergreen sprigs to decorate the huge fireplace's mantel in the lodge.

On her run to the store, Shelly picked up the honey and coffee creamers along with three boxes of Andes Mints, which she used as party favors by sprinkling them around the tables. A last minute search in the dusty storage closet produced several bags of silk flowers that Shelly rinsed off and laid out to dry on the counter in the camp kitchen. Within twenty minutes she had whipped up a trailing ivy vine dotted with rosebuds, and five mixed bouquets that she arranged in some cheap glass vases the cook provided for her. The vine worked nicely down the side of the tea cart, and the bouquets were placed throughout the dining hall to add spots of color.

Shelly was lighting the last candle on the dining room tables when Emma Jane, the former camp hospitality coordinator, stepped into the room.

"What's going on here?" she asked. Emma Jane was a large woman who wore her hair wound in a tight gray bun on the very top of her head. She was as fluffily round as a pillow and had always run the camp in an institutionalized, efficient manner. Having suffered a minor stroke a month earlier, she had been advised by her doctor to retire two years earlier than she had planned.

"We have a women's group arriving any minute," Shelly explained. "Looks pretty, doesn't it? I wanted to make a nice first impression."

"This isn't how we do things here," Emma Jane said. "Does Mr. Hadley know you've done all this?"

"No, but I'm sure he wouldn't mind. He has turned over a lot of the decision-making to me."

Emma Jane grew red in the face. "I told him I'd be coming back to work as soon as I got better."

Shelly didn't know what to say. It wouldn't do for the arriving conferees to be spectators to this conflict. "Why don't we go in the kitchen," Shelly suggested.

"I have to go to the lodge to start checking the campers in when they arrive."

"Actually, we changed the procedure. The women will come here first and have dinner. Our guys will unload all the suitcases off the buses and into the lodge for the conferees. Then the women will have an hour to check into their rooms before the evening meeting. It seemed a calmer way to start their retreat."

Emma Jane looked flabbergasted.

"May I get you something to drink?" Shelly offered.

"No," the woman snapped. "And don't think I don't know

about your coffee baskets. You can't fritter away the camp's money like that, and you know it. You haven't heard the last of this." She turned and strode from the dining room with clomping steps.

As the side door slammed shut behind Emma Jane, the front doors of the dining room opened wide. The voices of many women suddenly filled the room. Shelly rushed to the door to welcome the ladies. "Please come in and make yourselves comfortable. Sit anywhere you like. Welcome. Hi, nice to have you. Come in, please."

One of the camp maintenance guys had met the bus and had followed Shelly's instructions, informing the women to proceed directly to the dining room.

"Well, look at this!" Shelly heard the women exclaim as they entered. "It looks as if they're expecting company. It wasn't like this at all last year. Do you think we're in the right place?".

She kept smiling and greeting the guests, inwardly delighted that they liked the change in their camping experience. As soon as all the women were inside, a short, redheaded woman carrying a clipboard informed Shelly that she was in charge of this group and wanted to know what was going on.

"In the eight years our ladies have come here, we've never done it this way. We always check in first."

Shelly smiled her comforting smile and said, "We thought it might be more relaxing for your ladies to come to dinner first. Our staff will unload all the luggage from the buses. After dinner the women will have an hour to check in, and their luggage will be waiting for them in the lodge."

A startled look of pleasant surprise came over the coordinator's face. "How nice. We never thought of doing it that way."

Over the speaker system, Shelly heard soft harp music begin to play. The women lowered their voices and settled around the dozens of round tables. The lights overhead were dimmed. Shelly turned toward the kitchen door to see her sister standing by the light switches, smiling and waving.

Since Mr. Hadley wasn't there, Shelly stepped over to the microphone at the front of the dining hall. In her polished, flight attendant voice, she said, "Good evening, ladies. Welcome to Camp Autumn Brook. We realize you have your choice of camping facilities, and we appreciate your choosing to stay with us. To make your flight —" Shelly quickly caught herself, ". . . your stay more comfortable, we've rearranged the schedule slightly."

Meredith caught Shelly's eye and covered her mouth to show she was trying to hold back the giggles.

"Your luggage is being unloaded for you by our staff and will be available for you to pick up in the lodge after dinner. At that time you may also check in at the desk and receive your room key. We sincerely hope that you enjoy your visit. Dinner will be served momentarily."

A slight rumble of voices was followed by a spontaneous round of applause. Shelly slipped into the kitchen, where Meredith caught her by the arms.

"You were terrific! A natural. Listen to them applaud. This is fantastic!"

"People like to be pampered, I tell you."

"I guess they do," Jack Hadley said, coming up beside Shelly and Meredith. "I came hoofing it over here to bawl you out after what Emma Jane told me, but that would have been a mighty big mistake. You're exactly what we need around here, Shelly. Please tell me you'll come on full-time."

"I don't know," Shelly said. "Right now we need to serve dinner while it's still hot."

"I'll help," Meredith said, grabbing a white apron off the hook by the door. "So will I," Shelly said. "Hand me an apron."

"Oh, why not," Jack said. "Give me an apron, too, Meredith."

With six servers working the dining room floor, the dinners were all served hot to the delighted women. Emma Jane used to have them line up cafeteria-style. This seemed to go nearly as fast and allowed the conferees a chance to relax.

The compliments kept coming in, and Jack strutted around like a happy man. The women had spotted the coffee bar and were helping themselves to their choices of hot beverages. Everything ran right on schedule. The luggage was lined up neatly in the lodge, and Jack was in such high spirits he told Shelly he would check in the ladies.

Shelly and Meredith helped the kitchen staff clear the tables and put away the candleholders. "Back to routine tomorrow for breakfast?" Clyde, the cook, asked. "Or do you have some bright ideas about that, too?"

"No. For now we'll stick with our usual format. Will you let me know if you think of anything that would be helpful to you?" Shelly gave Clyde a friendly hug. "Thanks for being so flexible and willing to make all these last-minute changes."

"Anytime," Clyde said. "You are going to replace Emma Jane, aren't you?"

"I'm thinking about it," Shelly said.

"You have my vote," Clyde said. Coming from a somber man who usually said little, Shelly took that as a wonderful compliment.

"Is there any stroganoff left?" Meredith asked.

"Help yourselves," Clyde said. "And to the apple pie, too."

"This doesn't taste like the camp food I remember eating

190

when we used to come here as kids," Meredith said.

"That's because Clyde wasn't the cook then, were you, Clyde?" Shelly said, flashing him a smile.

"I've only been here two years."

"Well, I hope you stay another fifty. You're the best."

Clyde seemed to hold his head a little higher as he moved around Shelly and Meredith to start his kitchen cleanup. The two sisters sat on stools and ate their dinners off paper plates.

"I'm going to stick around to hear the speaker," Meredith said when they had finished. "I met her at dinner, and I've read some of her books."

"Do you think she might want to write a kids' book for you?"

"Maybe. I don't know. But that's not why I'm staying. I'd like to hear what she has to say. Do you want to stay, too?"

"I could. The only thing I didn't do yet today is chop some kindling."

"I did it," Meredith said. "The exercise was just what I needed."

Shelly couldn't help but feel content. Here she was, enjoying a once-in-a-lifetime friendship with her younger sister, living in the cottage of her dreams, and finding her niche on staff at this camp. A small corner of her heart, where her treasure chest of love for Jonathan had once stood, still ached. But now nothing was left in that corner except air. It might be that way for quite a while. Shelly wondered if she could live with that. Was she one of those people who was better suited to remaining single? She didn't know. And she didn't feel she needed to know right now. Tonight it was enough to bask in the glow of her first success at Camp Autumn Brook.

The two women said good-bye to Clyde and headed across the grounds for the chapel. The snow had not come yet, but it was certainly cold enough for it. They walked fast, huddled close together with their hands in their pockets.

"Brrr!" Meredith exclaimed. "It's going to be cold in our little nest when we finally do go home tonight."

"Do you want to go now?" Shelly asked. "We can."

"No, I really want to hear this woman speak."

They sat in the chapel's very last row and watched as the women came streaming in. They were all commenting on how cold it was outside and how good it felt to be in the warm chapel.

Shelly enjoyed being back in a place of worship. She had fallen out of the routine of going to church after she moved back to Seattle. At first she rebelled against her parents' expectation that she go to church with them every Sunday the way she had while she was a child. In Pasadena, she had attended a large church with an active singles and career group. But her dad's church was small and didn't have a separate class for her age group, so she told her parents she was interested in finding her own church in Seattle.

She had never even visited any other churches because of her crazy schedule. Sunday needed to be a day of rest, and she felt that dressing up to go to church for an hour was anything but restful. Meredith went to a Saturday-evening service at a large contemporary church and had often urged Shelly to go with her, but Shelly never felt like attending.

Sitting here in the cozy chapel, Shelly was reminded of St. Annakapella in Germany. She didn't know why she suddenly thought of that chapel except maybe because its door had been locked and she had never had the chance to see inside. She imagined it looked something like this chapel, with whitewashed walls that arched up to a point and a landing on which the podium stood. Shelly pictured St. Annakapella having an altar where this chapel had a baptismal tank with a stained glass window behind it.

Then her thoughts floated over to Jonathan and the confrontation they had had on St. Annakapella's steps. Because the backdrop was so dramatic, the encounter seemed more vivid in Shelly's mind. Later she had thought of so many things she should have said. She still had so many unanswered questions.

The most important words had been said, though. They had both said they were sorry, and Shelly knew she had been freed by those words from Jonathan. She felt certain her words had freed him as well. Now they both could move on with their lives.

The meeting began with singing. Sweet, soprano voices filled the snug chapel, claiming, as one voice, "Father God, we adore you. There is no one else who compares with you. May your name be exalted in our presence. Come, dwell inside our hearts and make us new."

For some reason, Shelly couldn't sing. All she could do was cry.

23

Meredith sang like an angel as she stood beside Shelly. Blinking quietly, Shelly tried to coax her emotions to behave. Finally she calmed them down by sitting with her eyes closed and listening to the songs the group sang. The praises echoed off the rounded ceiling and encircled the women, binding them together.

Then the speaker went up on the stage, and Shelly opened her eyes. She was surprised to see that the woman looked ordinary. Not that Shelly knew how an author should look, but since Meredith had wanted to meet this woman, Shelly had thought she would have a more dramatic appearance. The speaker's voice was ordinary, too. As were her outfit and her hair. The woman prayed and then began her message.

There was nothing ordinary about her words.

The topic was one Shelly could have taught in her sleep: Adam and Eve in the Garden of Eden, hiding from God because they had lost their innocence and were ashamed.

"I believe," the speaker said, "that within the heart of every woman, the Lord God still comes, walking, as it were, in the cool of the evening. He knows exactly where we are. He knows everything that's happened, and yet he still comes. And when he comes, he asks us the same question he asked Adam and Eve."

There was a moment's pause.

"Where are you?" the speaker said in a whisper. "Where . . . are . . . you?"

Shelly felt her heart beating.

"I believe God will not give up until he gets us back. He comes walking in the cool of the evening, seeking us. Imagine that. He's giving us every chance to come to him as he calls out, 'Where are you? I want you back. Don't hide anymore. Come back to me. I won't give up because I absolutely love you.' "

Shelly had never heard God's love explained like that. It drew her to him in a way she had never felt before. Maybe God was more than just a "mighty fortress" standing afar, looking down on her. The concept rocked her in that quiet room.

"Isn't it interesting," the speaker said, "that when God chose to begin a relationship with humans, he placed them in a garden? He could have given them beachfront property or placed them high on a mountain. But he put them in a garden. And when Christ rose from the dead, it was from a garden tomb. Do you remember the first person he spoke with after he came back to life? It was a woman. Mary Magdalene. Do you remember what happened?"

There was a bit of a pause. Shelly tried to remember.

"Mary thought he was the gardener."

Shelly flashed back to the man she had supposed to be the gardener in the Hilsbach cemetery who had asked her, "Who are you looking for?"

"We don't always recognize the Lord God when he comes walking in the garden of our hearts, do we? Mary thought he was the gardener, and she said to him, 'Where is he?' Isn't that amazing? When God made man and woman and they failed, he came to them asking, 'Where are you?' After he made the way for us to receive eternal life through his Son, it was as if God, the relentless lover, finally heard an echo from his first question when this woman said, 'Where is he? I want him back. I won't rest until I find him.' "

The words penetrated deeply for Shelly. Like Eve, she had been hiding from God for quite some time. Like Mary, something inside her desired to call out to him.

"What I love the most about this reunion is that all Jesus had to say to cause Mary to want to run into his arms was one simple word. All he said was, 'Mary.' He called her by her name, just as he calls each of us by name. If you have your Bible, please turn with me to Isaiah 43, the end of the first verse."

Pages rustled. Shelly was ashamed to realize she didn't even know where her Bible was.

" 'Fear not, for I have redeemed you; I have called you by your name; you are mine,' " the speaker read aloud to the group. "Talk about a relentless lover! He redeemed you. He called you by your name. He wants you back."

Shelly felt her mouth going dry.

"I'd like to do something a little different tonight as we close this first time together. I feel as if many women here need to respond to whatever it is God is trying to say to them. I don't usually do this, but I'm going to give what some of you might know as an altar call."

Shelly's heart pounded even more fiercely. Her dad's church never had altar calls. Those were only for the emotional worshipers at what he described as the more "free-spirited" churches. Shelly didn't think she wanted to stick around and watch a bunch of sobbing women go wailing down the center aisle and crumble on the stage. She considered getting up and slipping out, but it was as if the pew had glue on it.

"I don't know why I feel so compelled to do this," the speaker said. "But I want God to be free to come tonight and walk into the garden of your heart. When he calls you by name, will you respond? For some of you that might mean coming out from behind those bushes and admitting you've been hiding from him. Tell him you're ashamed or afraid or whatever it is that sent you there. He already knows. Tell him. You'll never be free until you speak honestly to him and say, 'I'm sorry. Please forgive me.' And he will, of course. He always hears, and he always forgives."

Some of the women adjusted their positions in the pews. Shelly thought she heard someone sniffling.

"I'll close in prayer," the speaker continued. "Then I'll step to the side. We'll stay in this chapel in a discipline of silence for the next twenty minutes and wait on God."

As the woman prayed, Shelly could feel her pulse rising up into her throat. This was it. She had to do something. She couldn't ignore God any longer. He wanted her back.

Shelly remembered standing next to Jonathan in the meeting room of the church in Heidelberg. He had looked at her with his eyebrows slightly lifted, waiting for her to respond. That's when she began to understand the pain she had caused her best friend after leaving him all those years before. She had wanted to fall into his arms and tell him she was sorry. Everything inside her had urged her to grab hold of him and say, "Jonathan, I'm back. I want you back."

She had restrained herself with Jonathan, unwilling to make a scene, and had stifled her emotions. Tonight was different. Shelly knew she had to respond to God. She felt herself make her way down the side aisle to the front of the chapel. As she knelt on the first step, she was oblivious to anything or anyone around her. With her eyes closed, hands folded, and head bowed, Shelly silently formed her prayer.

"God, I'm sorry. I've been hiding from you. I've tried to do everything my way, and I haven't sought you at all. Please forgive me. I want you back."

The tears began to form a steady stream down her hot cheeks. "I love you, God. I surrender everything to you. Thank you for not giving up on me."

Before she could form an "amen," she felt an arm around her shoulder. She supposed it to be Meredith's. When Shelly opened her eyes to smile at her sister, she found that the comforting arm belonged to the speaker. She was kneeling next to Shelly, shoulder to shoulder, tears racing down her own cheeks.

Shelly smiled and whispered, "Thank you."

The woman leaned over and kissed Shelly on the temple and whispered, " 'I have loved you with an everlasting love; I have drawn you with loving-kindness.' Jeremiah 31:3."

Shelly closed her eyes again and let the verse sink deep into her spirit. She became aware of others around her, kneeling, crying softly, whispering prayers. The comforting arm left Shelly, but she still felt bolstered inside. A clean, fresh feeling swept over her like a gentle wind. She lingered only a moment longer, then rose and walked to the back of the chapel where Meredith was waiting for her.

The two sisters embraced and said nothing. They walked back to their cottage arm in arm, as the promised snow began to fall, blanketing their world with its precious white.

The next morning, Shelly woke early and went looking for her Bible. She found it on her bookshelf and crawled back into bed, eager to find the verse in Jeremiah that the speaker had whispered to her last night. She read Jeremiah 31, then 32 and 33. She kept reading and found a pen so she could underline some of the verses. The more she read, the more she found to underline, as if it had been written for her alone.

One of the verses had a cross-reference back to Jeremiah 15. There she found a verse that made her laugh aloud. She read it again as she underlined it.

"Are you having a little party in here, and you didn't invite me?" Meredith said, tapping softly on the door and pushing it open.

"Listen to this," Shelly said. " 'Your words were found, and I ate them, and Your word was to me the joy and rejoicing of my heart; for I am called by Your name, O Lord God of hosts.' "

Meredith looked at her warmly, but she was obviously confused as to why such a revelation was funny.

"I can't explain it," Shelly said. "I've read chapters and chapters this morning. It's as if I've never seen this stuff before. I'm eating it up."

"That's great," Meredith said. "I hate to pull you away from your feast, but did you need to be at camp early this morning?"

"No, breakfast was as usual. Why? What time is it?" Shelly reached over and turned her alarm so she could see it. "Nine-fifteen! Yikes! I better get out of here."

Just then the phone rang, and Meredith went to answer it. The airline was calling Shelly in for a flight that left at noon. She had to scramble to get ready and make a call to Mr. Hadley to let him know she wouldn't be in for the rest of the women's conference.

"I understand," he said. "I sure hope you'll consider our offer, though. These women have been raving about the conference, saying it's the best they've ever had."

Shelly hung up and grabbed her travel bag. She really didn't want to go. Joining the women's group to hear the speaker once more was much more appealing. Shelly smiled. She didn't even know the speaker's name, but her message had changed Shelly's life. She was back together with God and knew his love in a way she never had.

An almost giddy feeling followed her down the island road as she headed for the ferry. The stark winter sun shone through the thin veil of clouds. Even though the sun was weak, it had managed to melt the snow. Shelly hummed all the way, feeling light and content.

On the flight to Phoenix, she smiled and gave an extra bit of care to each of the passengers. Her happiness seemed to bubble over. When the plane landed, she stood by the door next to the cockpit and bade all the passengers the customary "Bye-bye." One of the passengers, a large man who had ordered a hot and spicy V-8 when she came around with the beverage cart, stopped and smiled back at her before exiting. She had felt generous and had given him the entire can to drink.

"You look like a woman in love," the man said. His breath nearly knocked her over. Shelly wished she hadn't given him the whole can.

"Thank you," she said with a laugh. The truth was she did feel in love, in love with God for the first time in her life. How could she have grown up in the church and missed this?

During her stay at the hotel, Shelly didn't watch TV that night. Instead she started to read Psalm 1 and didn't stop until after eleven o'clock when she could barely keep her eyes open. She put a marker in her Bible at Psalm 134 and fell asleep with a smile on her lips.

Her return flight left Phoenix at six-forty-seven the next morning. Shelly didn't feel as tired as she should have after getting only five hours of sleep. She returned with the same crew and ended up having a conversation with one of the women who used to fly Sunlit out of San Jose. According to her, rumor had it that the airline was going on the block at the end of the month. That could mean termination for all employees and rehiring at the discretion of whoever bought them out.

Instead of feeling panicked, Shelly felt calm. *Look how God has taken care of you so far. Six months ago you thought everything was going to fall apart, but your life didn't collapse. You moved into your dream cabin, you have an awesome friendship with your sister, all your bills are paid off, you have money in the bank, you went to Germany, and you have another job offer. God, you are so good to me! How could I ever doubt you? Whatever happens, I'll thank you for it.*

After Shelly's flight arrived at SeaTac, she drove back to Whidbey Island in the pouring rain. The main road to Camp Autumn Brook was closed for repairs, so she had to take a detour that took her around the perimeter of the island. In the backed-up traffic she tried to see between the sloshing windshield wipers what was holding things up. It seemed that all the island traffic had been reduced to two lanes on this, the only available road.

Shelly never came this way since it was farther than the main road. She hummed contentedly to herself and thought about what she would tell Mr. Hadley. It seemed right and logical for her to go ahead and take the position at the camp, but something made her want to hold back. She couldn't figure out what it was.

Looking out the window at the driving rain, Shelly noticed a video-rental store and thought it might be fun to get something to watch tonight, but she remembered she was reading a book and was eager to finish it. Then she remembered the book was the Bible, and she laughed aloud.

Who would have believed I would turn down a movie to read my Bible?

Outside the window she noticed a restaurant's white twinkling lights. The sign above the door read, "Rondi's." Without using her blinker, Shelly turned right into the parking area where more than half a decade ago she and Jonathan had parked their bikes.

24

"It's really coming down, isn't it?" the waitress said after Shelly was seated at a small table by the window. The round tables on the patio, where she and Jonathan had sat, were being pelted by the steady rain.

"I'd like some tea," Shelly said. "And maybe a sandwich. Do you have turkey?"

"Sure do. You like a salad to go with that?"

"No. But do you have any soup?"

"Tomato bisque," she said. "The tomatoes are from Rondi's garden."

Shelly smiled when she remembered last time the raspberries had been from Rondi's garden.

"Sounds perfect. And I'd like some cream and sugar for the tea."

"Ah, a real tea drinker. I'll bring you a pot of Queen Victoria then. It's the real thing, leaves and all. I'll bring you a strainer. Rondi orders this from Murchies in Victoria."

Shelly was about to tell this newsy waitress that she wasn't a purist when it came to a proper pot of tea, but she had just gotten spoiled over the years with adding flavorings to her hot drinks and she didn't care for straight coffee or tea anymore. It didn't matter. The woman was off to place the order.

She returned shortly with a small, china teapot and all the necessary trimmings for a proper tea experience. Shelly thought she should have ordered scones instead of tomato soup and a turkey sandwich. But the food came to her table in a few minutes, and it all tasted good. Sitting back to sip her tea and to think, Shelly watched the pattern of the raindrops on the window.

She remembered something Jonathan's mother had once said when they were young. The day was rainy like this, and they were at Jonathan's house. His mom was helping them make cookies, which Shelly adored doing even when she was young. But her mother rarely had time for baking, and her older sisters didn't have the patience to help Shelly.

Jonathan and Shelly were sitting at a tiny kitchen table next to the big picture window that looked out on the sloped backyard. The rain was coming down in sheets, and Shelly and Jonathan were contentedly licking the electric mixer's beaters.

Mrs. Renfield looked over at them and then stopped, as if she were trying to see something more clearly. A smile graced her wide mouth, and she said, "You two are like a couple of raindrops racing down the window together."

Shelly and Jonathan turned in sync and looked at each other for meaning to his mom's statement. Then, shrugging in tandem, they turned back to their beaters and licked away. The moment was made memorable by Jonathan's mom, who laughed so hard her glasses slid off her nose and landed in the bowl of cookie dough.

But her statement was what Shelly remembered now. "Two raindrops racing down the window together," she repeated quietly. *Not together, Mrs. Renfield. Did it disappoint you, too, when I left? I'm sure you'll enjoy Elena as your daughter-in-law. You'll probably be eager for them to give you lots of grandbabies since I know you always wanted more children after Jonathan.*

Shelly finished the last of her tea and silently prayed for Jonathan. She prayed God's blessing on him and his future marriage. She prayed for Elena's and Jonathan's parents and then started to pray for her parents. Shelly paid the bill, leaving a generous tip, and slipped back into the slow-moving flow of traffic. It took nearly forty minutes to reach home, and she prayed the whole way.

"Oh, good. You're home." Meredith said as Shelly quickly closed the door behind her and took off her soaked jacket. She removed her wet shoes and put on a pair of slippers waiting for her by the door.

In the living room, a hearty fire blazed. Meredith was upstairs in her loft office, which was open to the entryway. She looked down at Shelly and said, "Do you want to go on a road trip with me next week?"

"A road trip? Is this for your work?"

"Yep. It's a prospective author in Oregon. Should take us about six hours to drive down. Are you up for it?"

"I don't know," Shelly said, making her way up the spiral stairs that led to Meredith's office. "How long will you be gone?"

"A day or two. I know you have the camp, and you're still on call at the airline. I must be crazy to ask you, but I checked into airfare, and it's ridiculous what they want me to pay for a Seattle to Eugene flight."

"What about Seattle to Portland?" Shelly asked, carefully moving a stack of papers from "the big flop chair," as Meredith called it. Shelly sat down and tucked her feet under her.

"I checked into that, but I would still need to drive almost three hours to get there from Portland; so I might as well drive the whole way. I just hate going places by myself."

"You always have," Shelly said.

"I know. So how about it? Do you want to go with me? I'm not above begging or bribing."

"It's only for a day, right?"

"I think so. We would drive down early on Monday morning and be back by Wednesday afternoon. You could still be here in time for dinner at camp on Wednesday, if they have a group coming in."

"That's not a problem," Shelly said. "And that's why I'd consider going. No groups are coming in until that weekend. They wouldn't need me at all during the week."

"What about the airline?"

"Looks like it might be sold next week. I don't expect to get too many calls, but I could take my beeper anyway. I could always catch a flight out of Eugene."

"This is a yes?"

"It is a . . . probably."

"All right! Wanderlust girl hits the road again. It'll be fun. Maybe we can even stop by Aunt Jane's cabin on the coast."

"Wait a minute. You're turning this into an all-week event."

Meredith sat back in her desk chair and propped up her feet on a three-foot-high stack of manuscripts. "Why not? You just said you don't have to be back until the weekend. I can work anywhere. Have laptop, will travel."

"Yeah," Shelly teased. "Laptop, cell phone, portable fax. You're a streamlined traveler, all right."

"Hey, I am. You even said so after Germany."

"You're right. You were award-winning in your compact packing for Germany."

"Germany!" Meredith said. "How could I forget? Big news today from Jana and Mike. I printed out their E-mail. Here, read this."

Shelly took the piece of paper and read the tidy little letters in a row across the paper.

"They're pregnant!" Meredith squealed out before Shelly had even finished the first line.

"So I see. How exciting for them; that's great." Shelly was about to hand the letter back when a line at the bottom of the page caught her eye. It said, "We also lost all our staff at the base in Belgium; so Mike has been there the last four days. It doesn't look as if we'll have new staff arriving until the summer; so we may have to shut down the youth club's meetings until then."

Shelly didn't say anything to Meredith. Her sister must not have noticed. But Shelly thought about it for the next few days. If all the staff in Belgium had left, that meant Jonathan and Elena were no longer there. What had happened? Were they married? Did they move back to Akron? That's probably where the wedding was, which would perhaps explain why Shelly didn't receive an invitation.

No matter how she explained it away, it still hurt. For five years she hadn't known where he was. Boulder, Colorado, was her only clue, and then there he was in Belgium. She could almost handle that he was marrying Elena so long as Shelly at least knew where he was. Now he was gone again.

She considered a dozen different ways to find him. A letter to Mike and Jana would most likely reach him eventually. Or she could E-mail Jana and ask for Jonathan and Elena's address, saying she wanted to send them a wedding gift, which would, of course, be true.

She prayed about it, telling her heavenly Father that she wanted to do what was right and best. All week long she had been devouring the Bible, looking not for answers but beyond that. She wanted to know the heart of him who holds all the answers. It struck her that so much of her life she had seen prayer as the way to ask for blessings, the way a child asks Santa Claus for a gift.

That old paradigm was shattered in this growing love relationship that had begun between Shelly and the Lord. Now she sought not the blessing but the Blesser, not the gift but the Giver.

Friday morning she decided to ask Meredith if she could use the computer to send an E-mail before she went over to the camp. Meredith set it up for her, and Shelly typed a short note to Jana, congratulating her on her pregnancy and asking for Jonathan and Elena's address.

As an explanation to Meredith, who was bound to read it before she sent it out, Shelly said, "I've had them on my mind for days. I want to send them a wedding gift and wish them well. Do you think I'm doing the right thing?"

"Of course. Any communication you have with Jonathan is okay by me. I only wish there wasn't an Elena in the picture. I know you say you're fine with it, but I still wish —"

"I know," Shelly said, cutting her off. "But take my advice, Meri, and don't go there."

Meredith tapped a few keys and sent the electronic mail zinging over the phone wires to the other side of the world. "A sister can still make a wish, can't she?"

"Let me know when you hear back from Jana," Shelly said, traipsing down the stairs and ignoring Meredith's question.

"I will. I promise. The very second I receive E-mail back I'll tell you."

Shelly headed over to the camp through a light drizzle. She needed to give Mr. Hadley an answer about taking the position. They had a meeting set for Monday, but she needed to talk to him today so she and Meredith could start on their trip early Monday. The only difficulty was that Shelly still didn't feel settled about agreeing to take the job. It made sense for a long list of reasons, but every time she prayed about it, a cloud of hesitancy moved in. She remembered something she had read in Psalms about God leading the children of Israel through the wilderness by using a cloud by day. Shelly looked around at the hovering puffs of mist and thought, *If God led them around with a cloud, did that mean the children of Israel were in a fog all the time?*

The silly thought made her smile. But it also reminded her that maybe she wasn't the only one who ever felt as if she were walking around in a fog instead of floating on a cloud.

When she met with Mr. Hadley, she told him what was on her heart. "I can't explain it, but I don't have a clear answer for you. I don't feel right about making a commitment yet. Could you give me another week to pray about it some more?"

"That's no problem. We've had a couple of applications come in, and now we know more clearly what kind of person we want to run the show. Your changes to the setup have made a world of difference, and that means a lot."

Shelly told him about taking off with Meredith for the next week, and that was fine with him, too. "It's a good week to go," he said.

"That's what I thought, since there aren't any groups coming in."

"Not that," Mr. Hadley said. "It's Valentine's Day on Monday. You and Meredith shouldn't be stuck here in the woods like a couple of spinsters. You should get out to meet people."

Shelly knew he meant well, but it was a bitter comment to swallow.

When they loaded up Meredith's Explorer on Monday, it was still dark. Shelly remembered Mr. Hadley's comment and shared it with her sister.

"Do you think we're turning into old maids?" Meredith asked once they were on the road.

"Maybe. It doesn't bother me as much as it would have a couple of weeks ago," Shelly said. "I mean, I want to get married someday, but I feel more content and fulfilled right now than I ever have. I know I'm still on an emotional high with God, but you know what? It's the most incredible thing that's ever happened to me. I've never felt so complete before."

"You'll get no criticism from me," Meredith said. "I love seeing what God is doing in you. I have to admit, for a while there I was kind of worried. You never went to church or seemed to have any interest in spiritual things. I prayed for you a lot."

Shelly stretched out her legs. "Thanks. God sure answered your prayers. He does that, you know."

"What? Answers prayer?"

"Yes. All the time. I never saw it before. He puts all the bits of life together like a mixed bouquet, and he knows what goes in where."

"I hope he includes a tall, dark, and handsome 'flower' in my bouquet," Meredith said with a laugh. "He'd better. I've been praying for one for the last three years."

"Anyone in particular?"

"Yes. I want the right one, the one God has picked out for me."

"Do you think," Shelly said, "that there's really only one man for us, or could we marry just about anyone and be happy as long as we're going by God's rules?"

Meredith paused before saying, "All I know is that there is a man out there somewhere for me, and the day I meet him, I'll know."

"Whoa! No room there for any sloppy mix-ups?"

"No."

Shelly had nothing else to say. They drove on, listening to music as Shelly thought about Jonathan. Meredith hadn't heard back from Jana yet, but she had brought her computer along; so Shelly might hear from Jana this week.

They made good time and didn't stop until they reached Portland. Meredith and Shelly both got out to stretch at a gas station. They forgot that in Oregon only the station attendants can pump the gas, but they were happy to let the uniformed guy perform his duty. They went next door to a small espresso bar to buy some wake-up coffee, and both ordered the Valentine's Day Mocha Special, which came with a chocolate candy heart.

"Nice way to start the day," Shelly said. "Someone to pump your gas and wash your windows for you."

"And," Meredith added, "chocolate for breakfast. I could get used to this place."

Shelly took a turn driving. The coffee woke her up, and she nibbled on a bagel from their bag of snacks. The sky was fully awake now and drenched in an aquamarine shade of blue. A few puffed-up clouds lazily made their way north as Shelly and Meredith continued to make their way south.

Humming along with the music and carrying on one of her running conversations with God, Shelly enjoyed the beautiful drive. A river swollen with Mt. Hood's cast-off winter white, raced beside the freeway. Towering evergreen trees made their magnificent presence known.

It wasn't until they were cruising through the flat farmlands of the Willamette Valley that Shelly realized she had better find out where to get off.

"Meredith? Are you awake?"

"Hmmm."

"We're passing a sign that says, 'Corvallis, next right.' How much farther is it?"

Meredith opened her eyes and squinted at their surroundings. She reached for a piece of paper on the seat next to them and looked up again. "We still have a little ways to go," she said, yawning. "Thanks for driving this stretch."

"I love it. It's a gorgeous drive. By the way, where are we going?"

"Didn't I tell you? It's a little town called Glenbrooke."

25

"Tell me about this author you're going to meet in Glenbrooke," Shelly said.

Meredith yawned and stretched her arms. "Her name is Jessica Buchanan. She's never published anything before, but she sent in some samples of her writing, and I think she has some great ideas. She said she liked our books, and that's why she contacted us."

"Isn't it kind of risky to put all this effort into someone who hasn't been published before?"

"Not if I know what I'm doing. Part of my job is to discover and develop new talent. I have to take some risks. She went to Oxford and was an English teacher at the high school in Glenbrooke. Those are pretty good foundational credits in my book."

Shelly pulled into a rest area about ten miles from Glenbrooke and shook her head. "It would seem to me that creativity has to count more than degrees when it comes to children's books."

"And that's what I'm trying to find," Meredith said with a bit of irritation in her voice, "creative people with whom I can work."

"Don't take what I'm saying wrong. I just could never do your job is all."

"Sorry," Meredith said. "I'm a little nervous."

"It'll be fine," Shelly comforted her.

Meredith took over at the wheel again. Shelly had nibbled away nearly all the snacks in their bag, leaving only the carrot sticks and two Kudos bars for Meredith. That seemed to suit her fine.

"Is she expecting you at a certain time?"

"No. I told Jessica I was driving down with my sister, and she said they had a guest room in which we could stay. The plan is for us to talk business tomorrow. I wanted to get here early so we could scout around. Maybe find a couple of antique stores."

"Sounds good," Shelly said. "Do you think Jessica would be offended if we stayed at a hotel instead of her guest room?"

"I don't know. Why?"

"Well, what if she lives in a real dive? I've been offered the hospitality of many well-meaning people over the years, and I personally prefer hotel rooms."

"You live in hotel rooms."

"Not anymore. But I'm used to them. They're familiar."

"Let's do this," Meredith said. "We'll roll into Glenbrooke, find her address, and decide if we want to stay there or not."

"Just by the outside," Shelly added. "None of this going inside and then saying we want to leave. It's rude."

"Okay. So we drive by and give it a thumbs-up or a thumbs-down. I'll let Jessica know I've arrived, either by ringing the doorbell or by calling her after we've checked into the local motel."

"Right," Shelly agreed. "Then you and I go 'tiquing, and you have your meeting with her tomorrow."

"Sounds like a plan."

"And none too soon," Shelly said. "Did you see that sign?

Two miles to Glenbrooke."

The road began to twist and turn uphill as they covered the last few miles into Glenbrooke. Houses appeared here and there, tucked behind thick overgrowth and giant cedar trees.

"Cute place," Shelly said as Meredith entered the main part of town and slowed her car way down. "That looks like a promising lunch spot, The Wall Flower. And an antique store only three doors down. Good choice of authors, Meri."

"We don't know that. This could be the biggest mistake of my career."

"Or the best move. You don't know."

"These directions are kind of strange. Can you figure this out?"

Shelly coached her sister through the center of town and past charming houses lined in a row with primroses growing in their window flower boxes. The directions took them up Madison Hill to a breathtaking Victorian mansion. A wide porch with a swing fronted the home, and a loop of smoke tousled itself out of the chimney to disappear into the blue sky.

The two sisters looked at each other.

"I think it's a thumbs-up," Meredith said.

"I think we must have the wrong address," Shelly smarted off. "Your author didn't mention to you that she lived like a princess, did she?"

"No. Jessica seemed normal on the phone."

"Maybe it's her parents' house."

"No, she said she was married." Meredith pulled the keys from the ignition and gave herself a quick look in the rearview mirror, fluffing up her hair before going in. "I should have stopped to put on some makeup," she said.

"You look mah-velous, dah-ling," Shelly teased. "Come on. I can't wait to meet this woman."

They got out and immediately heard the barking of dogs. Two golden retrievers stood at the top of the stairs, guarding the front door.

"Do you think we should get back in the car?" Meredith said. "What if they come after us?"

"These guys look friendly. Aren't you," Shelly said, addressing the dogs with her calming voice. "You're just two big fur balls, aren't you?"

They stopped barking. With tongues out and tails wagging, they responded to Shelly's calming words.

"Piece of cake," Shelly said, thrusting her hands into the pockets of her suede jacket. "Man, it's cold out here."

The front door opened, and a delicate-looking woman with shoulder-length, honey blond hair stepped out onto the porch. She was very pregnant.

"Hi. Are you Jessica?" Meredith said cautiously as she and Shelly started up the steps.

Shelly guessed that Jessica hadn't mentioned to Meredith that she was expecting, otherwise Meredith wouldn't have seemed so shocked.

"Yes?" Jessica was obviously surprised to see them as well. The dogs laid down, huddling close to Jessica's feet as if they were trained to protect her.

"I'm sorry to drop in like this. I know we should have called. I'm Meredith Graham from G. H. Terrison Publishing. This is my sister, Shelly. We arrived a little early. I wanted to make sure I had the right place."

"Yes, yes, welcome," Jessica said, her expression brightening.

Shelly noticed that Jessica had a slight scar on her upper lip that curled up when she smiled. "Please come in. I'm hosting a little Valentine luncheon. I'd love it if you two could join us."

216

Another car, with a woman driver, came up the driveway.

"Oh, good, Lauren's here. I asked her to come early and help me set up," Jessica said.

A slim woman with short, light blond hair stepped out of the car and waved to the three of them on the porch. As soon as her car door slammed shut, the dogs rose and began to bark again.

"It's okay; it's only Lauren," Jessica said.

The dogs took off down the steps and joyfully greeted Lauren, jumping up on her long, floral shirt.

"Cut it out, you guys. They smell the cat hair," she called out to Jessica, who was clapping her hands to get the retrievers to return.

They charged back up the stairs in their eagerness to obey. As the brutes slammed their broad sides against Jessica's legs, Shelly watched Jessica wobble and reach for the doorjamb to balance herself.

"Hi," Lauren said, coming up the stairs. "I'm Lauren."

"I'm Meredith."

"I'm Shelly."

"Nice to meet you," the blue-eyed woman said, extending a hand. "It's cold today, isn't it?"

"Yes, we were noticing the same thing," Shelly said. She turned to look at their hostess, as a hint that they were ready to go in. Jessica stood frozen in place, her hand still clutching the doorjamb. Her face had gone pale, and her eyes were wide.

"Jess?" Lauren said, immediately reaching for her arm. "Are you okay?"

"I think my water just broke."

No one said a word. Shelly had been through training in flight school and was the first to go into action. "Are you in any pain?" Shelly asked.

"No."

"Okay, then let's do this: Meredith and I will help you down the stairs nice and slow. Lauren, would you mind grabbing a jacket for Jessica? We're going to take you to the hospital. Is that okay with you?"

Jessica nodded.

Lauren rushed into the house.

"Kyle!" Jessica said as Meredith and Shelly offered an arm to steady her. She didn't seem weak, only dazed. "I need to go call Kyle."

"I'll get ahold of him," Lauren said, handing Jessica's coat to Meredith when they were halfway down the stairs. "I'll tell him to meet you at the hospital." Lauren turned, but when she took the top stair, she tripped and fell with a wail on her way down.

The dogs started to bark.

"You okay?" Shelly asked over her shoulder.

"I think so."

"I'm okay," Jessica said, walking slowly and holding her belly with her hand. Shelly let go of Jessica's arm and said, "Why don't you put her in the back seat, Meri. I'll check on Lauren."

Shelly took the steps carefully. They were slick, and she could see how Lauren stumbled. Lauren was still sitting down. She had a pained expression on her face.

"I twisted my ankle," she said. "I feel ridiculous."

Shelly carefully touched Lauren's ankle and tried to bend her foot up. She remembered a passenger on a trip to San Diego a few years ago who had tripped entering the plane and had said it was nothing when, in fact, his ankle was broken. By the time the plane had landed, he couldn't put any weight on it.

"Why don't you come to the hospital with us? We can call Jessica's husband with the cell phone."

A sudden, sharp cry came from the back seat of Meredith's Explorer.

"When is Jessica due?" Shelly asked, offering Lauren her shoulder and helping her walk slowly down the stairs.

"Not for three more weeks. Ouch."

"Try not to put any weight on it, if you can help it. Why don't you sit in the front seat? I'll ride in the back with Jessica. That way you can direct Meredith to the hospital."

Lauren was barely in the front seat when Jessica released another cry. This time she tried to stifle it.

"It's okay," Shelly said, getting into the back seat and draping Jessica's coat over her in her propped-up position. "You can scream if you want. Just don't panic."

Jessica tried to laugh, but it came out in a cough. She began to draw deep breaths in through her nose and exhale through her mouth. Meredith pulled around the circular drive and headed down the road at a fast clip.

"I'll try not to hit any bumps," Meredith said. "Which way to the hospital?"

"Turn right at the first stop sign," Lauren said. "When you pass the fire station, turn left. It's not far."

"Do you want to call anyone?" Meredith said. "My cell phone is right here."

"Oh, good." Lauren reached for it and punched in some numbers. "Kenton? Hi. Get Kyle. We're on the way to the hospital. Jessica's water broke. . . . No, she's okay. . . . Yeah, I'll see you there."

Shelly reached over and took Jessica's hand when she could tell by Jessica's expression that another contraction was coming over her. The contractions seemed close together. Jessica's fragile, long fingers wrapped around Shelly's, and as a wave of pain rose within her, Jessica squeezed Shelly's hand with more ferocity than Shelly would have guessed possible for a woman of Jessica's stature.

"My back," Jessica moaned as the contraction diminished.

Meredith had already laid a blanket over the seat for Jessica. Shelly took the other car blanket from the storage space behind them and rolled it up like a long pillow. "Let's try this," she suggested.

Perspiration began to gleam across Jessica's forehead. Her coloring went pale again. "I think I'm going to be sick."

"Do you want me to pull over?" Meredith asked.

"No, keep going," Shelly urged. She was immune to the sight and sound of people's air sickness. She reached for the large plastic bag that had held their carrot sticks earlier that morning. "Use this, if you need to. I'll crack the window for a little air."

Meredith seemed to hit every bump in the road. Rolling her window down an inch, Lauren looked as if she might get sick as well. Shelly reached for a box of tissues on the floor of the back seat, ready for Jessica to vomit. But she didn't. She kept her chin up and kept breathing.

"Do we still have some bottled water up there, Meri?"

"No, I drank it all."

"That's okay," Jessica said. Her eyes were closed, and her jaw seemed to be clenching. "Here comes another one." Her breathing deepened. Shelly reached for her hand, and again Jessica gripped it like there was no tomorrow.

"We're here!" Meredith announced.

"Go around this side to the emergency entrance," Lauren suggested.

Meri drove over the bump into the parking lot so fast that both Shelly and Jessica let out a cry.

"Sorry!"

"There's Kyle and Kenton," Lauren said. "Honk your horn so they'll see us."

Jessica took a deep breath. Shelly patted Jessica's moist face with a tissue. "You're doing great," Shelly said calmly. "We're at the hospital now. Are you ready to move?"

Jessica squinted her eyes and nodded her head. Her mascara had smeared and ran in tiny rivulets down her flushed cheeks.

Shelly quickly dabbed the dark streaks away. With her most tender smile, she said, "It won't be long before you're holding that little miracle in your arms."

With a weak smile, Jessica said, "Thank you."

A dark-haired man had rushed to the car and was opening the back door before the car came to a complete stop. Another man with the same strong, defined jaw and broad shoulders hurried toward them with a wheelchair.

"It's okay, honey, it's okay, just breathe. That's it. Nice steady breaths," the first man said, taking Jessica into his arms and slowly helping her from the car. "Where's that wheelchair? Kenton, get over here! Breathe deep, Jess. How far apart are the contractions? You're going to be okay. Breathe, now. Slow, even breaths. Quicker. I mean, slower. It's okay, Jess. You're going to be okay."

"Kyle, relax!" Jessica said, lowering herself into the wheelchair. "I'm fine. Now take me in there, and let's go have a baby."

26

"I can't take this anymore," Meredith said, pacing the living room floor of Kyle and Jessica's Victorian mansion. "I have to call the hospital."

"They asked us to wait here," Shelly said, putting down her magazine and getting up to poke the smoldering blaze in the marble-hearthed fireplace.

It was after six o'clock, and for the past four-and-a-half hours, Meredith and Shelly had held down the fort at the empty house of their host and hostess. The mansion was as gorgeous inside as it was out. The living room, or parlor, as Shelly called it, offered them cozy, overstuffed chairs and a couch covered in a soft pink, floral pattern. The facade on the tiered ceiling reminded Shelly of the beautiful ceiling in Jana and Mike's place in Germany.

"I can't believe how nervous I feel!" Meredith said. "We drive up for my first face-to-face author meeting, and she goes into labor."

"She didn't do it on purpose," Shelly said dryly.

"I know. But I can't believe how responsible I feel. We can't turn around and go home now. I wish we could do something."

"Pray that the mom and baby will be all right."

"I have been," Meredith said.

The front door opened, and Lauren called out, "Hello? Anyone home?"

"We're in here," Shelly said. She and Meredith hurried to meet Lauren and her boyfriend, Kenton, as they entered. Lauren was on crutches with her foot in a cast.

"Oh, no!" Meredith said. "It was broken?"

"Yes. I feel so ridiculous!"

Kenton put a supportive arm around her and gave her a hug. He looked at Meredith and Shelly and said with a proud smile, "It's a boy. Travis Gregory Buchanan."

"That's wonderful!" Shelly and Meredith both started to ask questions at the same time.

"Mother and son are doing fine," Kenton said. "We're still not sure about the father. He was hyperventilating last time we saw him."

Shelly and Meredith had learned earlier at the hospital that Kenton and Kyle were brothers. The two sisters could appreciate the special brand of ribbing they gave each other.

Lauren giggled. "I've never seen Kyle like this. He's a paramedic. That's actually how he and Jessica met. She was in a car accident, and he rescued her. Today I think he was the one who needed a little rescuing!"

"The baby is okay, then?" Shelly asked.

"Get this," Kenton said. "He weighed in at seven pounds four ounces and twenty inches long."

"There's nothing premature about that baby," Shelly said.

"No kidding," Lauren added. "If she had gone to her due date, he would have been a bruiser! The doctor said it was a good thing he came early because Jessica was able to deliver naturally. If she had gone a few more weeks they might have had to do a cesarean since she's such a small-boned woman.

And her labor was only five hours, which they said was very fast for a first baby."

"Do you want to come in and sit down?" Shelly asked. She had noticed that Lauren didn't look too comfortable propped up on the crutches. "Not that it's my place to offer."

"Why don't we go in the kitchen," Kenton suggested. "Have you two eaten yet? I'll find something for us. Kyle probably won't be home all night. He asked us to make sure you two felt at home."

They followed Lauren as she hobbled into the kitchen and found a chair in which she could sit and prop up her foot.

"Do you think Kyle would mind if I plugged in my laptop?" Meredith asked. "I just need to retrieve my E-mail."

Kenton and Lauren acted as if Meredith had said something funny or magical. They caught and held each other's gaze, keeping the connection for a long time, as if no one else existed.

"Sure," Kenton said, slowly turning back to Meredith. "Do you know where the library is? That's Kyle's office. You can use that room for privacy, if you like."

"Thanks." Meredith left.

"Have you both moved into a guest room yet?" Lauren asked. "There are a couple to choose from. My favorite is the one downstairs at the end of the hall. I call it the geranium room."

"Thanks," Shelly said. "We did find it and put our stuff there. I hope it's okay that we took ourselves on a tour. This is a beautiful home, and the nursery is adorable."

"They just finished it last weekend," Lauren said. "Good thing! Kyle has been working full speed on this camp he's developing, and Jessica had to chain him to the nursery so he would paint it."

"Chain *whom* to the nursery?" Kenton asked.

"Excuse me. Chain Kyle along with the man of my dreams to the nursery," Lauren said with a smile to Kenton. "Kenton's a champion with a paintbrush. It's one of his many fine attributes."

"Tell me about this camp," Shelly said.

"Kyle and Jess own some property outside of town," Kenton said. "It's a great piece of land along Heather Creek. He's developing it into a retreat center. Even has its own little waterfall."

"Really?" Shelly said.

"It's no Multnomah Falls," Kenton said. He looked at Lauren, and the two of them shared another secret smile. "But it's coming along. He hired a guy last week to develop the layout of the camp. They haven't gotten all the permits cleared yet, so the only thing they can start working on is the ropes course; you know, a rock-climbing, rappelling, tree-to-tree kind of recreation setup. Kyle will probably offer him the position of director once the camp is up and running."

"Is Kyle looking for any other staff positions?" Shelly wasn't even sure why she asked. She had an ideal setup at home. Why would she want to move here and work at a camp that wasn't even started yet? It must be the adventurer in her, she decided. If she were to start a camp from level one, she would do a lot of things differently from the way Camp Autumn Brook had been set up.

"It's not that far along," Kenton said. "The ground is cleared for the main lodge, but like I said, the permits haven't passed. I don't know when he's going to start hiring." He opened the refrigerator and had a look. "There's some little frilly sandwiches here," Kenton said, pulling out a glass plate covered with clear wrap. The sandwiches were cut in heart shapes and rested on lace doilies.

"Those were for the party," Lauren said. "I hope Ida got here in time to catch everyone and tell them it had been canceled. I took a half-day off from school. I teach high school English. Jessica and I had this big plan to host a Valentine's Day party for some of the women in town who don't have sweethearts. We wanted to do something special to let them know they were loved. I feel bad we had to cancel."

"I'm sure they all understood," Kenton said, reaching for one of the copper-bottomed pans that hung above the island stove. "All you'll have to do is tell them it's a baby shower, and they'll be back next week. You might even be able to use the same sandwiches."

"I don't think so, honey," Lauren said.

Shelly couldn't help but think she would have qualified for an invitation to Jessica's valentine luncheon since she didn't have a sweetheart. She also thought it would be fun to come here for a baby shower for Jessica.

"I'm sure eager to see the little guy," Shelly said. She felt connected with him even though she had just met Jessica.

"He's beautiful," Lauren said.

"Handsome," Kenton corrected.

"Okay, Uncle K.C., he's handsome. He looks like his daddy and his uncle," Lauren said. "The doctor was saying that Jessica could come home tomorrow, if she wanted to. I'm sure Jess and Kyle would want you and Meredith to stay."

"I don't know what Meredith's plans are now," Shelly said. "I'm just along for the ride. We both felt a little awkward, dropping by at such an inopportune time."

"Are you kidding?" Lauren said. "Jessica thought you were angels from heaven who came down to minister to her. You were amazing, Shelly, the way you knew what to do and got her to calm down. The scene would have been disaster on wheels if it had been up to me." Lauren laughed. "I mean, look! I couldn't even get to the phone to call Kyle without disaster finding me."

"You do keep your guardian angels busy," Kenton said in a gentle, teasing voice.

Lauren didn't seem to take offense at his words. She beamed at him, and he looked as if he caught the warmth and held it.

"You know, you two don't have to stay here and entertain us," Shelly said. "We can manage fine. You probably had plans for tonight, didn't you?"

"We were going dancing," Kenton said with a half-grin. "But Wren suddenly changed her mind, for some reason."

Wren, what a sweet nickname. Shelly let out a tiny sigh. *God, I'm delighted that you have called me by name and that I'm yours. But what about this feeling? It's Valentine's Day. I have no sweetheart to call me by a tender nickname, and that makes me want to cry.*

"Omelets sound good?" Kenton asked, extracting ingredients from the refrigerator.

"It's his specialty," Lauren told Shelly from her chair. "Kenton is good at many things. Omelets are at the top of the list."

Kenton straightened up and looked at Lauren over the top of the refrigerator door. "Why, thank you, my love."

Lauren smiled and caught his gaze once more. Still smiling she quipped, "How do I love thee? Let me count the ways. I love thee for every room you paint and every omelet you make."

As they looked at each other, Shelly thought she could almost see the sparks, like tiny, heart-shaped bursts of love, coursing through the air between them.

"I'm going to check on Meredith," Shelly said, suddenly

feeling as if she were interrupting something between Kenton and Lauren. She backed up and went down the hall to the office.

The door was closed. Shelly tapped on it lightly and then opened it and went in. Meredith was on the phone. When she saw Shelly, she covered the mouthpiece with her hand and said, "I'll just be a minute."

Shelly knew that was her sister's way of saying she wanted privacy. Closing the door behind her, Shelly headed back to the kitchen. She quietly pushed open the swinging door that separated the kitchen from the entryway and noticed that Kenton wasn't at the stove whipping up omelets. He was standing in front of Lauren, who sat in her immobile position with upturned chin and a face that glowed, making her much more beautiful than Shelly originally had thought she was.

Kenton took Lauren's face in his hands, leaned over, and placed a kiss on her lips as if he were sealing some promise. Shelly knew that kiss. It was the kiss she had rehearsed a hundred times in her mind, the kiss she had planned to give Jonathan last October, the kiss that said, "I'm my beloved's, and he is mine." Shelly's kiss remained within her, unspent. Kenton had just broken the bank.

Feeling like an intruder, Shelly slowly backed up and let the door silently close. Part of her wanted to linger, to vicariously enjoy this couple's love that was in full bloom. It was too beautiful to turn away from. She stood for just a moment behind the closed door.

"My Wren," Shelly heard Kenton say, "I cannot, I will not wait another day, another hour. You are the other half of my heart. I've waited patiently, as you asked. Please say that my wait has come to an end. Take me as your husband. I want you for my wife."

Shelly bit her lower lip and closed her eyes. She silently

called out, *Lauren, don't be coy. Gather those rosebuds he just tossed at your feet, or you'll be sorry forever!*

"Hi," Meredith said, coming into the entryway from the study.

Shelly jumped.

"Sorry to startle you. What's happening?"

Shelly put a silencing finger to her lips and directed Meredith into the parlor. "Well," Shelly said, folding her arms across her middle and trying to play it cool. "Let's see. Jessica had a baby. You knew that. Lauren broke her foot. You knew that." She tapped her index finger on her chin and said, "Oh, I know. Kenton is in there, proposing to Lauren. You probably didn't know that."

"Are you kidding?" Meredith's eyes grew wide. "How romantic. On Valentine's Day! Did he give her a ring?"

"I wasn't watching!"

"Well, you better sit down because I have news for you."

"What?"

"Sit down."

"No, just tell me."

Meredith shrugged and said, "Okay. I received an E-mail from Jana."

"Oh, good. Did she send you Jonathan and Elena's address?"

"No."

"Why not?"

"Because there is no address for Jonathan and Elena. Jonathan and Elena broke up."

27

Shelly stumbled back and plopped down on the pink-flowered couch in Kyle and Jessica's living room.

"I told you to sit down," Meredith said. She went over and sat next to her sister. "Jana said a guy named Tony from Akron came to see Elena at Christmastime."

"Tony?"

Meri nodded.

"Tony the mechanic. She was trying to fix me up with him."

"Well, he's no longer available," Meredith stated flatly. "Two days after Tony arrived, Elena broke up with poor 'Johnny' and went back to Akron with Tony."

"You're making this up."

"No," Meredith said, holding up her hand like she was taking a pledge. "It's all on the E-mail."

"I just can't believe this. Jonathan must have been shattered."

"It wouldn't be the first time," Meredith said flippantly.

Instantly, the tears sprang to Shelly's eyes.

"I'm sorry," Meredith said. "That was cruel. I shouldn't have said that." She slipped her arm around Shelly and apologized again.

"No, it's true. I deserved that. Jonathan is the most tenderhearted, loving man I know. He didn't deserve to have his heart broken even one time. How will he ever trust another woman again?"

"I think I know how he can learn to trust again. I think you should write him," Meri said.

"I thought you didn't have his address."

"You asked for Jonathan and Elena's address. That one doesn't exist. Jana did send me an E-mail address for Jonathan. You want to write him? I left my computer on."

Shelly numbly followed her sister into the large study and compliantly sat in the leather chair behind the great mahogany desk. The screen of the laptop computer glowed like a night-light before her.

"I don't know what to say."

"Open up your heart to him," Meredith said. "Let him know what you think and feel. Let him know he is welcome back anytime. That's your gift, Shelly. You have a welcoming heart. You can put complete strangers at ease. Look how you were with Jessica this afternoon. Jonathan is no stranger. He is your very best friend. Tell him you still love him."

Shelly's stomach muscles felt tight as she absorbed her sister's words. She knew Meredith was referring to Jonathan, but so much of what she said corresponded to the way Shelly felt about the Lord and how she had responded that night at camp by opening her heart and surrendering to him.

Her fingers began to tap out the message that was on her heart.

Jonathan,
   I heard from Jana today that you and Elena are no longer together. I'm sorry, my friend. I don't know what else to say.

Looking up at her sister, Shelly said, "I don't think this is such a good idea."

"It's a very good idea. Keep writing."

"I don't know what to say."

"Tell him how you feel."

Shelly gazed at the rows of floor-to-ceiling bookshelves that lined the softly lit room. She stared at the computer screen. The only thing that came to her mind was the crazy memory of when they had baked cookies at his house that one rainy afternoon when they were so young.

I feel as if I am, and maybe always will be, what your mom said so long ago. Do you remember when she told us we were like two raindrops on the window?

I'm feeling for you for what you must have been going through these past few months. Please know that, in some inexplicable way, I'm the other raindrop racing down the window beside you. You'll always be my best friend.

"It's not going to win any awards," Shelly said.

"It's just right," Meredith said.

Shelly hesitated before writing the salutation.

"Go ahead," Meredith said. "Sign it 'love.' "

Shelly wanted to say something more than love, because what she and Jonathan had shared for so many years was, in fact, much more than love.

Always,
Shelly Bean

"Just click on 'send mail,' and it's off," Meredith said.

"I don't know." Shelly reread the letter and thought it sounded sappy. "Maybe I should take my time and write something that makes more sense."

There was a knock on the study door, and Kenton entered. "I don't mean to disturb you," he said, "but I'm going to get at those omelets now, in case you two want something to eat."

"We didn't mean to disturb *you,*" Meredith said with a knowing twinkle in her eye.

Kenton smiled. "You overheard?"

"Well, a little," Shelly said.

"Just so you know, she said yes," he stated calmly. "I had big plans, of course. Dinner, dessert, a romantic drive along the coast. Life sort of took a curve around here today. I knew if I didn't get on my knees before the day was over, my heart would burst. I'd planned what to say over and over."

"That's wonderful!" Meredith said.

He smiled. "She said yes."

"So you said," Meredith commented.

A lump stuck in Shelly's throat. She pictured Jonathan planning their bike ride and dinner all those years ago. He would have been just as happy and content as Kenton if only she would have said yes. But that was past. She was determined to move forward.

"Congratulations," Shelly said. "I'm very happy for you both."

"Are you okay?" Kenton said, looking at Shelly more closely.

"She's trying to decide whether or not to send an E-mail to the man she loves."

Kenton took long-legged strides over to the desk. Shelly froze when she saw his intense gaze on her. He stopped in front of the desk, reached over, and with a kindly, brotherly expression, he grasped her hand and said, "You must send it."

Shelly was almost afraid to do anything else. "Okay," she

said, clicking on the "send mail" box. A few seconds later, it was gone. Now she had the excruciating pain of waiting for his reply. She couldn't imagine how people ever did it years ago when all they had was "snail mail" to send out the pulse of their hearts.

Shutting down her laptop, Meredith followed Shelly and Kenton back into the kitchen.

"Tell me more about this camp," Meredith said. "Can we go out there tomorrow?"

"Sure, if you would like."

It flashed through Shelly's mind that Meredith wasn't in the kitchen when Kenton mentioned the camp earlier. How did she know about it? She let the thought float away when she looked at Lauren.

Happy tears glistened on her face. "Did he tell you?" she asked.

"Yes! Congratulations!" Meredith said. "This has been quite a day around here!"

"Could you hand me the phone?" Lauren asked. "I want to tell Jess."

"She already knows," Kenton said.

"How could she know?"

"I told Kyle at the hospital. I showed him the ring."

"Oh, let's see your ring," Shelly said. She and Meredith admired the lovely diamond set in a Black Hills gold setting. "That's beautiful. So unique. I love it," Shelly said.

"Do you mean to tell me that you told your brother before you asked me?" Lauren said.

"Yes."

"What if I would have said no?"

"I knew you would say yes this time." Kenton cracked another egg into the silver mixing bowl and beat it with a wire whisk.

A new hope rose inside Shelly. She didn't know Kenton and Lauren's love story, but apparently he had proposed to her once before, and she had turned him down. They looked as if that delay in their relationship hadn't adversely affected their love at all. Was it possible that she and Jonathan might be able to get together again? Would he hold out a ring in his hand to her once more?

"Then let me at least call my mom and my brother," Lauren said.

Shelly handed her the phone, and Lauren dialed a long string of numbers. "Hi, Jake? It's Lauren. Is Brad there? He is? With Alissa? Well, would you tell him to call me tonight when they get back? . . . Thanks . . . You too, 'bye."

Suddenly all the names Lauren had just used rang a bell with Shelly. "Alissa? Brad? Did you say Jake?"

Lauren nodded. "He's my brother's roommate."

Shelly's mouth dropped open. "You're Lauren!"

"Yes."

"Lauren Phillips!"

"Yes."

"You're Brad's sister! The one who . . ." Shelly was about to say, "The one who always has funny, disastrous things happen to her," but she caught herself in time. "I can't believe this! I'm Shelly Graham. I was Alissa's roommate in Pasadena!"

Both the women let out a scream and gave each other a hug.

"Did I miss something?" Meredith said.

Kenton tilted the mixing bowl and coaxed the whipped-up eggs into the hot pan.

"I guess this is one of those 'had-to-be-there' things. What do you like in your omelet? Some mushrooms maybe?"

Shelly and Lauren chatted at full speed while Kenton

whistled and flipped his omelet in the pan like a pro.

"Oh, my mom," Lauren said. "I forgot to call my mom!" She pressed some more numbers on the remote phone. Shelly understood Lauren's exuberance and went over to the stove to watch Kenton work.

"This is perfect," Meredith said, taking a bite of his first creation.

"It's a little browner than I like on the underside." Kenton checked the flame and turned it down before starting his next omelet.

"It tastes wonderful," Meredith said.

"Did Jana say anything else in her E-mail?" Shelly asked.

"Like what?"

"Like where Jonathan was living now. You didn't say."

"Oh, didn't I? He's back in the States. I'm sure he'll let you know exactly where when he E-mails you." Meredith walked away with the plate in her hand and poured herself a glass of milk.

Later, as Shelly lay awake in the geranium room, she wondered about Meredith's illusiveness. The room was quiet except for the rhythm of Meredith's metered breathing. Shelly couldn't help but question whether Meredith knew more than she had let on. What if Jonathan was back in the Seattle area? Meredith would have told her, wouldn't she?

Shelly's heart and mind filled with questions about Jonathan. Had he already read her E-mail? What would he think of it? What if he didn't want a romantic relationship with her again? She hadn't exactly come on strong in her letter. She tried to remember what she had said. He could interpret it as an old friend being concerned or as someone being vulnerable and opening up her heart.

Turning onto her side, Shelly felt certain she was going to drive herself crazy working through every possible scenario in her mind. Then it occurred to her: *You haven't prayed about this, Shelly.*

With a huge sigh that released all her anxieties, Shelly started to pour out her heart to God. God knew where Jonathan was. He knew what was going to happen.

Shelly pictured herself in a garden saying to the gardener, "Where is he?" And the Lord God was saying, "I'm right here." She took that to mean she shouldn't work herself into a frenzy trying to hunt down Jonathan or trying to figure out what was going to happen. It was enough that God was with her every second. He wanted to be her first love, before any human's. In that deep peace, Shelly fell asleep.

The next morning, Meredith woke her and kept urging her to get going. "What's the rush?" Shelly said.

"I thought we would check out that camp Kenton mentioned."

"Okay. I'll pull on some jeans, and we can get going."

"Don't you want to take a shower?"

"Do I need to?"

"I don't know," Meredith said. "It seems like a good idea to shower."

"To tromp around in the dirt? You're acting wacky this morning; you know that, don't you?" Shelly grabbed her clothes in a mound and headed for the shower. "I'd like to check your E-mail before we leave."

"Okay," Meredith said. "Hurry."

Shelly didn't hurry. She took her time. The shower had become her favorite place to pray, and she had lots to pray about this morning. After the shower she sat down with her Bible, eager to read several chapters since she hadn't read any during their busy day before. While she was praying last night she realized how much she had missed her morning reading.

"What are you doing?" Meredith said, coming into the

guest room with her coat on, all set to go.

"Reading. What's your rush?"

Meredith had an exasperated look on her face. Shelly remembered that look from childhood. It meant, "If you don't let me have my way, I'm not going to play with you the next time you ask me to."

"It's a gorgeous day outside," Meredith said. "I'd like to do more than sit around here. I want to see what there is to see. Come on. Let's go. Grab your coat, and let's get out of here."

"You always did manage to get your own way," Shelly muttered as she went for her coat.

"Well, if I do it's only because it's for your own good!"

Shelly laughed at her whining sister's logic.

28

Knowing how persistent Meredith could be once she put her mind to something, Shelly didn't even try to argue with her sister this morning. Meredith started the car's engine, and Shelly said, "Wait. I forgot to check the E-mail."

"I checked it while you were in the shower. There wasn't anything."

"Are you sure?"

"There were letters," Meredith said, "but none for you."

"Oh."

Meredith powered down the driveway as if she was in a hurry to get somewhere. When she hit a bump at the end of the drive, Shelly held on to the handle by the door and said, "Whoa, Meri! We're not going to the hospital this morning. You can slow down!"

Meredith flashed her sister a coy smile.

"What was that for?"

"Nothing."

"You're acting awfully strange. What's going on?"

"Nothing, really," Meredith said, sobering. She turned left.

"So, when did you decide we needed to see this camp?"

"I just thought you might like to have a look since you're

into camping and conference centers lately. You even said last night after you brushed your teeth that you would be curious to know more about Kyle's camp."

Shelly couldn't argue. She looked out the windshield at the pale blue, winter sky. Streaks of silver clouds were rising in the distance. But for the moment, the sun held court.

"Are you sure it's okay that we go out there?" Shelly asked.

"Yes. This is Glenbrooke. Kyle and Jessica don't even lock their front door. There will be no 'keep out' signs or anything."

Shelly didn't say anything the rest of the way, holding close her own thoughts about the adventure of starting a camp from the ground up. The idea was appealing, but this would have to be some setup to persuade her to leave Camp Autumn Brook. Shelly thought about how understanding Mr. Hadley had been, even when she delayed making her decision about going full-time.

"This is the place," Meredith said, coming to a halt on the dirt road and putting down her paper with the directions. "Let's go exploring."

"What's to explore?" Shelly said, looking out at the large meadow and cleared field before them. Markers were in the ground with bits of yellow plastic strips. To the right was a forested area with a trail that led into the thick overgrowth.

"I thought somebody said there was a waterfall," Meredith said. "I love waterfalls. Let's go find it." She was already out of the car.

Shelly got out and looked around. The setting was peaceful. She could imagine a majestic lodge right there in the middle of the clearing. The meadow should be left as it was, which would provide glorious views from the lodge windows. She could imagine this field bursting with spring wildflowers in about a month. It would be gorgeous, she was sure.

"This way," Meredith urged, standing at the head of the trail that led into the shaded forest. "I think the waterfall is down this way."

Shelly joined her, and they crunched through the twigs of this primeval forest. Shelly's spirit began to lift as she felt something vaguely familiar about this forest. She stopped and closed her eyes, drawing in the fragrance of the green around her. In the treetops, a squirrel chittered loudly, and suddenly she remembered. The wooded trail on the way to St. Annakapella.

Opening her eyes and looking around, Shelly couldn't help but smile. These woods contained a soft sacredness. What was it her grandma had said? *All you ever need to know about St. Annakapella is that you were drawn closer to God through his creation on your journey to it.*

"You're here, aren't you, God?" Shelly said, barely above a whisper. "I know you are. And I'm here for you. You are my beloved, and I am yours. I don't want to ever stop falling in love with you."

Overhead, a small, brown bird started to sing its heart out. The squirrel chittered back fiercely. Shelly smiled.

"Thank you, Father God, for never giving up on me. Thank you for pursuing me."

"Shelly," Meredith called from down the trail, "are you coming?"

Reluctantly Shelly left her moment of communion and shuffled down the trail. Meredith was standing at a crossroads.

"We should go to the left, I think," Meredith said.

"But I can hear water running," Shelly said. "It sounds as if it's coming from the right."

"It might be," Meredith said, coaxing Shelly along by pulling her to the left. "But let's check out this trail first and

241

then come back and go that way."

Shelly stumbled along after Meredith for about eight feet, and then she stopped. "Okay. What's going on?"

"What do you mean?"

"Meri, I know you. You are a woman on a mission. What is it you're not telling me?"

Meredith let out a sigh. "Okay, okay. I never was good at keeping secrets."

They stood in a patch of sunlight that poured through the trees. The faint sound of hammering echoed through the forest.

Meredith gave her sister a hapless grin and shrugged her shoulders. "Promise me you'll hear me out."

"I make no promises until you tell me what's going on."

"Jana told me a little bit more in her E-mail than I let on."

"Like what?"

"Like where Jonathan is living."

Shelly's eyes opened wider. "Where?"

"You're not going to believe this."

"Try me," Shelly said, raising her voice. She never did like Meredith's cat and mouse games.

"Right here."

"Right here," Shelly repeated, motioning to the forest around them.

"It's all too bizarre," Meredith said. "Jonathan lives in Glenbrooke. He was hired by Kyle to develop this camp. He's working here, right now. I found out from Jana's E-mail. I called Kyle at the hospital last night. He said Jonathan would be working here this morning."

"You know," Shelly said, putting her hands on her hips, "you may think this is a very funny little game of love tag, but I have news for you, Meri: These are real people's lives you're messing with. Why didn't you tell me all this? Did you think it would be fun to play a prank on us? Were you trying to shock me the way I shocked Jonathan in Heidelberg?"

"No!" Meredith stated emphatically. "Nothing like that. I was probably all wrong, and if so I apologize, but when I read Jana's E-mail, and she said Jonathan was in a little town in Oregon called Glenbrooke, I couldn't believe it. I wanted to run and tell you, but then I remembered how difficult everything was between you in Heidelberg."

"So? You don't have the right to try to arrange meetings."

"I wasn't. I was hoping you would once and for all admit to yourself and to Jonathan that you love him and you want him back. I don't know why that's been so hard for you to say. All these months I've wondered what would have happened if you had opened up your heart to him that morning at the marketplace. Would he still have announced his engagement if he knew you loved him?"

"You can't make speculations like that in real life, Meredith. It's not like that. God is the one who orchestrates those things."

"I don't doubt that. Look, God brought you and Jonathan to the same place halfway around the world once, and now he's brought you both to Glenbrooke at the same time. That has to be God! But God's not the one I'm worried about."

Shelly adjusted her position, vaguely aware that the echoing of the steady pounding most likely was coming from a hammer that was held in the hand of her only true love. She suddenly felt nervous and unsure of what to do or say if and when she saw him.

"You're the one who hides, Shelly. That's why I forced you to write that E-mail last night. You have to tell Jonathan how you feel. How else is he going to know that you want him back?"

Shelly glanced down at her feet, which had grown cold

standing in the damp, molding leaves on the trail. She knew her sister was right. In the same way it had taken her so long to admit to God that she needed him and that she wanted an ongoing love relationship with him, Shelly had a hard time admitting the same thing to Jonathan.

"I know you mean well," Shelly said. "And you're probably right about some of your reasoning. But I need a minute to think this through."

"Jonathan doesn't know you're here," Meredith said. "He'll probably be shocked again when he sees you."

"No doubt."

Meredith gave Shelly a lopsided smile. "I know I probably had no business doing this matchmaking. I apologize if I messed things up. I just wanted to see this brick wall between the two of you finally crumble."

Shelly let out a deep breath. "I know, Meri. Me, too."

"So go already," Meredith said, motioning with her hands for Shelly to shoo on down the trail. "The last hero left on this planet is within your grasp."

Shelly cleared her throat and moistened her lips. She headed down the trail, checking her coat collar and fluffing her hair off the back of her neck. She had worn it down long and straight this morning. The soft water from the shower had made it extra silky.

Feeling her heart pounding in rhythm with her steps, Shelly walked out of the forest and into a small clearing where the trail led up into another forest. At the entrance of that trail was a large tree from which dozens of ropes hung. Shelly could see a platform about twenty feet up in the tree and boards nailed to the trunk leading up to the structure.

She couldn't see Jonathan, but she could hear him pounding. Shelly moved to the side bushes, not completely sure she was ready for him to see her. At the base of the bushes she noticed a contraption that looked like something Jonathan would come up with. A taut cable hung just above her head and ran up to the platform in the tree. It looked like a more sophisticated version of the zip line Jonathan's dad had once rigged at their tree house so they could slide down it. Jonathan had called it their "Tarzan rope," and both of them had put in many hours of flight time, zipping down that line.

Shelly reached up and gave the cable a little tug. Then, puckering up her lips, she whistled — two short, one long.

The hammering continued.

She tried again, this time louder and longer.

Jonathan stopped hammering. She could see him now, stepping out of the shadow and to the edge of the platform. He had on jeans, a ragged gray sweatshirt, and a carpenter's tool belt around his waist. He looked down but apparently didn't see Shelly. Stepping out of the bushes, into the open area, Shelly faced Jonathan unashamed. She whistled again. Two short, one long. Surely Jonathan would remember what that meant: "Come here. Come to the window. I'm waiting for you."

The instant Jonathan saw her, he froze.

29

"Hi," Shelly called up.

Jonathan paused. "Hi," he answered after a moment.

"Did you get my E-mail?"

"What E-mail?"

"I sent you an E-mail yesterday. I guess you didn't get it."

"No."

"Oh."

"What are you doing here?" Jonathan said, adjusting his stance.

"Well, I'm . . . ah, talking to you," she answered coyly.

"But what are you doing here?"

Shelly cleared her throat and called up, "Jonathan, I found out yesterday that you and Elena broke up. I'm sorry."

He didn't say anything.

"I was actually already in Glenbrooke. Meredith came to meet with Jessica Buchanan, and I came along for the ride. I didn't know you were here. Meredith had to drag me out here."

"Drag you out here?" Jonathan repeated.

"Not drag me to see you. I mean drag me out here like a surprise because she didn't tell me you were here until just a few minutes ago."

He was too far away for Shelly to be sure, but it seemed the shocked look had dissipated and his familiar grin was returning.

"I'm glad you're working here and developing this camp," she called out.

"Is that what you came out here to tell me?" Jonathan called.

"No." Shelly paused and took a deep breath. "I came out here to tell you that I want you back."

He didn't move. Shelly couldn't blame him. Jonathan had enough reasons to distrust women. Yet she couldn't stop the words that sprang to her lips. "Don't you understand what I'm saying?" She held out her arms as if pleading with him. "I love you. I want you back. What's the matter, Jonathan Bean? Are you a scaredy-cat?"

In one motion, Jonathan grabbed the handles of the pulley at the platform and pushed off with his legs. As Shelly watched, her best friend came flying down the zip line toward her. His feet hit the ground less than a foot away from her, and his brown hair showed the tousled evidence of his heroic entrance. With searching, gray eyes, he scanned her face.

Shelly stood still, hoping her welcoming smile was making up for her sudden loss of words.

Jonathan pulled off his gloves, and with his rough right hand, he reached over and gently touched her hair, slowly smoothing it to the very ends. His cool hand returned to cradle her cheek and draw warmth from her flushed face.

Shelly kept her gaze on his lips, waiting for them to move and bring her the words she needed to hear.

Slipping his hand beneath her hair and holding the back of her neck, Jonathan moved closer. Before Shelly could convince her eyes to close, Jonathan kissed her with a kiss that was not like any kiss Jonathan the teenaged boyfriend had ever given her. This was a kiss that pledged undying devotion to his first love, a kiss that took Shelly's breath away and threatened never to return it.

They pulled away slowly. Shelly tried to breathe. She opened her eyes and saw that Jonathan seemed to be having the same difficulty. They smiled and wrapped their arms around each other.

"I love you," he whispered in her ear.

It's likely that the birds were singing in the forest the entire time Shelly had been standing there, but she didn't notice them until this minute. Under this enchanting canopy of praise, Jonathan and Shelly held each other for a long time.

"So, if Meredith brought you here, where is she now?" Jonathan said, slowly pulling away.

"Here I am," a voice perked up from the shadows of the forest.

Shelly jumped. "Meredith!"

Jonathan laughed. "Once the sneaky little sister, always the sneaky little sister."

"I couldn't leave and not know what was going to happen! That slide down the rope was very impressive, Jonathan. I actually started to cry. You guys make the most romantic, adorable couple I've ever seen."

Jonathan and Shelly exchanged glances and both shook their heads at Meredith's exuberance. Without planning it, they each reached for the other's hand and gave it a squeeze.

"I suppose we should head over to the hospital," Jonathan said. "I want to ask my boss for the rest of the day off."

They walked back to the car, hand in hand, with Meredith leading the way down the trail. "I wasn't trying to be nosy, you guys. You know that, don't you? I mean, I just wanted to know everything worked out okay."

"It did," Jonathan said.

Shelly gave his hand a squeeze. It felt good to be back with him again, side by side, hand in hand, and to feel free, with nothing to hide. They walked through the forest, their stride matching the other's step. Shelly looked down and noticed a tiny glimmer of brilliant blue along the trail. Letting go of Jonathan's hand for a moment, she stooped to pick up the treasure. It was a tattered feather, long and spindly and of bright blue hues.

"Isn't it beautiful?" she said, showing her find to Jonathan, who was smiling his approval.

"Yes, beautiful," he agreed. He wasn't looking at the feather. He was gazing at her.

Shelly felt as if the glowing inside her heart must surely have reached the outer layers of her skin by now. Her face had to be a rosy tint. She didn't care. She loved it. She loved being here with her beloved and feeling his gaze of approval on her.

Jonathan opened his arms, and she again happily fell into his embrace. "My Shelly Bean," he murmured into her hair. "Don't ever let go."

"I won't," she whispered back.

Never were more sacred vows spoken in this hushed forest.

"Hey!" Meredith called from down the trail. "Are you guys coming or what?"

"Or what," Shelly and Jonathan both stated at the same time and then laughed. They slid their arms around each other's waists and walked together.

Meredith drove her Explorer to the hospital, and Shelly and Jonathan followed in his truck. He explained that it was actually Kyle's truck.

"How did you end up here in Glenbrooke?" Shelly asked.

"A college student named Bill came over during Christmas break. He told me about this millionaire in Oregon who wanted to start an orphanage in Mexico and a camp in Oregon. I was curious about the camp, and then the next day, Elena gave me her Dear John letter."

Shelly was about to tease him and say, "Wasn't it a Dear Johnny letter?" But she bit her tongue and listened.

"I guess I should tell you right up front that I cared deeply for Elena. It didn't surprise me as much as it should have when Tony showed up, though. She talked about him all the time. The thing was, she and Tony had been high school sweethearts, just like we were. She had gone off to college and then decided to go out on the mission field. The Belgium outreach program we were with was recommended to her by her youth pastor."

"You don't have to tell me this if you don't want to," Shelly said.

"No, I want you to know. It's important. I saw in Elena her desire to grow and to travel and to be all that God wanted her to be. That was the first time I understood why you needed to take off and do your own thing after high school. When my parents married, it was so different."

"Mine, too," Shelly agreed.

"My mom never even went to college. She found her fulfillment in marrying my dad and making a home for him. She molded her life around his."

"That's not always such a bad thing," Shelly said. Her mind had been filling with all the ideas she had of how she could easily mold her life around Jonathan's at this new camp. She would have an area of specialty in which she could use her gifts, yet they would be together, working side by side. The arrangement was completely different from the way things would have been for them five years ago.

"You're right," Jonathan agreed. "Sometimes it's a good thing, when it's a partnership. Elena and I had a partnership in youth ministry, but we were more linked in our common purpose than we were in the heart. That's why it was easy for her to go back to Tony. He had a piece of her life and heart that would never be mine to share with her."

Shelly wondered if it was harder for Jonathan to talk about this than he made it seem.

"What I learned in all this was that you and I had something unique and very special. I wanted to call you immediately and beg you to come to me." Jonathan had pulled onto the main road, and the bumps had smoothed out. Shelly took off her seat belt and moved next to him on the bench seat.

"So why didn't you call me?"

Jonathan put his arm around her. "I had what I would call a shakedown by God. During New Year's I spent three days on a personal retreat at a monastery. It was the most profound experience of my life. I didn't speak to anyone for three days and ate only bread and water. All day and night I just prayed. God was so real to me. He made it very clear that I was to leave Belgium and that I wasn't supposed to call you. He would work that out."

Shelly was amazed, thinking of how God had been drawing them back together even when she had no idea what was going on. If Jonathan had called in January, she didn't know how she would have responded. It's possible her reaction would have been quite different.

"Then everything started to happen at once," Jonathan went on. "The military base in Belgium cut back on personnel, the other guy on staff resigned, Elena was already gone, and so it was just me. I called Kyle and asked about the camp."

"Kyle's a millionaire?"

"Apparently so," Jonathan said. "He and Jessica have been unbelievably kind to me. They flew me out here in January for a few days to see what I thought of the camp plans. We hit it off immediately and spent some time praying through everything."

"Kyle and Jessica are Christians, aren't they," Shelly said.

Jonathan nodded.

She had never liked it when people labeled others as Christians and non-Christians because she always thought that was up to God to determine. But she had sensed something different about Kyle and Jessica even in all the frenzy. She suspected that Lauren and Kenton also lived out a relationship with God.

"I flew back to Belgium, packed my bags, and arrived here two weeks ago."

Shelly tried to remember what had been happening in her life two weeks ago.

"I knew right where you were," Jonathan said. "I called your parents, but I asked them not to say anything."

Shelly was amazed. "They didn't. Of course, I haven't seen them in a few weeks. It probably made it easier on my mom not to have me around, if she had to keep a secret."

"I was going to come for you," he said with a chuckle. "I even found a guy on Whidbey who had a white horse. I was going to rent it from him and come riding up to your Tulip Cottage and take you away."

Shelly giggled at the thought. "Why didn't you?"

"Aside from your parents never knowing when you were home, as I prayed about it, it seemed the Lord was telling me to wait. I didn't know why until today." He squeezed her shoulder and pulled her close.

They were at the hospital now. Jonathan parked the truck. He turned to Shelly with that unstoppable grin on his face. "You're beautiful, you know."

Shelly felt herself blushing.

"I will never forget that morning at the flower stall. You have no idea what you did to my heart."

"I know, Jonathan," Shelly said with a sigh.

Meredith tapped on the truck's window and cheerfully waved for them to come into the hospital with her.

"Go ahead," Shelly called out. "We'll be there in a minute." She turned her attention back to Jonathan. "I wanted to apologize to you for that. It must have been miserable for you with my clinging all over you and here you were about to announce your engagement."

He reached over and touched her silky, brown hair. "You weren't clinging to me at all. That's what made it so hard. You were just there. You didn't ask for anything or try to change anything. I didn't know how to deal with that. I guess I wanted you to tell me you hated me or tell me you loved me. Anything! But you didn't say anything."

Shelly swallowed hard, tilting her chin toward the roof of the truck. She suddenly remembered the last time they had been in a borrowed truck together and how awful that moment had been. This was their redeemed time.

"Jonathan, I held all those feelings too tightly in my heart. When I saw you, I wanted to run into your arms and never let you go. I didn't know how to express that because I'd buried my true feelings for so long."

He touched her cheek softly as she spoke.

"I don't know that I could have done or said the right things six months ago," she continued. "Some amazing things have happened to me since then, and I feel as if, for the first time in my life, I really know what love is."

Jonathan pulled back slightly, his eyebrows raising. "You're not going to tell me you met somebody, are you?"

Shelly laughed softly, "Actually, I did. I met God. Really met him. I know him differently than I ever did as a child. A deeper realm of love has been opening up to me. I didn't have that six months ago. I also started working part-time at Camp Autumn Brook. My position at the airline has all but dried up. It's as if God was making you wait so that he could do all these transformations in my life."

Jonathan's eyes were fixed on Shelly's. He prayed aloud, "Father God, thank you. Thank you for giving us back our first love — for you and for each other."

Shelly smiled. "I love you, Jonathan Charles Renfield. I've always loved you, and I always will."

"And you know that I love you. I always have, and I always will."

"I know," Shelly whispered.

Jonathan was leaning forward, about to kiss her, when another tap on the window interrupted their perfect moment. It was Kyle, grinning from ear to ear and looking as if he had had too much caffeine. "Open the door," he called out, motioning with his hands.

When Jonathan did, they could see Meredith next to Jessica who was in a wheelchair, holding a little bundle in her arms.

"Come see my boy," Kyle said, his face beaming.

Jonathan and Shelly quickly slid across the seat and gathered around Jessica. She lifted the soft white receiving blanket, and there was the most precious, tiny face Shelly had ever seen.

"Oh, he's beautiful!" Shelly cooed.

"Handsome," Kyle corrected her.

They all laughed, and Kyle reached over to give his wife's shoulder a loving squeeze.

"You two are welcome to come over," Jessica said.

Shelly and Jonathan looked at each other. He put his arm around her shoulders and drew her close. "We might be by later. Right now we have some plans to make."

"So Meredith tells us," Kyle said.

Jessica smiled at Shelly and gave her a wink that sealed their friendship. "I hope your plans involve Glenbrooke," she said.

"I would say there's a pretty good chance of that," Shelly said, flashing her smile at Jonathan.

Kyle tucked Jessica's coat around her and said, "We'll see you later on at home then. You are taking the rest of the day off, aren't you, Jonathan?"

"If you insist," Jonathan said.

Meredith gave a wave to Shelly and said, "See you guys." One of her contagious giggles spilled over as she said, "I am so happy you're back together!"

Jonathan opened the cab door for Shelly, and she slid over to the middle of the seat. He got in and started the engine.

"Well? We have a full tank of gas and the rest of the day to ourselves. Where should we go?"

Shelly knew the years of her restless journey had come to an end. God had performed some miracles she never would have expected. The rest of their lives now spread before them like a field of clouds, fluffy and white, without a single footprint to mar the welcoming vastness. Planting a kiss on Jonathan's ruddy cheek, she answered with a full heart, "Anywhere at all in this whole wide world, my love. As long as we go there together."

Dear Reader,

As I write this, five crumpled autumn leaves watch me from the corner of my desk. When I gathered these small treasures, they were vivid shades of topaz, amber, and ruby. Now their frail, thin arms are curled up and they've turned a dull shade of brown. All the fire and life has gone from them.

What were the words from Robert Herrick's poem? "This same flower that smiles today, tomorrow will be dying."

I collected these leaves last fall from some intriguing places. One came from a cobblestone path surrounding Heidelberg castle. Another was waiting for me on the steps of a church built in 1509. And my favorite, a deep burgundy leaf, fluttered my way in a shadowy, moss-scented wood leading to St. Annakapella.

For months these leaves have silently sat here, reminding me of those sweet, adventure-filled days in Germany. And now they're crumbling into dust.

I thought of these leaves when I wrote the section in Clouds in which Shelly confronts her spiritual struggles. I thought of Adam and Eve and how they stitched together thick green leaves in an attempt to cover themselves in God's presence. I thought of how quickly the once-green leaves must have shriveled, proving themselves inadequate for the task.

Just like Adam and Eve and Shelly, I'm learning that we can never cover up or hide anything from God. He's right here. Always. He's relentless in His pursuit of us. Everywhere we go, He's already waiting for us. We are His first love and He's not about to give us up.

This kind of love is beyond my understanding. It's vast and unchanging. It's quiet and intimate. It's demanding and precise. It's God.

Oh, that we might come out of hiding, put aside all our inadequate "leaves" and surrender to His love! Then we can freely "sing to God, sing praises to His name; lift up a song to Him who rides upon the clouds."

Always,

Robin Jones Gunn